THE ROAD TO GARRETT

THE Road TO GARRETT

—A *Two-Lane Wyoming* Novel—

SUZIE O'CONNELL

SUNSET
Rose
BOOKS

ISBN-13: 978-1-950813-10-0

For the friends who truly are.

———————— *Chapter One* ————————

"WHAT ON EARTH was I thinking?" Annemarie groped her way down the treacherously steep, inky black stairwell, placing her feet more carefully when she knocked loose a cascade of crumbling concrete debris. As she descended, the air became stale with lung-clogging must and mildew. Her hand brushed a dangling cobweb, and she shivered. The basement was bad enough fully illuminated, but even with her eyes wide, there was nothing for them to see but blackness that provided the perfect canvas for her imagination.

Her skin crawled at the thought of the giant brown spiders she knew lurked down here.

Don't think about them. She snorted. *Yeah, right.*

She located the flashlight hanging from the rough-sawn beam to which the breaker box was screwed. Clicking it on, she located the tripped breaker for the kitchen and dining room—how sad was it that she knew them all now without needing to decipher the faded, curling labels?—and reset it. Warm light flooded the basement from the bare bulb directly above the trap door in the tiny dining room. "Utterly brilliant move this was, Garrett."

"Mom, are you okay?"

She glanced up to see her sandy-haired son peering over the edge of the trap door. His blue eyes were wide, and she flashed her most reassuring smile. "I'm fine, pumpkin. Just a tripped breaker."

"You didn't see any *monsters* down there, did you?"

"Nope." She glanced to her left as she climbed out of the basement, spied an eight-legged creepy-crawly staring at her from the crack in the foundation, and suppressed a shudder. *No monsters. Just really big, ugly spiders.*

She reached the top of the steps and lovingly stroked her hand through Cody's silky hair. *This is all for him, and it will all pay off for him someday. I hope.*

"TJ says there's monsters down there. And ghosts."

"Well, he's wrong. And he's a liar who only said that to scare you."

"But—"

"Don't listen to TJ, Cody. Just because he's your half-brother, it doesn't give him any right to be mean to you. Go on back to your drawing and forget about ghosts and monsters."

Cody wandered into the living room and plopped on the floor amid the sheets of printer paper, coloring books, crayons, and markers scattered across the scarred pine floor.

After four months living here, tripped breakers were nothing new to him. Their cabin's old wiring simply couldn't handle the load of modern appliances, and she tripped a breaker at least once and frequently two or three times a day. This fear of monsters was sudden and new, however, and she needed to have a talk with TJ's mother. At eleven years old, TJ was plenty old enough to know better than to bully a kindergartener. Or maybe she shouldn't bring it up. Knowing Sandy, she'd probably encourage it.

She followed Cody into the living room and kissed the top of her son's head before she returned to the kitchen to finish dinner. While the noodles boiled and the spaghetti sauce simmered, she washed and cut ingredients for salad, gazing out the west-facing window toward the sheer wall of the Absaroka Mountains and the sprawling sagebrush plain between them and her son's barren ranch. The five hundred acres were a gift from his father and grandparents, and she wondered now if she hadn't put herself and Cody into a bind they'd never get out of in her attempt to get Thomas Grant Jr. to take responsibility for his son. Even sixty miles north, five hundred acres would've been incredibly valuable, but here it was worth next to nothing. Five hundred acres of sagebrush, thin, brittle scrub grass, rock, and dust. It was too far away from the river to be irrigated without punching a new well, which she couldn't afford, and the single spring on the property wasn't large enough to do much with.

At first, she'd been floored by the suggestion of land as a means of seeing to Cody's well-being. The offer was well intentioned; it had come from Tom's parents—Thomas Sr., who had a good if gruff heart, and Ginny, whose amazing strength, stubbornness, and kindness Annemarie had dearly missed these last seven months—but the selection of the land had been up to Tom, and he'd picked the driest, most unproductive corner of the massive Grant Ranch to bequeath to his bastard son.

Message received loud and clear, she thought with a scowl. *And I was dumb enough to take it.*

She'd known almost nothing about ranching or working with cows, and until she'd officially taken possession of the land a year and a half ago, she had still been able to count the number of times she'd been on a horse on her fingers. She hadn't learned nearly enough in the time since to make her believe she could find a way to make this work… and yet, she'd given up her small house in town to move into this even smaller cabin miles away from anyone with the thought that it would be easier to manage things if she were on site and that the money she'd save on rent could be put toward improving operations. Her first four months in the cabin didn't give her much hope that the latter would be happening any time soon; all that rent money hadn't gone toward the ranch but rather into cleaning supplies, paint, used stove and refrigerator, and more repair supplies. The repairs she'd made last summer had barely been enough to make it livable. It still needed so much more to make it feel like home.

At least calving, which had ended just two days ago, had gone much better this year. She'd lost two calves and a heifer last year. This year, she hadn't lost any. That was something wasn't it?

Sighing, she returned her attention to meal prep. When the spaghetti was done, she called Cody in to wash his hands for dinner. She set the table while he stood on his step-stool at the sink singing the hand-washing song her mother had taught him the last time they'd made it home to Alcova for a visit—six months ago. Annemarie was certain her parents thought she was nuts for trying to make this dusty ranch turn a profit rather than selling it, and they were most likely right, but there was something she wanted here for Cody that he wouldn't have without this ranch—roots. In contrast to the Garretts, who were scattered across the country, the Grants had worked this land for generations, turning the high mountain desert land into a rich ranching empire. It didn't matter that Tom refused to acknowledge that Cody was part of it. This was her son's heritage, and if she had to work herself into an early grave so he could have it, so be it.

Is it really all *for Cody?* a cunning, venomous voice whispered.

As she glanced out the window again toward the main compound of the Grant Ranch, her traitorous heart fluttered. Despite everything, a faint glimmer remained of the naïve girl she'd been six and a half years ago when Tom Grant had sauntered into the restaurant where she'd waited tables to pay for college. He'd looked like he'd walked straight off the set of a cowboy romance, so devastatingly handsome with rich dark hair and fiery dark eyes topped off with a crisp black Stetson and the supreme confidence of someone who never failed to possess what he wanted. And during his two-month stay in Laramie to care for his uncle who'd undergone open heart surgery, he'd wanted a woman half his age to make him feel young and virile again in a way his high-maintenance wife couldn't.

Of course, she hadn't known then that he was married with two kids.

And she hadn't found out *that* piece of rather important information until she'd tracked him down to tell him he had another on the way.

He'd done a flawless job of hiding the evidence. No wedding ring. Not even a telltale tan line or indentation of one. No pictures of kids in his wallet. No phone calls from home even when they'd spent the night at his uncle's. She'd since figured out that the uncle had played along. Thomas Sr. wasn't shy about sharing his distaste for Tom's self-serving inclinations, and she suspected he hadn't spoken to his brother in over two decades because Steven was the same breed of selfish swine as Tom.

She'd been sucked in like a simpering fool by his devilishly attentive charm and lavish praise of her plans and aspirations. He was a womanizer of the highest level, and he'd known all the things to say and do to conquer her reservations. He'd made her believe she was valuable… and then, when she'd informed him of the result of their affair, he'd shown her just how worthless to him she truly was.

A small hand tugged on her pants leg. "Mom? Are you okay?"

She glanced at him and smiled. "Of course I am, pumpkin."

"But you're crying again."

She touched her cheek with her fingertips, surprised when they came away wet.

"How come you're sad?"

She wiped the tears like they didn't matter. Because they shouldn't. She shouldn't be crying at all over Tom Grant. He wasn't worth it. "I was thinking sad things again, but I promise to put them away. Come on over to the table, and we'll eat and talk about happy things. Like maybe you and me going for a ride tomorrow after I get off work."

"Can we? Really?"

"Sure we can. And maybe we'll invite your grandpa to come with us."

The delight that splashed across his face at the mention of Thomas Sr. made every heartache and frustration of the last year worth it. *That* was what she wanted for her son, that connection.

As they ate, she listened to him chatter about their horses and his excitement over the impending arrival of Diamond Dot's foal, who was due any day now.

Given the chance to go back and do it all over again, she might change the circumstances if she could, but she wouldn't stop herself from getting involved with Tom Grant because the result of that union—this beautiful, bright-eyed boy—was her whole world.

When dinner was done and the dishes were washed, dried, and put away, it was time for bed. Annemarie stepped into Cody's tiny bedroom and flipped on the light.

Nothing happened.

She doubted a burned-out bulb was the problem because she'd just replaced it three days ago, so she tried the teddy-bear lamp on the dresser. It remained troublingly dark, too. While Cody brushed his teeth, she descended into the basement again, but none of the breakers were tripped. She reset the ones for that side of the house anyhow, eliciting a yelp from her son when the light in the bathroom briefly darkened, then returned to Cody's room. It was still dark.

"I guess we read our story by flashlight tonight," she sighed as she climbed into bed beside him. She clicked on the flashlight she kept on his dresser beneath the teddy bear lamp.

He was out like the lights before she finished the story, and she kissed his forehead, then tip-toed out of his room. With a sigh, she snatched the cordless phone off the kitchen counter and dialed the main house of the Grant Ranch, praying Thomas picked up. No such luck. Tom answered.

"It's Annemarie," she said quickly. "Is Thomas around?"

"No. It's Monday. He's over at George's."

Right. Monday was "Bullshit Night" at the Sage Flats Ranch. She swallowed, willing her trembling hand to still. "I have an electrical problem. Can you spare Jack for a couple hours tomorrow?"

"No, I can't. If you have an electrical problem, call a damned electrician."

"I can't afford one right now, Tom. Please, can't you—"

"Not my problem, and no, I can't. My family has already done more than enough for you and your son."

"Done enough for me and my son? He's *your* son, too."

"No, he isn't."

"I didn't ask for any of this, Tom. I just—"

He hung up on her. She gripped her phone so tightly her knuckles ached, and she tipped her head back, closed her eyes, and counted to ten so she didn't hurl the thing across the living room. The last thing she needed was to wake Cody up or to give herself one more thing she couldn't afford to replace.

With her eyes burning and her chin quivering, she took a deep breath and dialed the one friend she had in this corner of Wyoming. With pencil and notepad in hand, she waited for Jamie to answer.

"Hello?"

"Hi, Jamie. It's Annemarie."

"Hey. Is everything all right?"

"Sure. I hope I didn't wake Caleb."

"No. That kid sleeps like the dead. What do you

need?"

"An electrician. A while back, you mentioned one who'd done some work for your parents."

"Yeah. Gabriel Collins. Dad says he's the best. Hang on. Lemme get his number."

Annemarie wrote the man's name down, amused. Her mother would approve of his angelic name.

After a short pause, Jamie was back on the phone. "Ready for it?"

"Yep."

She jotted the number under the name, thanked Jamie, and promised they'd get their boys together again soon. When it warmed up, Annemarie hoped to have Caleb and his mother and his new stepdad out to go riding. That'd be as good for her as it would be for Cody, who would undoubtedly be delighted to spend a day riding the range with his best friend.

The idle daydream was a stark reminder of how she'd exiled herself out here. It couldn't be healthy.

She set the phone on the counter, tore the sheet off the notepad, and stuck it to the refrigerator door with two of Cody's colorful magnetic letters. Her eyes skimmed over what she'd written. Even if her electrical problem turned out to be a quick fix, it would still be expensive. And what if it wasn't something small? How was she going to afford it?

Suddenly, everything crashed down on her like a landslide. She crumpled to the floor with her back against the fridge, curled her arms around her knees, and sobbed silently. If ever she'd needed a shoulder to cry on or someone to tell her everything would work out, it was now, but she had no one.

She was miserably, achingly alone.

Chapter Two

"THANKS AGAIN, GABE. Sorry you had to clean up Halverson's mess, but I got tired of waiting. This'll be great for the guests."

"This isn't the first time I've had to come along behind him and pick up the slack." Gabe shrugged. "More money for me."

"Speaking of money, I'll drop a check by your office tomorrow morning, if that's all right."

"That's fine. Just drop it in the mail slot if I'm not there."

Gabe glanced at his watch. Four-thirty. Running the wires for the new theater system in the attic of the Masons' bed and breakfast and cleaning up Halverson's mess of an installation had taken longer than he'd expected. He should probably call Ms. Garrett and reschedule for tomorrow.

Instead, he bid farewell to Matthew Mason and drove north out of Cody toward the Garrett Ranch. The drive to and from her place alone would add at least an hour to his day and who knew how long it would take him to locate the problem if the woman's wiring was in the kind of shape her description led him to suspect, but he ignored his weary body's complaints and turned up the radio.

He'd be lying if he said he wasn't curious about the young woman the Grants had mysteriously given five hundred acres to. She kept to herself, so no one knew much about her other than she was relatively new to town—she'd hired on as an accountant in Stan and Delanney McCoy's office a year and a half ago—and had a young son. Curious though he was, that wasn't the reason he couldn't bring himself to reschedule. The weary resignation in her voice when she'd called first thing this morning had strummed his heartstrings like a fine guitar.

Following her directions, he turned left off the highway onto the paved road that ran between the sprawling Grant Ranch and its considerably smaller southern neighbor, the Sage Flats Ranch. After a mile, he turned right onto Grant Ranch Road, which was only paved for the first twenty yards until it passed through a massive log gateway adorned with an exquisite metal sign proclaiming the lands beyond to be the Grant Ranch.

He knew there was some serious money tied into this operation, but as the Grant Ranch employed its own maintenance crew, he'd never been called out to do any electrical work, and what he'd heard about the ranch's wealth didn't come close to the truth of it. His family's spread at the feet of the Owl Creek and Absaroka Mountains near Meeteetse was a drop in the bucket compared to this place. The compound, comprised of the main house, at least a dozen employee cabins, several barns and silos, and an enormous indoor arena, was easily five times the size of his family's, which had only a main house, his two eldest brothers' houses, a couple cabins for visiting family, and one big barn.

Longing stirred. It didn't matter how long he spent away from it; ranching would always be in his heart.

"Not in the cards, though," he murmured.

The road flirted with the river for a mile before he came to the intersection Ms. Garrett had noted, and he turned right as instructed. Gravel pinged the undercarriage of his truck and crunched beneath the tires in a long-familiar and cherished song as the road twisted and dove and climbed through the gullies eroded into the plain by snowmelt and runoff.

Gradually, the road narrowed and deteriorated, forcing him to reduce his speed, and a mile and a half from the intersection, it curved sharply to the left and his truck rumbled jarringly over a cattle guard. The fence post on the left bore a hand-painted wooden sign announcing his arrival to the Garrett Ranch. He figured he was less than half a mile from the highway now, and judging by the angle of the road, it would take him all the way out to the highway. So why the wandering route across the Grant

Ranch?

He turned left onto the driveway just beyond the cattle guard.

Driveway was a loose term. It was barely more than a pair of parallel ruts through the sagebrush choked with flattened, winter-dead grass that was the only sign of recent use. She hadn't been living here long—a few months at most. The track started down a shallow, narrow gully littered with the sun-silvered skeletons of dead cottonwoods, and when it leveled out and widened, the small cabin Ms. Garrett called home came into view beside a spring-fed pond all of twenty feet in diameter. It was idyllic with a copse of young cottonwoods, willows, and quaking aspen clustered around it and the cabin—a beautiful oasis in the middle of the sagebrush and desert.

The cabin itself was a quaint, whitewashed log structure that probably dated back to the very beginnings of the Grant Ranch prior to Wyoming joining the union as a state. It was in need of a lot of work, but it showed some minor improvements like fresh, cheerful sky blue and sunny yellow paint on the shutters and trim and flower beds recently tilled and waiting to be planted.

What was a young mother doing out here so far from… anyone?

There was no vehicle parked in front of the cabin, so he continued down the trail to see if maybe Ms. Garrett had parked down by the small barn. She'd given him permission to go inside if she didn't make it home from work before he arrived, but he'd never liked entering someone's house when they weren't home; it seemed too much like an invasion of privacy.

Sure enough, there was an older pickup parked by the barn, so he pulled his truck in beside it and climbed out. The unmistakable sounds of a horse in trouble had him jogging inside. He located the horse—a paint mare in labor—and a young woman with a sweaty, smudged face and blood-smeared hands in one of the barn's two stalls. A little boy he guessed was her son perched on the rails of the stall with tears brimming in his big blue eyes.

The woman glanced up when she heard Gabe's approach, and the worry widening her eyes was a punch to his gut. Something was wrong with the delivery.

"Ms. Garrett?" Gabe asked.

She nodded. "You must be Gabriel Collins. The electrician."

The catch in her voice triggered a primal need to alleviate her concern, and he climbed over the railing to join her in the stall. "Yes, ma'am, but Gabe will do. What's going on here?"

"She can't seem to get the foal out. I thought I could try to pull, but I can't even feel the foal."

"Is Diamond Dot and her baby gonna be okay?" the little boy asked.

"I hope so," Gabe replied before Ms. Garrett could. "How long has she been in labor?"

"I don't know. She was acting funny this morning before I went to work, so I put her in here and called Jim to ask if he could check on her a couple times today, but

I called him again as soon as I got home and found her like this—fifteen minutes or so ago—and he's been tied up with calving all day."

Gabe glanced over the mare, noted the gleam of sweat and the labored breathing and didn't waste time asking who Jim was. The worry in Ms. Garrett's eyes ignited into panic when the horse folded her legs and lay down in the straw with an exhausted groan. Gabe shed his button-up shirt and draped it over the railing beside the boy and offered the kid a reassuring wink.

He recognized the problem quickly upon closer inspection—the placenta had separated prematurely and was being pushed out first, blocking the foal. Gabe strode to the sink across the barn from the stall, hoping that the new bottle of hand soap sitting on the upturned bucket beside it meant it was operable. Cold water spilled from the spigot, and he quickly scrubbed his hands and forearms and the blade of the Leatherman he always kept on his belt.

"If you haven't already called your vet, I suggest you do it now," he remarked as he climbed back into the stall and started cutting away the placenta, careful to avoid nicking the foal.

"I called her before I called Jim. She should be here any time. I actually thought it was her when you came in. Um… do you know what you're doing?"

"This ain't my first rodeo, Ms. Garrett. We had this happen with a couple of our mares, and since I was the one on foaling duty both times, I got to be the one who helped."

"And did everyone… survive?"

"Yes, ma'am, they did. But I don't know how long she's been like this, so you might want to do a little praying, if that's your thing. Even if it isn't, it probably wouldn't hurt."

"Is Diamond Dot's baby hurt?" the little boy asked. "How come he isn't coming out?"

"I don't know if he's hurt or not yet, squirt," Gabe replied, "but the stuff that fed him and helped him grow in his mama's belly came out first and he's stuck behind it. Don't you worry, though, okay? We'll get him out, and hopefully he'll be just fine."

"You're gonna do your best to help them, right, Mr. Collins?"

"You bet I am."

He cleared the placenta out of the way, and as soon as that was done, he slid his hand into the birth canal, ignoring Ms. Garrett's grimace and her son's gasp of concern. He found the foal's front hooves and let out a breath of relief. The little guy was facing the right direction and still kicking. With a firm grip, Gabe pulled with the mare's next contraction, and the foal's nose appeared.

"I know you're tired, mama," he murmured, "but we're almost there. Just a couple more."

She responded to his voice, and with a low groan, she gave a big push. He pulled with it, and the foal's head, neck, and shoulders appeared.

"Atta girl, Diamond Dot."

The barn door opened just as the next contraction hit, and Gabe didn't pay any attention to anything but the task at hand until a forty-year-old woman he knew well was standing beside him.

"Fancy meeting you here, Sparky. Guess I'm going to owe you another dinner for doing my job, eh?"

"About time you got here, Terri," he grunted, now supporting most of the foal's weight. "The party's almost over."

"So I see. Need a break?"

Gabe gave one final tug, and the foal came free. "Nope."

He lowered the newborn horse to the straw and let Terri take over, lingering several minutes while the veterinarian cleaned the colt's nose and gave him a quick preliminary examination. Assured the foal was all right, he stepped out of the stall and over to the sink to wash the blood and amniotic fluid from his hands and forearms. A faint smile played upon his lips as the old relief and awe filtered through him. Thank God he hadn't called to reschedule.

Ms. Garrett joined him at the sink, holding out a towel. His shirt was tossed over her shoulder. No longer distracted by a struggling mare, he became acutely aware of her. She was pretty enough smudged and grimy, more adorable girl-next-door than blatantly beautiful—the type of woman he'd always found most appealing—petite and just shy of five and a half feet tall. Long, light brown hair was pulled back in a practical braid, and she had the kind of big blue, innocent eyes he'd never had much success resisting.

"Thank you," she murmured. "I don't want to think what would've happened if you hadn't arrived when you did."

"It was my pleasure, Ms. Garrett."

"Please. Call me Annemarie."

"Yes, ma'am."

She held his shirt out to him, and after he realized his T-shirt was stained beyond salvaging, he tugged the hem free from the waistband of his jeans and asked, "Do you mind?"

"Not at all," she replied and politely averted her gaze.

He stripped out of his dank, gritty T-shirt and dampened a corner of the towel to wipe away the worst of the sweat, grime, and afterbirth.

As he was stuffing his arms into the long sleeves of his denim button-up shirt, Annemarie glanced at him. Her cheeks flushed prettily, and she hastily looked away again but not before he saw her lips curve into a smile that made his pulse jump and his own face heat uncomfortably. More than once while he buttoned his shirt, her gaze shifted covertly to him. No sign of a wedding ring on the hand she held out to take the towel, and he'd heard no rumor of a boyfriend.

She's a client, he reminded himself. *Single or not.*

Still, it was interesting to consider the possibilities, even if she *was* somewhere in the neighborhood of eight or ten years younger than him.

"Terri," he called to the vet.

"Hmm?"

"Do you need a hand here or can I get started on *my* job?"

"I've got things covered here," Terri replied, rising to her feet with a broad grin. "You did good, Sparky. Guess those ranching skills aren't as rusty as you always say."

"Thank goodness for that," Annemarie commented. "Looks like you'll need to add one foal delivery to my bill."

The resignation he'd heard this morning returned to her voice, and the effect it had on him was even stronger this time around. "No charge for that. I'm just glad I was here to help."

"Thank you." Her voice was so quiet he barely heard her. More loudly, she asked, "Can I at least feed you since it's highly unlikely now that you'll get to eat before midnight otherwise?"

"If you're sure you don't mind, that'd be great."

"You quite possibly just saved the life of my horse's baby. Believe me, I definitely do *not* mind. Terri, why don't you come up to the house when you're done here, and I'll feed you, too."

"I'd love to, but I have another horse to check on before I get to go home tonight. Can I take a rain check?"

"Always. Come on, Cody."

The boy, who was in the stall with Terri watching

everything she did with intense curiosity, slipped between the rails and led the way out of the barn. The tears had long ago dried up, and now he bounded ahead of his mother and Gabe having put the fear of losing his colt far from his mind. Oh, to be able to forget the heartaches and the worries so easily.

"So, you know Terri?" Annemarie asked.

Gabe nodded and held the barn door open for her and her son. "She's my neighbor. And I wired her new veterinary hospital a few years ago."

"Ah. Cody seems like every small town. You know the kind—where everyone knows everyone else. I'm still getting used to that."

Sunset was just fading from the sky when they stepped outside, and Gabe's watch said it was just after six. The longer days of spring and summer couldn't get here soon enough. He was tired of the cold and dark, and the unseasonable warmth in the evening air was *not* helping.

"It's not as bad as some towns, but yes. I've always appreciated that."

"You're from Cody?"

"Technically, I'm from Meeteetse, but close enough. I went to school in Cody. Mind if I move my truck up by the house? It'll take me a lot less time to get this done if I don't have to pack my tools up the road."

"Of course."

They moved their trucks up to the cabin and headed inside.

The front door opened into the living room. To the left was the kitchen and dining room, and to the right were the two tiny bedrooms and single bathroom. Like the exterior, the interior was dated and in need of renovations, but it was tidy, and Annemarie had decorated it simply in such a way to make the U-shaped structure look like a charming country cottage instead of the run-down homestead cabin it was. He wondered if she'd chosen the motif because it suited her or because it suited the house.

As she led him across the living room to Cody's bedroom at the front of the house, he noted a distinct lack of clues that might indicate she had a boyfriend. An instinctive and uninvited satisfaction surged, and he chided himself for it, but that did nothing to lessen it. He might not want a big family like his parents and siblings, but that didn't mean he wanted to be a bachelor the rest of his life, and since turning thirty-one last May, the understanding that he wasn't getting any younger had been nagging him almost as incessantly as his mother.

"Like I told you this morning," Annemarie said, "everything in the room is dead. The light, the outlets… everything."

Gabe nodded and squatted to investigate the outlet right inside the door. The telltale stink of melted plastic gave him a pretty good idea of where to begin.

"Do you mind if I leave you alone to work so I can get dinner going?" Annemarie asked.

"Not at all, but would you mind showing me where the breaker panel is first?"

"Oh, yes. Sorry. It's in the basement. Come on. I'll show you."

He followed her into the dining room and descended through the trap door she propped open, ducking his head so he didn't conk it on the low timbers. The foundation was concrete—crumbling with age in places but newer than the cabin, which he guessed had been moved from somewhere else. Before turning off the power to the cabin's bedrooms, Gabe familiarized himself with the visible wiring. He was neither pleased nor surprised to note that the cabin appeared to have been wired entirely with repurposed extension cords. He and his old boss had come across more than a few jobs like this, usually outbuildings on ranches and farms.

"There's a right way, a wrong way, and a ranch way."

How many times had Gus muttered that in the years Gabe had trained under the grouchy old master electrician? More than he could count.

He climbed out of the basement. In the kitchen, Annemarie was rolling out what appeared to be homemade pizza crust. He nodded to her as he passed by. Cody, who'd been sitting at the dining room table coloring, trailed after him and sat on the bed to watch intently as he unscrewed the suspect outlet and lifted it out of its box. Sure enough, the wires behind it—more extension cord— were melted.

"What happened?" the little boy asked.

Gabe showed him. "The wires got hot and burned

through."

"But why doesn't the light work?"

"This is the first outlet on the circuit, and with these wires burned, the electricity can't get to the light or any of the other outlets. It's a bit like your train over there. If you remove a section of track, the train can't get to the other stops, right?"

"Oh! Kinda like our road, too. It washed out this fall, so now we have to go through the big ranch. I wish we could fix it so we didn't have to go by Tom and Sandy's house, but Mom says we can't afford to get it fixed."

Washed out? Well, that explained the meandering route Annemarie had sent him on across the Grant Ranch. The remark about Tom and Sandy Grant made him curious and the part about not being able to pay to have the road fixed confirmed a suspicion that had been forming throughout the evening, but he left both topics alone. "Yes, just like that... except that the electricity can't simply go around."

Gabe cut the melted section of cord out and had a new outlet wired and in place in a handful of minutes. Cody kept up a stream of questions, comments, and compliments, and Gabe's face ached from smiling by the time he replaced the outlet cover. The boy's animated chatter made the job a pleasant one. "All right. Time to turn the power back on and see if I did a good job."

Cody followed him to the top of the steep, narrow stairs to the basement, and Gabe hesitated at the sudden fear in the boy's eyes.

"What's wrong, squirt?"

Cody chewed his lip, staring into the dark maw of the basement with rounded eyes. "I don't want the ghosts and monsters to get you."

"I didn't see any down there before, but just in case, I'll keep my flashlight in hand so I can bop them on the head if need be. Okay?"

The boy nodded solemnly, and Gabe swallowed a chuckle as he descended the stairs. If Cody thought this was serious business, he would treat it with the same caution. He turned the breaker on and asked Cody to go see if his bedroom light was on. Rapid footfalls marked the boy's sprint across the house and then his return.

"It's on!" he called.

Gabe joined him in the dining room, holding his hand out for a high-five as he ascended the steps. Cody's small hand slapped his, and the boy flashed him a grin before turning serious again.

"No monsters?"

"Not a single one."

Satisfied, Cody raced into his bedroom, and Gabe let out the chuckle he'd been holding in.

"Your son is adorable, Ms. Garrett. Annemarie." He shrugged. "Sorry. Habit."

Her lips lifted briefly. She slid the pizza into the oven and twisted the nob on the timer to set it before she faced him, leaning against the counter with her arms folded across her chest. Almost like she was hugging herself. It wasn't his place, but he wished he could ease the worries weighing on her, to find a way to coax an open smile from her. He imagined she'd be downright beautiful without that shadow of heartache in her eyes.

"I hope he wasn't too much of a pest while you were working. I should've told him to leave you alone, but I had my hands full, and you didn't seem to mind…."

"I didn't mind at all. I have over two dozen nieces and nephews."

Her brows shot up. "Big family?"

"Six older brothers and one younger sister, and they all have between three and five kids."

"But you don't have any of your own?"

"Not yet." He leaned against the wall across from her, crossed his ankles, and hooked his thumbs in his pockets. For a moment, he studied her with narrowed eyes. "You sound surprised."

She glanced sharply at him, then shrugged, but she flicked her gaze over him again.

"Do you want the good news or the bad news first?" he asked.

"Good. Maybe it'll soften the blow of the bad."

"Cody's room has electricity again."

"And the bad?"

"This cabin desperately needs to be rewired and brought up to code."

"I was afraid of that, but… *how* desperately?"

"Desperately enough that I'm almost surprised this place hasn't burned down. As far as I can see, whoever wired it used nothing but extension cords."

Her face paled, and she hugged herself more tightly as she lowered her gaze to the floor.

"Five minutes ago, I was relieved because Terri stopped by on her way out and said she wasn't going to charge me for Diamond Dot's delivery because you did most of the work before she even got here," she murmured. "I can't afford to have this place rewired."

The hitch in her voice and the resignation in her wide blue eyes when she met his gaze touched a deep corner of his heart, and he offered her a sympathetic smile even though she wasn't looking at him to see it. "I need to clean up my mess and get my tools stowed in my truck, but let's see if we can work something out after."

He strode away, intentionally denying her the chance to discuss the matter while his bad news was still so fresh in her mind. *Let her absorb it for a while before I hit her with what it'll cost.*

Besides, he wasn't sure what kind of deal he was willing to entertain. Even with a price break, he didn't think she'd be able to afford it. A payment plan might work, but how far out would they have to set the pay-off date to make the payments manageable for her? It would take a solid week to rewire her cabin, and he hadn't yet factored in materials. He couldn't take that much time away from his full-paying jobs, especially if he decided to give her a price break. That didn't mean he couldn't give up some of his off time. It wasn't like he had an active social life. He spent most of his evenings and weekends at home alone or out at his family's ranch when he needed to scratch that particular itch.

One thing was clear. He had to find a way to help her. His conscience wouldn't let him ignore her even if he were inclined to try. And he wasn't.

You're never going to get rich if you keep giving people breaks, he could almost hear old Gus grumble.

Maybe not, but there are things that can make a man far richer than money.

He stepped into Cody's room to retrieve his tools. The little boy was thoroughly engaged with his Legos, building what appeared to be a multi-colored barn complete with an attached corral.

"Glad to have your lights back on so you can play in here, huh?" he observed. He set his tools aside and joined the kid on the floor. "Whatcha building?"

"A stable for Diamond Dot and her new baby."

Gabe picked up the toy horses that looked just like Cody and Annemarie's mare and her foal. "I should've guessed. Have you and your mom thought about what to call him?"

Cody shook his head. "I think I want to call him Angel even though it's kind of a girl's name."

"Why Angel?"

"'Cause you came like an angel and saved him, and your name is Gabriel, and that's an angel's name, isn't it?"

Gabe stared at the kid, and it took him a second to reply. "Yes, it is, but how did you know that?"

"My Grandma Garrett told me. She loves the angels."

"She's never been much on religion," Annemarie said, leaning against the doorjamb, "but, yes, she does love the angels."

How long had she been standing there? Long enough to have heard most of his conversation with her son, he guessed. He had no idea what she thought of it—her expression was unreadable—but she didn't disapprove. A glimmer of surprise played across her face, and it was the only hint of emotion in her expression.

"Grandma says we all have a guardian angel looking after us," Cody remarked.

"I haven't seen much to make me believe she's right."

Annemarie said it so quietly that Gabe didn't think she'd meant either him or her son to hear it. When he met her gaze, she flinched and her face reddened. Nope. He wasn't supposed to have heard.

"Pizza's up," she said gently before turning on her heel and striding away.

Gabe glanced at Cody, but the boy's eyes were wide with confusion. No information there, either. He rose to his feet and gathered his tools in one hand, offering his other to Cody. "C'mon, squirt. We'd best go get cleaned up for dinner."

All through the meal, Cody chattered away about Diamond Dot's foal. He was so adorably animated that Gabe couldn't help but smile. And the pizza was amazing. Forget frozen pizza. Even his favorite pizzeria in town wasn't going to be nearly as appealing after this. He offered to help clean up dinner so Annemarie could get Cody ready for bed. She hesitated, uncertain.

"Please," he pressed. "You didn't have to go to all this trouble. I would've been happy with chicken nuggets."

She laughed softly, and for the first time, he got a glimpse of the brilliant spirit beneath the strain. Either she wasn't used to someone openly helping her or she wasn't used to accepting it. Maybe both.

"Go take care of your boy. I may be a terrible cook, but I make up for it by being a pro at washing dishes."

A little more laughter and a little wider smile.

At last she gave in.

She'd already washed all the dishes she'd dirtied prepping the meal, so there wasn't much to wash, and he finished long before Cody was out for the night. He returned to the dining room to ponder what kind of deal he and Annemarie could work out. There was only one solution he could see—a services trade. Electrical for bookkeeping. She *was* an accountant after all.

The idea made him squirm. He kept his own books for a reason, but logically, that was a task it would be more beneficial to farm out to someone else. Of course, logic wasn't the problem.

She'll only have access to the books, not the accounts. Besides, she's not Leigh.

Now that he was finally free and clear from *that* fiasco—financially, at least—he could afford to give a struggling single mother a break. The lingering emotional impacts would take longer to recover from, but maybe striking a deal with Annemarie would be a good step toward healing those wounds, too.

"Gabe?" she called. "Would you come here for a minute?"

"Sure."

Still pondering his options, he joined Annemarie in her son's bedroom. The kid was tucked in and ready for bed.

"Cody has something he'd like to ask you," Annemarie said.

"What do you need, squirt?"

"Will you come out again to visit? Please?"

Wow. Not what he had expected. "Uh…."

He looked to Annemarie, but she wasn't any help and only regarded him with what he thought might be hope. It was so faint that he couldn't be sure.

"I can't make any promises, but I'd love to." He cleared his throat and shifted his weight. "It would, uh, be great if I could check on Diamond Dot's colt in a few days and see how he's doing. If your mom's all right with that."

She nodded.

"Good night, squirt."

"Good night, Mr. Collins."

"My friends call me Gabe."

"Does that mean… I'm your friend?"

"You bet it does."

"Okay. Good night, Gabe."

After Cody was asleep and dreaming of horses,

Gabe and Annemarie adjourned to the dilapidated front porch to take in the night air still clinging to the day's warmth while they talked business.

"I can't ask you to work out a deal with me. Not after everything you've done for me," she said quietly. "And I don't think I could afford even a very generous, long-term payment plan."

"First of all, you didn't ask. I offered. Secondly, I think we can come up with a deal that doesn't include money."

"What can I possibly give you in return?"

The way she eyed him was so comical that he nearly choked trying to contain his laughter. "Nothing like what you're thinking, Ms. Garrett, and please don't take that as an insult."

"Annemarie," she mumbled, lowering her gaze in a futile effort to hide the blush that colored her cheeks in a most enchanting way. Relief splashed across her face, but so did something else. Something he thought might be a hint of disappointment.

"I'll get it eventually, I promise."

Shaking her head, she let out a huff of laughter. "I'm sorry. I don't know where that thought came from. You've been nothing but polite and professional. I guess I'm just used to dealing with a different kind of man."

What an odd explanation. Her expression became guarded again, and he filed the comment away for later. "Anyhow…. Regarding this proposed business arrangement, you're an accountant, right?"

She nodded.

"Would you be willing to trade some bookkeeping for electrical work?"

"What about the supplies you'll need?"

"I'll cover it. Let's make this easy. I'll put a dollar amount on my services and the materials, and we'll use that to determine your side of the trade based on what you would make if I walked into your office and hired you. How's that sound?"

"Perfectly reasonable. And a much better offer than I think I'd get from your competition."

"I'll need to figure out my costs—what materials I'll need, your preferences, how long this job will take—but it's far too late to do that tonight. Would you mind if I stop out again on Wednesday? We can settle on the details of our deal then, too."

"That would be great. I can't thank you enough."

"You already have. Dinner was delicious." He strolled out to his truck with Annemarie walking beside him almost as if she wasn't ready for him to leave yet. He certainly wasn't ready to go even though it was now half past eight. "Do me a favor, though, will you?"

He turned to face her, and she waited expectantly for him to elaborate.

"Invest in a couple fire extinguishers if you don't already have them."

"Are you always so thoughtful of your clients?" she inquired with a note of playfulness entwined with gratitude.

"I try to be."

He climbed into his truck, tugged his Collins Electrical ball cap on his head, rolled down the window, and leaned out. Tipping the bill of his hat, he said, "Good night, Ms. Garrett."

"See you Wednesday, Mr. Collins," she returned with more of that enticing mischief twinkling in her blue eyes. "Any special requests for dinner?"

"You're going to feed me again?"

"It's the least I can do. So…?"

"Like I said, I'm happy with chicken nuggets."

She laughed this time—a rich, musical sound that invited him to join her. "Good night, Gabe."

"Good night, Annemarie."

As he drove away through the rapidly cooling Wyoming night, he smiled. He had an inkling that by the time he was finished rewiring her cabin, he'd gladly do it all for free.

Chapter Three

ANNEMARIE SET A BELGIAN WAFFLE in front of her son and settled into her chair to enjoy her own. She cut a bite-sized piece and speared it with her fork, then pushed it idly through the syrup, staring out the dining room window at the cheerfully bright morning. It was a deception, that brilliant sunshine that looked so warm and tempting. When she and Cody had walked down to the barn just before sunup to check on Diamond Dot and her foal—the name Angel had stuck—they'd left footprints in the frost on the grass beside the road. And the forecast called for a high of only thirty-five. Warm compared to last week's highs in the twenties, but she was ready for spring.

Thinking of their new horse, she smiled. It was Saturday at last, which meant Gabriel Collins would be here soon to start rewiring the cabin. She'd been looking forward to seeing him again since their laidback discussion on Wednesday evening about her preferences for outlet and switch locations and lighting styles. His offer was beyond generous, and maybe she could blame her excitement on gratitude for his unbelievable kindness and the relief that her electrical problems would all be solved soon… but that wasn't the half of it.

She was far more excited to see the man himself.

A knock sounded on her front door. She dropped her fork on her plate, jumped out of her chair, and went to answer it with a wide grin and a noticeable bounce in her step. There was only one person it could be, and she yanked the door open still smiling.

Gabe stood on the other side with two coils of yellow-coated wire hanging from one shoulder, a red metal toolbox in one hand, and a cordless drill in the other. How had he managed to knock?

"Good morning. Come on in," she greeted a little too breathlessly, stepping back to give him room to walk inside.

"Good morning to you."

"Gabe!"

The clatter of silverware on porcelain and the groan of a chair being shoved back from the table followed Cody's excited greeting, and half a second later, he zipped around the corner hiding the dining room from the living room and launched himself at the electrician.

"Hiya, squirt," Gabe greeted with a wide grin as he leaned down to wrap the boy in a one-harmed hug. "You going to be my big helper again today?"

"Can I?"

"As long as your mom doesn't mind."

Both the little boy and the big one looked to her expectantly, and her heart lurched. Cody had spent only a handful of hours—maybe eight total so far—with Gabe, but he had taken to the man like she hadn't seen him take to anyone outside her family but his teacher, Caleb's mother Jamie, her new husband Tad, and Ginny Grant. She could add Thomas Sr. to the short list of people he adored, but it had taken him weeks to warm up to the gruff rancher, not hours.

Annemarie tilted her head. Aside from the blue eyes, her fair-haired little boy looked nothing like Gabe, whose hair was so dark it was almost black, but those matching, hopeful grins triggered an impression of father and son—an impression she'd never once gotten with Cody and Tom even though Tom *was* his father.

Suddenly, she couldn't breathe.

No. She couldn't think like that. She'd let hope blind her once before, and look how that had turned out. Besides, she didn't even know if Gabe had a wife or a girl-friend. Other than the few appreciative glances she'd caught, he'd made zero moves on her, and she knew all too well that even if he had, it didn't mean he was single. Tom certainly hadn't let his marriage stop him from pur-suing her... or who knew how many other women.

She swallowed the lump in her throat and somehow managed to say with a level voice, "Fine by me as long as you remember Gabe's here to work and not to entertain you, Cody."

"I won't forget, Mom. I'll be a big help."

She ruffled his hair with a fond smile. He was a good boy, and pride in him momentarily overwhelmed her. "Finish your breakfast first. I'm sure it'll take Gabe that long to get everything ready, anyhow."

After Cody returned to the table, she glanced up at Gabe. He stared in the direction of the dining room with one corner of his mouth lifted.

"He's quite a friendly little guy."

"Not usually. Consider that a compliment, because he's normally pretty shy."

"It's all my nieces and nephews. They've turned me into a sucker, and every kid I've ever met has this remarkable sucker radar."

Laughing, she replied, "So that's what it is. You remembered to bring some bookkeeping for me, right?"

"I surely did."

Once breakfast was done and cleaned up, Cody wandered off to help Gabe, and Annemarie settled in at the dining room table to tackle Gabe's books. Despite what he'd led her to believe Wednesday, he was remarkably adept at keeping his own books. She had very little work to do, mostly entering in receipts for the last week and verifying that he'd earmarked the correct amount for income taxes. It took her less than two hours to familiarize herself with his books and update them. Their deal was stacked overwhelmingly in her favor. Surely he had to know that. So why had he made the offer?

People that generous didn't exist.

Her family would've gone to great lengths to help her if she would've let them, and had the situation been reversed, she would've done the same for them. Because that's what families were supposed to do. Gabe didn't have that reason. He was little more than a stranger and had no obligation to help her.

Maybe not such a stranger.

A constant stream of conversation floated up to her through the trap door. She couldn't believe her son had followed him down into the basement that terrified him so he didn't miss out on anything Gabe was doing. She paused in her work to listen as Gabe explained how the breaker box worked.

"Annemarie?" he called.

"Yes?"

"I need to turn the dining room and kitchen off."

"Thanks for the heads up."

With the familiar clicks of breakers being switched off, the bulb over the trap door went dark. Cody didn't let out so much as a yelp.

Guess he's over his fear of monsters in the basement.

Moments later, he clambered up the stairs with a big grin on his face. Gabe appeared right after, and it wasn't until he'd retrieved his ladder from his truck and set it up beneath the access panel to the attic that it dawned on her why he'd turned off the electricity to this side of the house.

Half a second after that realization, it became clear she wasn't going to get any work done while he was in here. He appeared to be inspecting the lay of the house and the existing wiring at the moment, and that should have bored her, but she was riveted. The graceful movements of his body, the effortless strength he exhibited when he hoisted himself into the attic and then lowered himself onto the ladder a few minutes later....

Good lord, the man was a pleasure to watch.

Dressed as he had been that first day in jeans that hugged narrow hips and long, muscular legs and a denim button-up shirt with the sleeves rolled up not quite to his elbows, Gabriel Collins was an exquisite specimen of masculinity.

Tom exuded that same unquestionable virility, too, but as far as she could tell, that's where their similarities ended. Tom's confidence had a haughty edge while Gabe's kindness and generosity softened her impression of him and perfectly matched his physical grace. Taller and broader than Cody's father, he had the potential to be intimidating, but there was too much warmth in those striking blue eyes, and they sucked her in.

Stop it, she scolded herself, forcing her gaze away before he caught her staring. *Of course he looks good in comparison to Tom. Just about any man would at this point.*

Abruptly, she snatched the cordless phone from its base on the counter and marched into the living room to call Jim. She hated to bug him on his day off, but going over their arrangements for the livestock auction this Friday would get her mind off the attractive electrician and onto something that would hopefully put some much-needed money in the bank.

Just when she thought the call would go to Jim's answering machine, the ringing stopped and she heard a clatter followed by cursing. Finally, the ranch hand answered.

"Jim, it's Annemarie."

He swore again, and she steeled herself for bad news.

"I was about to call you."

"Oh?"

"I have to cancel on you. Again. I *just* got home from an emergency at the Grants'." Jim sighed. "I'm sorry, Annemarie. I am."

"Cancel on me? Not the auction. Please God, Jim, don't tell me you can't…." She let her voice trail off, unable to say the words. Tom. He had something to do with this; she just knew it, felt the cold rejection and seething fury churning in her gut that always came when Tom tried to block her. "What kind of emergency?"

"Johnny got stomped pretty good by a bull after slappin' it on the ass this morning while he and Cam were out feedin'. They just hauled him away in the ambulance. Looks like his back might be broke, but even if it ain't, he'll be laid up for weeks, most likely. Goddamned fool's lucky to be alive for bein' so stupid."

Sounds like something Johnny would do, Annemarie thought with a scowl. "I don't mean to sound insensitive, but why does that mean you have to back out on me?"

"Johnny was supposed to haul cattle to Torrington

same day you need to have yours to the auction."

"Can't they find someone else?"

"Not on such short notice. And why would they when they have another hand with a CDL?"

"Yes, why would they?" she murmured.

Jim wasn't being thoughtless, only conveying the Grants' thought process, but it was one more slap in the face and one more not-so-subtle reminder that Tom couldn't care less about her or their son.

"I'm sorry, Annemarie," Jim said quietly with genuine regret in his voice.

She couldn't help but believe he was sincere, and he often worked so many hours above and beyond his regular duties at the Grant Ranch to help her that she couldn't entertain even the tiniest shred of anger at him. She wanted to ask if he would come work full time for her, but she couldn't afford to pay him, and just like everyone else, he had bills to pay.

"I know. We really need that money."

"I know you do, darlin', and I know it doesn't really help, but I admire your spirit."

"I, uh… I'll call later to see if there's any news on Johnny. I *do* hope he'll be all right."

She ended the call as quickly as she could without being rude as her heart lunged in her chest. Her breathing was too rapid and shallow, so she snatched her coat from its hook by the front door and slipped outside before either her son or Gabe noticed her distress.

Hugging herself to ward off the bite of the frosty

morning, she sat primly in the rickety rocking chair. It creaked loudly as she pushed against the weathered planks of the porch with her toes.

What was she going to do now? She and Cody *needed* the money her bred heifers and yearling bulls would've brought in at the local auction, but there was no way she'd be able to get them to it now.

Closing her eyes, she forced herself to take deep, measured breaths and concentrated on the icy breeze that caressed her cheeks. The sun was pleasantly hot where her body wasn't in the shade of the roof, and she imagined it warming away her worries.

It didn't help. Not really. As soon as she opened her eyes again, the problem would still be there, and her skittering pulse and the acid of panic still simmering in her stomach reminded her of that. She shouldn't have moved out here from town. She shouldn't have taken the land. She shouldn't have given into her stubborn pride and moved across Wyoming in the first place. There was no way she'd be able to make this work—not the ranch, not Cody's connection to his roots—no matter how badly she wanted it for her son. All she was doing was digging them into a hole so deep they'd never be able to climb out. She should cut her losses and sell the land now.

"Even if I could," she muttered, wiping beneath her eye with her thumb as a solitary tear slipped her guard, "I won't. This is Cody's."

But maybe, if she could find a way to get their cattle to auction, she should sell off the whole lot, put the money in the bank, and move back to town. Then, when Cody was old enough to decide if he *wanted* to be a rancher, it would be his choice and not his mother's stubborn, hare-brained whim.

Guess that means there's no point in Gabe finishing his job.

As soon as the thought crossed her mind, she killed it.

Maybe this whole mess was her idea, but there was one thing that made her believe it wouldn't be so easy to just pack up and move back to town. The horses. Cody loved them, and now that Diamond Dot's foal had arrived, she doubted he'd want to leave them. Maybe she could board those two at least on a ranch closer to town—no way would she ask the Grants to do it—but that would cost money, eating away at whatever savings she might be able to pile up from selling the cattle and their two other horses. She might be able to leave them out here and have Jim look in on them, except that without her here to make sure that happened, Tom was likely to find every excuse to keep Jim from coming over.

She braced her elbows on her knees with her hands wrapped around her head and let out a muffled growl that came out more like a whimper.

Old hinges screeched, reminding her that they needed to be oiled or replaced.

Cody squeezed through the narrowly open front door, his eyes round with worry. He crawled into her lap and snuggled into her with his skinny arms clamped around her neck. She hugged him tightly, at once comforted by the warm weight of him and more deeply aware that she was failing him.

"Are you okay, Mommy?" he asked in barely more than a whisper.

"I'm fine," she lied.

He met her gaze with those big blue eyes. She hadn't fooled him. For one so young, he had a remarkable ability to sense lies and when someone was hurting.

Movement near the door drew her attention, and she saw that Gabe had followed Cody outside. He moved as silently as a shadow; she hadn't heard him. *So much for sneaking out.*

"Annemarie?"

His quiet, deep voice was full of concern, and at the sound of it, tears burned her eyes. She wasn't ready to face him, but an overwhelming desire to be tucked in his embrace nearly pushed her from her seat. She barely resisted by tightening her arms around her son.

"Would you go inside and grab me a water from the fridge, pumpkin?" she murmured to Cody.

With a somber nod, he scooted off her lap and slipped inside.

Annemarie lifted her gaze to meet Gabe's and saw the same strain in his eyes that had been in his voice. She took a shuddering breath and shifted her gaze southwest toward the Grant and Sage Flats ranches, clenching her teeth to keep her chin from trembling. The promise of reassurance was so close, but she couldn't give in. She had to be strong.

"What's wrong?" Gabe pressed gently.

She wished he'd asked if everything was all right. The closed, less familiar inquiry requiring only a yes or no answer would've made it easier to lie.

Instead, she told him about Johnny's accident, Jim cancelling because he now had to drive cattle for the Grants in Johnny's place, and her fear that she was on the verge of losing everything. The words came faster and faster, running together as fear spilled down her cheeks in streaming tears. When Gabe offered his hand to help her stand, she had no strength left to resist. She let him fold her into his arms, burying her face against his chest as icy failure consumed her.

He didn't say another word, only held her as she cried quietly, and the warmth of his arms and the gratitude for his steady support gradually soothed away the cold inside and out.

It wasn't until almost a minute after her tears stopped that he leaned back and brushed them from her cheeks with his thumbs. The heat of his fingers against her neck and face warmed her in a very different way as well, and she nearly jerked back in shock, but it was too enjoyable and it had been too long since she'd felt anything like it. She couldn't help it. She leaned into him again.

"It's too short notice for me to rearrange my schedule or make time off," he murmured, the rumble of his voice as comforting as his arms, "but give it a few weeks, and I can drive your cattle for you. Torrington has an auction every week, and you're likely to get better prices there than here, anyhow."

Finally, she found the willpower to step out of his embrace. "I can't let you do that, Gabe. I already owe you more than I can ever repay."

The corner of his mouth lifted in amusement, but his brows dipped slightly. "How many times are we going to have this conversation before you figure out I'm not offering because I want something in return? Everyone needs help sometimes, Annemarie, and the beautiful thing about life is that it also gives us opportunities to pay that help forward, which I'm certain you will when you have those opportunities."

Cody returned then, cutting off whatever she might've said to try to talk Gabe out of giving up more of his time for her. The truth, though, was that the surge of hope at his offer had already killed what argument she could've made. She *needed* to get those cows and bulls sold. She took the water Cody held out for her, then picked him up.

"Are you okay now?" he asked.

"I'm better now. Thanks to Gabe."

The little boy beamed over his shoulder at the electrician, and Gabe reached out to ruffle his hair with a tender smile.

"You have an amazing little boy right here, Annemarie," he said.

"Yes, I do," she agreed, kissing Cody's cheek.

"I have an invitation for you, since I won't be out the weekend after next."

"How come you can't come out that weekend?" Cody asked.

"I have to help my family brand calves. And I thought you and your mom might like to come out to my family's ranch with me. It might be a nice getaway for you. I might've mentioned to my mother that one of my clients has a sweet little boy, and it sounds like my nieces and nephews would be delighted to meet you, Cody." Gabe gave Annemarie a wink.

"Oh, Mom, can we?"

"That sounds like a wonderful time. Cody could use some kid time, and I'd love to see your ranch in operation, maybe pick up some tips, if you're sure it's not an imposition."

"Believe me. With the whole family there, you two will hardly be noticed."

She met Gabe's gaze over her son's head and held it, hoping he would see every facet of her appreciation. "Thank you."

His head dipped once, subtly, as he turned away to head inside. He got the message.

Chapter Four

GABE DRUMMED HIS THUMBS on the steering wheel while he waited for the sea of black Angus to cross the road from the winter pastures near the Grant Ranch compound to the greening spring pastures closer to the river. Was Jim among the ranch hands driving the cattle? Probably.

After a week, the memory of Annemarie crying in his arms was still fresh. In the short time he'd known her—just shy of three weeks now—Jim had dropped the ball twice. Why didn't she just fire him? Maybe he worked for cheap and she didn't think she could find anyone else to work for as little. Whatever the reason, he hoped she wasn't paying the man for work he wasn't around to do, but he suspected she was smarter than that. And too broke. His heart ached for her, even though he had no idea, really, what had brought her out here. What the hell was a girl with a college degree and a promising career in accounting doing trying to operate a run-down ranch?

He'd tried not to dig into her life too much, but the inkling of curiosity that had spurred him into keeping his first appointment despite the late hour had blossomed into a driving force.

A tap at his window drew his attention, and a middle-aged woman with silver-streaked blonde hair smiled at him from the back of a pretty bay gelding. He'd never met her before, but he knew who she was—Sandy Grant, wife of Tom Grant, who had recently taken over operations of the Grant Ranch from his father, Thomas Sr. He rolled the window down and returned her smile. "Good morning."

"Good morning," she replied brightly. "It shouldn't be too much longer."

He could see that with his own eyes, but he thanked her anyhow.

She extended her hand. "Sandy Grant."

He shook it. "Gabriel Collins."

"You're headed out to the Garrett place again?" She glanced over his truck, and he suspected she recognized it. She'd probably spotted him driving out to or back from Annemarie's a few times.

"Yes, ma'am. I'm rewiring the cabin for Ms. Garrett."

"On the weekend?"

Something about the way she said it—one brow lifted and the hint of a sneer replacing her smile—struck him wrong, but again, he nodded. "It needs to be done, but I have a full schedule, so this is the only time I have to do it."

"How very noble of you."

She could've come right out and said she didn't like Annemarie, and it wouldn't have been as clear a message as the disdain dripping from her words. Gabe lifted his brows.

"Are you married?" she asked.

What the hell kind of question was that? He shouldn't answer, but the words were out of his mouth before he could stop them. "No, ma'am, I'm not."

"Good. I'd hate to see another wife lose her husband to that home-wrecking whore."

The remark was so unexpected and so absurd that his mouth fell open. There were a lot of pieces to the puzzle of Annemarie in that single statement, but right now he couldn't fit them together. Right now all he could do was stare at Mrs. Grant and sputter, "Excuse me?"

Surprise opened the woman's expression. "Oh, so she *hasn't* told you?"

"I'm her electrician, ma'am. That hardly makes me someone she'd confide in." *Not exactly true,* he thought, remembering again the way she'd felt in his arms, her slim body quaking like an aspen leaf in a breeze.

"She's already got her hooks in you just like she got them in Tom." She snorted, then glanced over him and then over his truck with its utility toolboxes and rack. "She's smart—I'll give her credit for that. Electricians make good money. Watch yourself, Mr. Collins. She's figured out she's not going to get my husband's ranch, so now she's set her sights on you."

Gabe ground his teeth as fury exploded. Sandy wasn't the first woman to limit his worth to the size of his paycheck, and reminding him of Leigh while insulting the woman he had held as she fell apart in a moment of hopelessness obliterated any sympathy he might've scraped together for Tom's betrayed wife.

Home-wrecking whore. A gift of five hundred acres, a few dozen head of cattle, and four horses. Annemarie's determination to make it all work for her son.

As all the pieces came together, Gabe swore. "I beg your pardon, but your husband is the one who broke his vows."

"Men are weak."

The generalized comment broke his hold on his temper, unleashing it to burn away the shock and revulsion. He gripped his steering wheel tightly enough to turn his knuckles white and ground his teeth.

Ahead, the herd was thinning as the last of the cows made their way across the road. He couldn't sit here and listen any longer, so he turned his gaze back to her and said sharply, "Not all men. Good day, ma'am."

He hit the gas, maneuvering through the lollygaggers with the confidence and ease of a lifetime spent on a ranch, and didn't look back as he reached open road. He slammed the gas pedal to the floor, spraying a few of the cattle on the fringe with gravel, startling them. It was rude, but no less rude than discussing private affairs and making blanket assumptions about an entire gender with a complete stranger. After that, he didn't give a damn about being polite.

There was far too much empty gravel road between him and Garrett Ranch, and he drove faster than was probably safe just to reduce the time he had to think about the revelations that had him reeling. If he'd connected all the dots correctly…

Cody was Tom Grant's bastard son.

Why hadn't he figured that out already? Tom Grant was a known womanizer, and Gabe knew of at least three occasions on which he'd been unfaithful to his wife.

The implications of that piece of information swirled around him, and he couldn't figure out why it mattered so much to him. He had no claim whatsoever on either Annemarie or her sweet little boy, and while their situation tugged at his heart, he could barely call himself their friend.

The anger boiling in his blood at Mrs. Grant's remarks told him that he needed to forget what he'd heard and maintain a strict business-only relationship with Annemarie Garrett. None of this was his business. He had a simple and uncomplicated life, and he liked it that way.

But it's lonely.

He didn't believe for a fraction of a second that he'd be able to walk away when his job here was done.

She's already got her hooks in you….

Maybe that was true. And just maybe he didn't give any more of a damn about that than he did about being considerate of an embittered wife.

The more he thought about it, the hotter his anger burned. Sandy's comments and insinuations about Annemarie's character—that she was a manipulative, husband-stealing gold-digger—didn't fit his impression of the pretty young mother. His gut hadn't warned him about Leigh until it was too late, but that was one slip, and he still trusted his own instincts over those with reason to be biased.

A black Chevy pickup with the Grant Ranch's brand emblazoned on its doors in gleaming gold was parked in front of Annemarie's cabin when Gabe pulled up, and he growled. A man in his mid sixties sat in the old rocking chair on the porch. Thomas Sr., no doubt.

Seething, Gabe skidded to a stop and jumped out of his truck, which lurched forward half a foot when he let out the clutch before the engine had fully shut off.

He stopped short when Cody burst out of the house with a broad grin on his face and his favorite toy horse in hand. Thomas Sr.'s expression softened when he took the horse from the little boy, nodding at whatever Cody said. His smile was gentle, fond even. But of course it would be, since all clues pointed to Cody being his grandson.

"Gabe!" Cody cheered when he spotted his new friend. He held out his arms expectantly, and Gabe leaned down to hoist him off the ground when the kid wrapped his arms around his neck. Twisting in Gabe's arms, the little boy said to his grandfather, "Gramps, this is Gabe. He's fixin' the wiring for us. Gonna make it so the lights stop turning off when they're not s'posed to."

Gabe set Cody on his feet. It didn't seem fair to ruin the moment for either Cody or his grandfather, so when Thomas Sr. started to stand, Gabe motioned for him to remain seated and held out his hand in greeting.

"Mr. Grant," he said. "I'm—"

"Gabriel Collins. I know. Call me Thomas, Mr. Collins."

With a nod, Gabe replied, "Gabe'll do, sir."

"Go fetch your mother, Cody," Thomas murmured to the boy. Then, after the door closed behind his grandson, he said, "You have the look of a man spoiling for a fight, Gabe."

"I guess I probably do." Suddenly, his entire conversation with Sandy snapped back into focus, igniting his temper all over again. With one hand clenched into a fist at his side and the other pointing warningly back toward the Grant Ranch, he said in a low, measured voice, "The next time your daughter-in-law calls Annie a home-wrecking whore in my presence, I will *not* be so polite."

"Annie," Thomas remarked thoughtfully. "I wouldn't have called her that, but coming from you, it fits."

At Thomas's words, Gabe realized he'd slipped in his anger and shortened Annemarie's name.

"I would apologize for whatever Sandy said to you," Thomas continued, "but she's a spoiled bitch, and I'm not in the habit of defending her or making up for her."

For the second time in less than ten minutes, Gabe's

jaw dropped.

"You're an intelligent man, so I'm sure you've figured a few things."

Nodding, Gabe said, "Cody is your grandson, and that's why you gave Annie this ranch."

"Tom gave it to her."

"Bullshit. Oh, I'll bet the paperwork says he had a hand in it, but I'm damned sure he didn't do it by choice. I've spent enough time out here now to have a feel for the dynamics."

Thomas only smiled.

"Why?" Gabe asked.

"Aside from the fact that Cody is my own flesh and blood, your Annie is something special. She reminds me of my Ginny. Strong but kind."

"I agree, but she's not 'my' Annie. I'm just her electrician. And maybe her friend, if she wants me."

The door screeched open, and Cody returned with his mother right behind. Thomas smiled up at her, and she returned it briefly before turning her attention to Gabe. Her whole face brightened, and his heart leapt.

Thomas chuckled. "We'll see about that."

"See about what?" Annemarie asked, glancing between Gabe and the rancher.

"How smart Gabe here is." Without giving anyone a chance to react, Thomas pushed to his feet and picked Cody up in a bear hug. He then embraced Annemarie before turning to Gabe to grip his hand while his eyes locked on Gabe's. "My bet is he's got a much better head on his shoulders than my idiot son. And a heart that's a damned sight more loyal."

With that, the rancher strode out to his truck and climbed in. Gabe caught sight of a smug, knowing gleam in the older man's eyes. After everything he'd learned this morning, Thomas's bold insinuation should have had his jaw even closer to the ground, but instead, Gabe chuckled. Thomas Grant, Sr. had a reputation for being gruff and sometimes surly, but he was also said to be fair. Gabe decided he liked the old man.

"What was that all about?" Annemarie asked, turning to Gabe.

"I don't know if that's a conversation you want to have with me, and even so, I'm pretty sure you wouldn't want to have it in front of your son. And anyhow, I have work to get to."

"Cody, can you go inside for a few minutes? I'll let you pester Gabe to your heart's content after I talk to him."

Gabe watched Cody disappear inside, then turned to his mother, who watched him with a frown. *Yeah, I didn't think you'd let me off so easy.*

"Gabe. What was that all about?"

Sighing, he said, "I had an uncomfortable and rather inappropriate conversation with Sandy Grant just now while I was waiting for cows to move."

Annemarie's expression darkened. There was anger in her eyes, and rightly so, but there was something else entwined with it that he didn't like seeing.

Defeat.

"What did she say?"

"More than enough for me to figure a few things out. Like the fact that Cody is Tom's son. And I'm guessing since the Grants gave you the land, you're sure beyond a doubt. Positive paternity test?"

She nodded, her shoulders drooping with that unspoken admission. "I didn't need it to know Cody was Tom's, but I wanted it so Tom couldn't deny it. What else did Sandy say?"

"I have no desire to repeat it, but I'm sure you can guess."

Again, she nodded, folding her arms tightly across her chest and refusing to meet his gaze. It was probably overstepping his bounds, but he carefully took her hands and unfolded her arms, then slipped his fingers under her chin and tipped her head up so she had to look at him. Her eyes rounded, reminding him how young she was. She was usually so strong that moments like this and last Saturday hit him hard.

"It pissed me off, Annie." He caught his lip between his teeth. He'd done it again. "I'm sorry. I didn't mean to call you that."

"I've always hated that name," she murmured. "Kids always used it to tease me, but when you say it…."

Her voice had turned husky, and instinctively, he brushed his thumb along the line of her jaw. When he replied, his own voice was thick and rough. "How do I say it?"

"I don't know. But I think I like it."

Abruptly, she cleared her throat and straightened, composing herself as if she'd suddenly realized how close they were to crossing a line. He mourned the end of that moment of openness and the promise of it.

"I'm sorry for what Sandy said. You've been such a… a wonderful help to me that I hate to think she's dragged you into my mess."

"Not your fault."

"Which part? That she unloaded that on you like an eight-gauge or that I slept with her husband?"

"I don't think that's what happened. I mean, I'm sure it happened, but I don't think it happened how she'd like me to believe."

"Why wouldn't you believe her? You barely know me."

"I know enough. And what I know didn't come from a bitter wife whose opinion is far from objective."

"And what do you know about me?"

"That you're a young woman who made a mistake and is doing her damnedest to make the best with the hand she was dealt. You were, what, eighteen? Nineteen?"

"Eighteen. Nineteen when Cody was born."

"Tom must've been close to twice your age. More than experienced enough to make a naïve girl believe whatever he wanted her to believe. I've lived in Cody a lot longer than you, Annie. Tom doesn't exactly have the cleanest reputation, and I'd bet my family's ranch that you weren't his first… indiscretion." He laughed softly. "You are the first, however, who's had the guts to make him pay for it."

"I don't know who's paying for it."

She said it so quietly that he almost missed it.

"That right there. That's exactly why what Sandy said pissed me off. She called you a gold-digger. Not in so many words, but that's what she wanted me to believe. I don't know a gold-digger alive who would take this place—" he gestured to the cabin and, with a sweep of his arm, the rest of her ranch "—and try to make a home here. Takes too much work."

"You sound like you've had some experience with them."

"Just one. And it was an expensive lesson to learn." He stuffed his hands in his pockets. "She wouldn't have agreed to exchange bookkeeping for wiring, like you did. She would've tried to manipulate me into rewiring her house for free."

His voice had sharpened, and Annemarie eyed him like she might a snarling dog. He should say something to comfort her, but he couldn't. They stood on a threshold he wanted to cross, and trying to soothe her would push him back from it.

"Let's just get everything out in the open right now. You're not a gold-digger, and if I were married or had a girlfriend, I'd *never* cheat on her. Everything clear enough? Because I don't want to start our friendship with any doubt."

She chewed on her lip, and after a moment, she

nodded. "What was her name?"

"Does it matter?"

"Well, you know all the intimate details about my life now."

"Not all," he replied. "But fair enough. Her name was Leigh Bennett. What about you and Tom? How did that happen?"

"Pretty much how you said. I was just starting college in Laramie, and he walked into the restaurant where I worked, larger than life. He made me feel smart and mature and wanted." She shrugged. "And I fell for it. It went on for a couple months while he was in town taking care of his uncle. I didn't expect anything serious to come of it. I was on the pill, but it failed. Ninety-nine percent reliable, but I was the one percent."

"What'd Tom say?"

"He refused to acknowledge that Cody's his son. When I saw the ad for an accountant here in Cody, I thought it was a sign. Obviously, I was wrong. I shouldn't have come here." She glanced over her shoulder toward the Grant Ranch and her lips lifted in a faint smile. "But even as hard as it is, I'm glad I did. I wanted Cody to have a relationship with his father's family, and maybe Tom is still as indifferent as ever, but Thomas…. He dotes on Cody. So did Ginny, before she died. I wanted Cody to have roots, and Thomas at least is giving him that."

"What about your family?"

"They all adore him, but we don't do roots. We tend to go where the wind blows us."

"And that doesn't appeal to you."

"It used to… until I had Cody. And I don't even like to admit this to myself, but maybe I wanted to make Tom pay however I could for making me feel so absolutely worthless." She sniffed and turned back to him but didn't meet his gaze. "I *am* sorry you've been dragged into this. I'm sure it's more than you ever wanted to know about a client."

"It's all right. I get the feeling you could use a friend right now, and that's a position I'm quite happy to fill. If you want me, that is."

"You're right. I could use a friend right now. And as far as that goes, I'd consider myself lucky to call you one."

Finally, she looked up at him, and her expression brightened. There was something more she wanted to say, but she held it back, and he figured she'd already told him plenty, so he didn't press her. Instead, he held open the front door for her and followed her inside.

As was their routine, Gabe got to work with Cody watching and helping where he could. He was particularly glad for the little boy's presence today. Cody's stream of questions and chatter kept his conversations with Sandy, Thomas, and Annie at bay. *That* was a nest of complications he wasn't ready to attempt untangling just yet.

Funny that he kept calling her that. It had a decidedly intimate feel to it, and while he was definitely attracted, he hadn't given himself a chance to consider if that attraction was something he wanted to act on. And the few times the idea of something more than a client-contractor or even a platonic friendship had crossed his mind, he had shut it down. Quickly.

He needed to do it again right now, or he would risk doing something stupid, like dropping the wire he was fishing through the wall. Or kissing Annemarie the next time she needed to lean on him for support.

Feeling eyes on him, he glanced over his shoulder to find Annemarie watching him from the couch. It wasn't the first time. She seemed to like watching him work almost as much as her son did, though she did so without the endless questions. Usually when he caught her, she looked away, but this time she smiled.

"Find this interesting?" he asked.

"Yes, I do. You make it look so easy."

"Practice." He returned his attention to his task. "Lots of it."

"Gabe?"

"Hmm?"

"Are you still okay with us coming out to your family's ranch next week?"

He stopped what he was doing but didn't look at her. Was he? "Why wouldn't I be?"

He heard the sigh she let out from across the room. Relief.

"I don't know," she replied. "I was worried that maybe what you heard today would make you feel awkward about it."

"Wouldn't matter much if it did. I promised you

and Cody a weekend away. Didn't I, Cody?"

"Yeah! But how come you have to go home to your ranch?"

"Branding."

"Oh, right."

Gabe turned toward Annemarie. "It's only going to be awkward if *you* make it so."

She nodded, shyly averting her eyes. Gabe nearly groaned as he fought the urge to sit beside her and gather her in his arms and hold her until she believed him.

He should walk away when the job was done. That would be the smart thing. But it was too late for that now. And the ease with which he admitted it meant there were some questions he'd need to answer before he risked his heart.

——————*Chapter Five*——————

THE ACRID STINK of singed hair and hide stung Annemarie's nose as the plaintive bawling of calves calling for their mothers drowned out the shouts and laughter of the men wrestling them down to be branded. She leaned against the corral fence with her arms folded on the top rail watching Gabe and his six brothers, eldest nephews, and brother-in-law work. Even at six feet tall, poor Andrew—the brother-in-law—was the smallest man in the crew. The Collins boys all stood between six-three and six-five. Even John, Gabe's father, was taller, having shrunk from six-four to six-two after a series of back injuries.

She tugged her heavy coat closer around her to ward off the chill wind soaring down out of the Owl Creek and Absaroka Mountains. The damp bite in the gray afternoon promised that the plumes of snow obscuring the peaks would soon descend on the narrow valley. The Collins

Ranch was barely four times the size of her spread, but it was considerably more fertile, watered by streams emptying snowmelt from the surrounding mountain ranges. The creeks were lined with dense thickets of willow, aspen and cottonwoods, and in between, hayfields and pastures sprawled. They were still gray with winter now, but in a few more weeks, they would be lush and green. It was so full of life while her ranch often felt unbearably empty and desolate.

Beside her, the only Collins sister—Delilah, Andrew's heavily pregnant wife—let out a howl of laughter when a calf escaped her eldest brother, Samuel. Annemarie grinned. The good-natured heckling between siblings reminded her forcefully of her brother, and she wished Robert and his family lived closer. They talked on the phone every week, but until she'd arrived at the Collins Ranch yesterday evening and been greeted by Gabe's siblings, she hadn't realized just how much she missed his face.

Annemarie glanced over her shoulder to check on Cody, but he was thoroughly entertained with half a dozen of Gabe's younger nieces and nephews. Ruth, the matriarch of the Collins clan, had them bottle-feeding bum calves in the pen next to the calving stalls while she cradled baby Joshua—Samuel's newborn grandson—in one arm with a relaxed confidence Annemarie was certain she would never possess herself. When she'd held Joshua at breakfast, she'd been as terrified of dropping him as she'd been of dropping Cody when he was that small.

It was odd to think that Gabe's brother was a grandfather while Gabe himself was unmarried and childless, but there *was* a fourteen-year gap between them.

"It's a bit overwhelming, isn't it," Delilah remarked. "Andrew didn't know what to make of this circus the first time I brought him home, either. He got used to it, and I'm sure you will, too."

It wasn't the first comment she'd heard alluding to a deeper relationship between her and Gabe. Not even close. She didn't think a waking hour had gone by without one of his brothers or his mother or father remarking on the unusualness of her presence on their ranch. Apparently, Gabe hadn't brought even his more serious girlfriends home to meet the family. What did that say about her?

"I'm sorry," her companion said when she didn't respond. "I try not to be as pushy as the rest of my family when it comes to Gabe's personal life, but my brother is different with you and it makes me curious."

Too shy and skittish yet to ask what that meant, Annemarie turned her gaze back to Gabe and his brothers and maintained her silence. No matter how hard she tried, she couldn't keep her eyes off him. The way he moved—with effortless power tempered by grace—fascinated her, and she was beginning to question whether it was only the insinuations of his family that made her hope there might be something between them or if she hoped because there really *was* something.

"How is he different?" she asked at last.

"He's protective of you and your son."

Annemarie repeated the word to herself, tasted it. It felt right. "Wasn't he protective of his girlfriends?"

"No, which I always thought was weird because he's always been the most protective of me. When Ezra and the rest would pick on me mercilessly, Gabe was always the one to tell them to shut up, and when I had a boyfriend in high school who tried to stake his claim on me at prom, it was Gabe who beat the piss out of him. Hence why he's my favorite brother. Maybe it's because I'm the only one younger than him, but I doubt it. It's just who he is."

Annemarie lapsed into silence, once again studying the man at the center of their conversation. There was so much she wanted to know about him, but it had been so long since she'd allowed herself to feel *anything* but anger and disappointment for a man that she wasn't sure where to begin. It helped that Delilah seemed willing to share information, but even so, she felt guilty for using Gabe's sister to dig up tidbits he might not want to share with her.

"Can I be honest with you?"

"Of course."

With a wicked grin, Annemarie turned to her companion and said, "Your brother is a very sexy man."

"Which one?" Delilah quipped with a wink. "I have seven, so you might need to be a little more specific."

Annemarie laughed like she hadn't laughed in a long time, deep and long. "Well, all of them are, but I was talking about Gabe."

"Yeah, he did get the best genes." The other woman

chuckled. "But I get the feeling that's not what you wanted to be honest about."

"No." She pursed her lips and returned her gaze yet again to Gabe. She winced when the calf he was holding kicked out with a hind leg and nearly clipped him in the jaw, but he dodged fast enough to avoid the strike. He caught the leg and held it firm while Andrew pressed the iron to the calf's shoulder. He was as good a rancher as he was an electrician, and she wondered why he'd left the ranch he so obviously loved.

"So… what did you want to be honest about?" Delilah pressed.

Annemarie chewed her lip, her eyes still trained on Gabe. "It's been a long time for me."

"What has? Sex?"

"That… and relationships in general." She cursed the heat that rose up her neck and crawled across her face.

"How long?"

"Cody's father. And I've come to the realization that it never qualified as a relationship."

"You can't be serious."

Annemarie nodded.

"But Cody must be almost six, right?"

Again, she nodded. "I learned a hard lesson, and one I'm in no hurry to repeat. But I like your brother." She hadn't meant to say it, but it was true, wasn't it? And it was liberating to admit it. "I haven't known him that long, really, but so far, he's been amazing. So kind and generous. But I thought that about Cody's father at first, too, although now that I have someone to compare him to, I wouldn't call him kind and generous so much as attentive and indulgent."

"Let me guess. He wined and dined you, fed you one pretty lie after another, and then left you saddled with a kid."

"More or less. Plus… he was married with two kids." Annemarie glanced at her companion and found Delilah staring open-mouthed at her. "I was young and stupid. So very stupid."

"I think you're being way too hard on yourself. Sounds to me like he knew exactly what he was doing, and you were just too innocent and trusting to see it."

"That's what Gabe said, too."

"Maybe you ought to listen to us. Especially Gabe. He knows what it's like to be deceived and screwed over by someone."

"Let me guess. Leigh?"

Delilah lifted a brow. "He told you about her?"

"He mentioned her. Why? Does he not talk about her?"

"No, he doesn't."

"Why not?"

"She let him know she was breaking up with him by maxing out his credit card and cleaning out his checking and savings accounts while he was in Thermopolis helping our brother Michael wire his new tire shop. It's a long story that still pisses me off, so if you want to know the juicy details, you'll need to ask Gabe. I don't want to have this baby right here in the pasture."

Annemarie tapped her thumbs on the corral rail. She was about to ask why Gabe had left the ranch when his sister spoke again.

"He had a blind spot where she was concerned, and she exploited it."

"Oh?"

"She was his first love—they dated all through high school. First loves have a strange way of sticking with us."

Was that why she hadn't been able to bring herself to start dating again after Tom? In a way, she supposed he was her first love. She could say without a doubt that she hadn't loved any of the boys she'd dated in high school. Not even the one who had become her first lover. And Tom *was* her son's father. She tilted her head as her eyes found Gabe again, and the term suddenly felt wrong. Tom was no more a father to her son than any bull who sired a calf. *Wham-bam, thank you, ma'am,* and that was the extent of it. Sire. That was the proper term for him. And that's how she'd think of him from here on out. Because a man who had been a stranger just a few weeks ago had already been more of a father to Cody than Tom had ever been.

Delilah squeezed her hand. "He's a good man, An-nemarie. He won't ever do what Cody's asshole father did to you."

"He's your brother. Doesn't that make your opinion of him biased?"

"Sure it does. I'm more likely to point out every single one of his faults."

"I might believe that if you hadn't already told me that he's your *favorite* brother."

"Favorite or not, it's my duty as his sister to make sure any woman thinking of getting involved with him knows what she's getting into."

"Is that to protect her… or him?"

"Him. He deserves a woman who'll love him for everything he is."

The first flakes of wind-driven snow spiraled around them, and Annemarie shivered as a few tickled her exposed neck. She turned up the collar of her coat and zipped it all the way to her chin before stuffing her unprotected hands in her pockets. With a start, she realized that the branding was done and the calves had all been turned loose to rejoin their mothers in the pasture. Gabe was almost to the fence where she and Delilah stood gossiping about him, and with those long strides, he reached them in no time. He climbed over the fence like it was nothing and dropped to the ground on the other side of his sister with equal ease. Tucking an arm around Delilah with a casual affection that made Annemarie miss her brother even more, he glanced between the women.

"You two seem to be getting quite friendly."

"What can I say? I like her. She may be a bit young for you, though, old man." Delilah winked at Annemarie. "I'm not sure you'll be able to keep up with her."

"You are barely a year younger than me," Gabe retorted. He inspected his sister's satiny dark hair. "Is that a gray hair I see?"

"No, it is not, you jackass."

Gabe chuckled and gave his sister a squeeze.

"In all seriousness…." Delilah swiveled to face him, and with her wrists crossed behind his neck, she leaned back in his arms and smiled sweetly. "You know I love you, but if you hurt her, I will castrate you myself."

She said it with that same innocent grin still firmly in place. Then she rose up on her toes and leaned around her big belly to kiss his cheek before she sauntered off to join Ruth and the kids.

Gabe stared after her for a moment, then turned to Annemarie with a brow lifted. "What was that all about?"

"Let's just say your sister is as easy to talk to as you are."

"Uh-oh. Should I be worried?"

"I don't think so. We talked about your family and her husband and baby-to-be… and about me… and you. She told me a little more about Leigh. Sounds like she didn't just go digging for gold but found quite a bit."

"That's a polite way to put it." His jaw clenched briefly and his eyes hardened, but then he sighed and the anger drained from his face.

"How did she do it? Steal the money, I mean."

"Her brother was the assistant manager of the bank where I had my accounts."

"How much did she take?"

"Close to a hundred thousand."

"Oh, my God, Gabe. Did you get it back?"

"Nope. By the time she was caught, there wasn't

anything to salvage. It took me four years to pay off the credit card, and I've only recently finished paying the money back to my savings."

He kicked at a clump of dirt with the heel of his boot, and it was close to half a minute before he met her gaze again.

"You think you were dumb to get involved with Tom? Believe me, I have you beat in the dumb department. She made it pretty clear that she didn't love me as much as I loved her when she headed off to college and dumped me within a month, but six years later, she came crawling back to me fresh from a divorce. She claimed her ex had abused her, told me if she'd just said yes when I asked her to marry me at graduation, we could've been living happily ever after and she never would've married her asshole ex. And like a fool, I fell for it and took her back."

"Was it true? About her ex?"

"Like I said, I was a damned fool."

Annemarie shook her head. "She played you. Just like Tom played me."

"If you say so." Gabe turned fully to her and rested an arm on the top rail of the corral. "I'm sorry I've been ignoring you and Cody. I'm sure you didn't expect to be dragged out here just to be left to fend for yourself against my family."

"There's nothing to apologize for, Gabe. I knew you were coming here to help out, and Cody's having a blast with your mother and your nieces and nephews. It isn't often that he is so free to just be a kid."

Frowning, he searched her face, and she quivered a little inside, both nervous and intrigued under his intent perusal. She felt exposed and vulnerable but also secure and valued.

"And how about you? Are *you* doing all right? I know my family can be a bit...."

"Overwhelming?"

"Yes, that."

"They were, at first. There are just so many of them, and none of them are at all shy."

Gabe chuckled. "I probably should've warned you, but I didn't think they'd be *quite* so obnoxious. I'm sure you've figured out that teasing me about being the only unmarried and childless sibling is a family sport."

"I have, and I'm glad you didn't warn me because I might have backed out of coming and missed this. It's nice to talk to people who aren't clients, and it's even better to hear them laugh... and to laugh with them. It gets lonely out at our cabin." She lowered her eyes to hide the shy smile that lifted her lips. "Of course, it hasn't been nearly so lonely out there lately."

"Don't let my family hear you say that or they'll be a hundred times worse."

"Um, Gabe?"

"Hmm?"

"What are we doing?"

"I'd say we're getting to know each other better."

"Obviously... but why?"

"Because we're friends?"

The way his voice rose to make that simple statement into a question sparked hope. Breathlessly, she asked, "Is that *all* we are?"

"For now."

His expression gentled even as his eyes lit up with a delightful sparkle, and the way he shifted his body closer made her heart trip over itself. The things he could do to her pulse just with a subtle shift in his expression....

"But I would like to take you out sometime soon."

"When?"

The question popped out of her mouth so fast that she blushed at her own eagerness.

"I was thinking next Sunday after I finish wiring your cabin." Gabe chuckled. "I guess that answers the question of whether or not you're interested."

He stuffed his stained leather gloves into his pocket and gingerly took one of her hands, pressing their palms together. The heat of his skin chased the chill from her fingers and spurred her heart into a gallop. Her hands looked so tiny and delicate against his despite the layer of calluses and fine scars she'd accumulated since taking over Garrett Ranch. What would those long-fingered, capable hands of his feel like gripping her hip or stroking down her back?

"I know it's been a long time since I gave a relationship a chance, and I suspect it has been for you, too," he was saying. The timbre of his voice had changed, roughened. "Maybe it's time we both took a chance."

She let out a small gasp when she met his gaze. A heady blend of vulnerability and confidence and hope filled his eyes, and instinctively she leaned into him, letting that emotion saturate her. Unable to trust her voice, she only nodded.

He threaded his fingers around hers and pulled her over to where his mother and the kids were finishing with the bum calves. He let go of her hand just long enough to hoist Cody to his shoulders—ignoring the pleas of his nieces and nephews for a piggyback ride—before taking it again. Annemarie gazed up at her son, noted his king-of-the-world grin, and gave Gabe's hand a grateful squeeze. Cody needed this. Needed to know that he could trust someone other than her and her family and that people outside their family could appreciate his beautiful soul.

"Are you still enjoying your stay?" Ruth asked as she joined Annemarie, Gabe, and Cody and walked with them after shooing her grandchildren into the house.

"Immensely, but it'll probably be a while before I can remember everyone and stop calling your kids and grandkids by the wrong names," Annemarie replied honestly.

"Don't worry about that. We're used to it." Ruth took Cody's hand and squeezed. "How about you, Cody? Are you having a good time?"

"Oh, yeah! It's fun bottle-feeding the calves. And the baby chickens and turkeys are so cute!"

"Well, you can come out here any time you like to feed them. Might be good for our herd of hooligans to have a gentleman such as you around more often. I know Jessen and Cole have been on their best behavior with you here, trying to earn some brownie points from Nana and Granddad. You're doing a great job with this boy of yours, Annemarie."

"Thank you," Annemarie said, "but he makes it pretty easy."

"I bet he does. Would you mind giving us girls a hand in the kitchen for a bit? The boys finished earlier than we expected, and we could use some help finishing dinner."

"I'd love to."

"I can help, Mom," Gabe said.

"No, you can't. *You* can look after that boy you got on your shoulders for a bit longer. I'm sure Annemarie will agree with me that he could use some boy time."

The knowing look Ruth gave her son and then turned on her made Annemarie think she was setting her up for a chance to see how Gabe interacted with Cody. As if she needed any more confirmation that they got along fabulously. Of course, with the possibility of a romantic relationship out in the open now, things had changed, and it might be that it was time to evaluate him not just as a friend to her son but as a prospective father.

There it was again. That was the second time this afternoon she'd slid Gabe into that role.

"If you don't mind, I'm sure Cody would love it."

"I don't mind in the least. C'mon, squirt. Let's go ride herd on your new friends. Think you can help me keep them out of the kitchen so your mom and mine can finish dinner in peace?"

"You bet I can!"

Gabe took off for the house at a jog, and Cody's laughter trailed after them. Annemarie's lips curved.

"If you're in the market for a daddy for Cody, Gabe's great with kids," Delilah quipped.

Annemarie squeaked and pressed her hand over her heart as if that could keep it from leaping out of her chest. "Good lord, Delilah. You scared the bejeezus out of me. For a woman due to give birth any day, you are remarkably light on your feet."

Gabe's sister laughed. "Or maybe you were just too absorbed by my brother."

"Well, his list of appealing attributes is quite a long one."

"Now, girls, you best not forget that that's my son you're talking about."

Ruth said it with the same teasing tone her daughter had used, and when Annemarie replied, her voice was thick with laughter. "Yes, ma'am."

The kitchen, when they entered, was already crowded. Gabe's six sisters-in-law had everything under control, so Annemarie positioned herself beside the island that separated the kitchen from the main living area to watch Gabe, his brothers and brother-in-law, father, and older nieces and nephews indulge the younger kids. Gabe seemed to be the favorite uncle, and though it would've been easy for her shy son to be forgotten in the chaos of his nieces' and nephews' demands for his attention, his focus was on Cody. She knew her son adored him, but it was undeniable now that the feeling was reciprocated.

Annemarie let out a long, slow breath, and for the first time since her son's birth, she opened herself to the possibility of something more than her lonely, financially precarious position, let herself pretend that this blissful sense of being a family with him and Gabe was her life.

Chapter Six

GABE LOUNGED IN ONE CORNER of his parents' giant U-shaped couch with his feet propped on the coffee table. Cody was curled against his right side and Annemarie sat on his left with her feet tucked under her and her knees pressed against his thigh. He was exhausted but more content than he'd been in a long time. Maybe ever.

Cody had been still for a while now, and glancing down at the young boy tucked against him, he was unsurprised to find the kid sound asleep. He shifted Cody's head from his waist to his thigh—only a kid could doze off with his neck in that awkward position—and combed his fingers through Cody's hair. He decided against alerting Annemarie just yet. She was too cute and too relaxed, and he was in no hurry to see the strain return to her eyes. Carefully, so he didn't attract her notice, he tugged the afghan from the back of the couch and draped it over Cody.

The only sound that disrupted the quiet was the crackling of the merry fire in the big stone hearth across the living room. The room wasn't silent because it was vacant. His parents and all seven of his siblings and their spouses were draped on the couches. The younger kids had been put to bed, and the teenagers and early-twenty-somethings had retired to the game room, but with eighteen adults, the room was still plenty full. It appeared that everyone else was as content to enjoy their drinks and this rare moment of peace as he was.

"Okay, I think I finally have everyone straight," Annemarie said, breaking the silence. She sat up straighter and pointed to Gabe's eldest brother. "Samuel was the first born."

"Thanks for not calling me the *oldest*," Sam quipped, raising his beer in acknowledgement.

"Your wife is Barb, and together you have Brandon, Joey, Mary, Jake, and Luke. Joshua—Brandon and Penny's son—is your first grandbaby."

"That's our crew," Barb replied, nudging her husband's foot with hers.

"Then came Isaiah, who's married to Deb. You two have Owen, Martha, and Charlie."

"Hank is our eldest," Isaiah corrected. "Owen is Ezra and Nancy's."

"Darn it," Annemarie muttered. "Sorry. I'll get it, I promise. Okay, so, Isaiah, you and Sam are the only ones who've stayed on the ranch."

"Not by choice for some of us," Ezra replied. "I

would've stayed, too, and I think Abe and Gabriel would've, but there's just not enough ranch for all of us. In fact, Michael, you're the only one who never had any desire to stay, right? Lilah, you would've, wouldn't you?"

Delilah shrugged. "I would've been happy to stay, but I'm just as happy running the bowling alley."

"All right, let me get back to this. Ezra, you and Nancy have the all-boy crew—Owen, Ian, Liam, Tristan, and Sean."

"That's us," Nancy remarked with a sigh. "One great big heap of testosterone, but as outnumbered as I am, I have no desire to try one more time for a girl."

"You can borrow ours any time," Emmanuel said.

"That's right. You and Linda have all girls," Anne-marie said. "Izzy, Beth, and Katie. And you're next after Ezra, right, Manny?"

"Yep."

"Abe, you were next, and you and Cindy have Mark, Zach, Sammie, and Cole. Michael and Karen, you have Jessen, Hannah, and Gail."

"Right you are," Michael confirmed.

"Next up is you, Gabe." She poked him playfully with a conspiratorial wink at his mother. "No wife or kids yet."

He chuckled, too amused that she was already picking up on his family's teasing to be annoyed. "That's me, the odd one out."

"And last is Delilah, who's married to Andrew. You two manage Yellowstone Lanes in Cody, and your kids are

Ryan, Christine, and Meghan with James due any day. And, except for Gabe—" she gave him a sidelong glance "—everyone's done having kids already."

"We were done after Meghan," Delilah said with a laugh, tugging on the hem of her sweater, which had inched up her belly a bit. "And then, surprise! What about you, Annemarie?"

"I've only ever wanted one or two."

"Gabe's never wanted more than one or two, either. Of course, the rate he's going, he's more likely to end up with zero."

Gabe rolled his eyes at the blatant hint.

"Let's talk about *why* Gabe's taking his sweet time," Ezra said.

"Let's not," Gabe said sharply. "Annie already knows."

"You're shittin' me. You already told her about Leigh? Well, hell, this is getting interesting."

"Stuff a sock in it, Ezra, before you ruin my good mood. I've already talked about Leigh too much today."

"No one here gives a rat's ass about Leigh," Sam said. "She's right where she belongs, anyhow."

"Where's that?" Annemarie asked.

"In a prison cell for felony grand theft. For at least five more years. Hopefully longer." Sam rose to his feet and looked pointedly at the rest of their brothers. "Before we put a sizeable dent in Gabe's good mood, I'm going to call it a night. Annemarie, goodnight, sweetheart, and if I don't see you and your boy before you leave tomorrow morning, it has been a delight meeting you."

"Goodnight, Sam. The feeling is mutual."

Sam reached across the coffee table and smacked Gabe's foot. "Sorry if Ezra pushed it too far again."

"He didn't."

The rest of his brothers and their wives vacated the living room soon after Sam and Barb, motivated by a stern look from Ruth. John waited a few more minutes before following his sons out of the room, leaving only Ruth, Delilah, Andrew, Annemarie, Gabe and a snoozing Cody to enjoy the peace that again descended. Andrew got up to toss another log on the fire in the big hearth. It was a particularly sappy piece, and it snapped and popped loudly. Or maybe it was just so quiet in the room that the sound only *seemed* loud.

"It was a good day," Ruth murmured. "A good weekend."

"Mmm," Gabe agreed. "Feels good to be tired after a long day of branding."

"I know I've said it at least a dozen times, Ruth," Annemarie said, unexpectedly resting her head on his shoulder, "but thank you for having Cody and me. We've had a wonderful time, and I wish you would've let me help more so we weren't such an inconvenience."

"Next time," Ruth replied. "The first time, you're a guest. After that you're family. Besides, with my crew, you and your boy aren't even a big enough drop to make a ripple in the bucket."

Annemarie laughed softly. "No, I guess not."

Andrew rose from the couch and kissed his wife. "All right, folks. Stick a fork in me because I'm done. I can't keep my eyes open, so I'll leave you ladies to harass Gabe in peace."

After Andrew departed, Gabe waited for his mother and sister to start in on him, but it seemed they were as happy to enjoy the quiet as he was. The weight of Annemarie's head on his shoulder slowly grew heavier until she jerked upright.

"I'm sorry. I guess I won't be staying up much longer, either," she mumbled. When she glanced at her son, her eyes instantly became more alert. "When did he fall asleep?"

"A while ago."

"You should've said something, Gabe."

"Why? He's fine, Annie. He's comfortable, and I don't mind."

"Are you sure?"

"Completely. Let someone else shoulder the burden for a little while and relax."

"I *have* been. Did you not notice me almost falling asleep on you just now?"

"I didn't mind that, either."

"So, if it happens again...?" She wiggled her brows.

He decided her liked her playful side and wondered what it would take to bring it out more often. "Fine by me."

"What if I decide to mimic my son and use your leg as a pillow?"

"Help yourself." He glanced at his mother and sister. They watched him with amusement twinkling in their eyes. "Don't even start."

Ruth held her hands up, but Delilah replied with a devilish grin. He almost wished he could convince Annemarie to stay awake to save him from his sister. Almost. He draped his arms on the back of the couch and met his sister's gaze head on. Her lips quirked. She'd leave him alone, but if Annemarie *did* fall asleep, it was on.

When Annemarie laid her head on his leg and smiled shyly up at him momentarily before she shifted onto her side facing the fire with her hands tucked under her cheek, he forgot about Delilah. It was everything he could do to stop himself from tucking her light brown hair behind her ear. Her willingness to cross the line first from acquaintance to friend and from friend to whatever this turned out to be surprised him, given her initial reserve.

Recalling how quickly she'd asked *when* after he'd said he wanted to take her out, he let his head fall back against the cushion. There was no stopping the smile that claimed his face, so he didn't try.

He almost nodded off himself, beckoned into the land of dreams by the weariness in his body and the saturating peace of the evening. His job was physical, but his body was used to that work. Today, he'd used muscles in ways he hadn't since branding time last year. They weren't sore yet, just taxed and leaden, but he was certain he'd be hurting in the morning. No one would hear him complain, though. As he'd told his mother, it was the best kind of tired to be, the kind that came with a sense of accomplishment. And to be back on the ranch he loved? Heaven. For the time being, he wasn't thinking of his full work schedule, finishing Annemarie's cabin, or any of the myriad of other things that usually plagued him. He was too tired, even, to give much thought to the possible complications of getting involved with Annemarie. He still hadn't worked through what those might be. Hadn't allowed it to distract him.

He'd have to work through them and sooner rather than later.

Not right now, though. He didn't have the brainpower for that kind of ruminating.

"Annie?" he whispered.

No response.

"She's out cold, Gabe," Delilah observed. "You just make too good a pillow."

"Never heard you complain about that, kid."

"You are barely a year older than me," she retorted, mimicking his remark that afternoon.

Ruth chuckled. "It warms my heart to hear you two teasing each other again like you used to."

"We never stopped, Mom," Delilah said.

"Gabriel did for a while."

He started to argue that he hadn't, then stopped himself. "I guess I did."

"You had a lot on your mind. And on your heart." His mother nodded her head at Annemarie. "I know it's early yet, and you barely know her, but I think she's going to be good for you. She *and* her boy there. Such a little cutie."

This time he couldn't resist. He gently fingered a lock of Annie's hair and pulled it back off her face. She didn't stir. Neither did Cody when he tucked the blanket around the boy's small shoulders. "I think so, too. I hope so, anyhow."

His mother and sister studied him with identical expressions—lips pursed, eyes narrowed, and heads tilted to the right. So much for being too tired to ponder the complexities of a relationship with Annie. Obviously, if they had picked up on something amiss, a hint of doubt had crept into his voice.

"Why wouldn't she be?" Ruth inquired. "She seems like a wonderful girl to me."

"Does this have anything to do with the fact that Cody is Tom Grant's son?" Delilah asked before Gabe could answer their mother's question.

"How the hell did you figure that out?"

"Uh, Cody *Grant* Garrett? She used the full name this morning when he was chasing the chickens trying to catch one to pet, and I put that together with the five hundred acres the Grants gave them. Seems pretty obvious to me. And it sounds like you've had confirmation that it's true."

He nodded. "She has proof. The kind even Tom can't refute."

"You sure you want to be a stand-in daddy to that cheater's bastard?"

Gabe bristled. It didn't seem right to apply that term to such a sweet boy, and he knew his sister didn't mean it how it sounded. "If it were just Annie and Cody, the only doubt I'd have would be about whether or not we have what it takes to last a lifetime. But there's a lot about her relationship with Tom that I don't know, and yeah, it scares me a little. I don't know if there's more to her decision to move to Cody than what she's said—that she wants Cody to be close to his roots."

"You think she might still have feelings for him?"

"I don't know. You spent most of the day talking with her. What do *you* think?"

"Well, she mentioned that there hasn't been anyone since him."

"Which could mean that she does."

Delilah regarded him with brows raised. "You don't believe that or you wouldn't have brought her home to meet your family. Anyhow, that's not the impression I got."

"Not the one I got, either," Ruth agreed. "She's been hurt, and maybe there's some residual attraction left, but she's too smart to ever act on it. She learned her lesson well. Just like you learned your lesson with Leigh. Would you ever take her back after what she did?"

"Never." He let out a long sigh. "That aside, there's the issue of having to deal with Tom. Maybe he's refusing to claim Cody now, but what happens if he changes his mind? If he wanted to fight for his son, he could win."

"I don't see that happening. For one, he already has

two kids with his wife. For another, I don't see Sandy *ever* agreeing to that."

Gabe snorted. "She's definitely not thrilled to have Annie so close."

"Of course not," Delilah retorted. "Cody is undeniable proof that her husband is a piece of shit."

"To hear her tell it, it was all Annie's fault."

"Gabriel."

His mother's quiet entreaty drew his attention, and it amazed him how that gentle smile of hers could still soothe him even though it had been a long time since he'd been her little boy.

"You took a big step bringing her here. It shows me that you're ready to give love another chance. Now it's time to take the next step."

"And that is?"

"Getting your brain to shut up so you can hear your heart. I know we've all teased you relentlessly this weekend, but it tells me a *lot* that you brought Annemarie out here for what has always been a *family* tradition."

"I get what you're saying, Mom, but I don't want to dive in head first. Last time I did that—"

"She is not Leigh," Ruth said sternly. "You're right to protect yourself, but there's a difference between protecting yourself and letting the past stand in the way. Keep your eyes open this time."

"You say that like you think there's something to watch out for."

"I can't say if there is or not because I am not you.

I don't know what will be wrong for you. Only you can know that. Your mind has raised some concerns, but now it's time for your heart to decide if they're real and if they're something you can deal with if they are." Ruth rose to her feet and ran her fingers through his hair before kissing the top of his head like she had countless times in his childhood. "It's a fine line between one kind of stupid and another—between protecting yourself from false love and throwing away what could be real love. I have faith you'll find it. Good night, Gabriel."

Gabe watched her go with his brows drawn together. Maybe it would all make sense when he was more lucid, but right now, he couldn't tell if she thought his doubts were baseless or legitimate. He dragged his hand over his face, then leaned back into the couch cushions and stared at the popcorn ceiling speckled with silver glitter he used to think looked like stars.

"Was she that ambiguous when you started dating Andrew?" he asked Delilah.

"If not worse. I guess ambiguity is better than Dad's 'go ask your mother'. It's something, at least."

"What do you think?"

"I think you're worn out from working your ass off today and that thinking about this tonight will only result in you tying yourself in a knot. I also think she's right."

"You're a big help."

"Okay, fine. How's this? I really like Annemarie, and even if nothing lasting comes of this, I agree with Mom. I think she'll be good for you."

Delilah sauntered away without another word. She turned off the lights on her way out of the room, leaving only the dying fire to illuminate the space that suddenly felt enormous without the rest of his family to fill it with chatter and laughter.

He briefly considered attempting to untangle his mother's conflicting advice but Delilah was right. He stretched out as much as he could without disturbing Annie or her son and knitted his hands behind his head. For a while, he stared at the ceiling, mesmerized by the play of golden firelight and shadow as the writhing flames slowly dimmed. Weariness pushed everything from his mind, and he let his eyes close. As he drifted off, he held on to the hope that this moment would be the first of many like it.

Chapter Seven

"WHY DID YOU WANT me to meet you in the barn?"

Annemarie looked over the back of her buckskin gelding. Gabe strode across the aisle of the barn holding up the note she'd tacked to the front door of her cabin. As usual, he was dressed in jeans, a long-sleeved, button-up denim shirt, and work boots. Her heart fluttered, remembering the first time he'd walked through that door. The image presented to her was almost exactly the same, except for the time of day and a pair of saddled geldings in place of a laboring mare, but so much had changed. The first time he'd walked into her barn, Gabe had been a stranger. He definitely wasn't now, and she was glad to see him for entirely different reasons.

"And why are River and Sundance saddled?" he asked, reaching her and Cody and the horses.

"We're going for a ride!" Cody piped before she

could reply. "Mom says it's too nice a morning to be inside working."

"It is," Gabe agreed. "But I really need to get the wiring finished. I don't like that it's taken me *this* long."

"We've lived in the cabin for five months now. A few more hours aren't going to make any difference." Annemarie led River out of the stall and handed the buckskin's reins to Gabe. "Besides, after the gray week we've had, Cody and I really need to get out and enjoy the sunshine."

He skimmed his hand over River's tawny neck with disappointment darkening his eyes. "Then go for a ride. I can work while you're out."

"Gabe. Your face right now says it all. Please come with us. Work can wait."

"Annie…."

"We'll make it a short ride. An hour or two tops. That should give you plenty of time to finish after, right?"

"Unless something goes wrong, which has happened more than once already."

"Just get on the horse."

Boyish. There was no other way to describe the grin that spread across his face because right then Gabe looked exactly like her son. Her face lifted to match. *I win.*

"Can I ride with Gabe?" Cody asked.

"If it's all right with him," she answered, "you're probably safer riding with him, anyhow."

"Come on over here, kiddo," Gabe said, waving the boy over. He lifted Cody into River's saddle and led the gelding out the big door.

Annemarie climbed into Sundance's saddle, guided the palomino outside, and held River's reins while Gabe closed the door. He wore his Collins Electric ball cap rather than the trademark Stetson both Tom and his father preferred, but the natural fluidity with which he swung into the saddle behind Cody screamed *cowboy*. They rode side-by-side toward western edge of Garrett Ranch, past the pasture where her small herd of black and red Angus grazed on the scattering of tender shoots of spring grass at last beginning to make an appearance.

Annemarie couldn't help but watch Gabe as he rode. He was entirely at home in the saddle, and he moved so seamlessly with the horse that she couldn't tell where he ended and River began.

A plastic bag had blown in from somewhere and snagged on a sagebrush, and when a faint breeze set it to flapping, River spooked and hopped sideways. Gabe sat it out with aplomb, soothing the startled horse with a quiet voice. Cody—safe in his arms—didn't budge, and Annemarie didn't have a chance to be afraid for him. Shaking her head, she let out a soft laugh. Despite her accumulating experience on the back of a horse, she'd never come close to that born and bred skill.

They continued north and west along the bench, and as the sun burned away the morning's lingering chill, Gabe tipped his head back and closed his eyes. The smile that played across his features was poignant and endearing, and helplessly enthralled, Annemarie took in the lines of his jaw and neck, let her eyes roam from broad shoulders down strong arms all the way over his long legs and back up. Sexy? Yes. Masculine? Definitely. Desirable? Absolutely, and in every way beyond physical. He belonged out here with a horse beneath him and the wide blue sky above.

"Fascinating," she said.

He opened his eyes and turned his gaze on her. "What is?"

"You. You're in your element." She tilted her head and regarded him with a thoughtful frown. "I saw it last weekend, too, watching you and your brothers branding. You're a gifted electrician, and it's clear you enjoy your work, but this is different. It's… spiritual. Does that make sense?"

"It does. When my grandmother used to try to get my grandfather to go to church, he used to say this was the only church he ever needed."

She thought again of how Gabe's confidence manifested itself in a quiet, unobtrusive way that was further softened by his innate kindness, and when she factored in the way he rode with her son leaning back against him utterly trusting and delighted, something in her settled. He didn't just belong out on a ranch. He belonged *here*. With her and Cody.

How could she feel like that when she'd known him a barely more than a month and they hadn't yet been on a real date?

"So, tell me, Gabe. If this was your ranch, what

would you do to improve it?"

He lifted his brows. What would he read into her question? Would he hear only what it was on the surface—a simple request for an informed opinion—or would he hear what was beneath it? He hesitated long enough that she suspected both, but he didn't question her.

"First thing I'd do would be to get a water diviner out here to help me find the best place to punch an irrigation well. Then I'd turn this bench into hay and alfalfa fields. The sage flats aren't likely going to be good for much. Too rocky and dry, and the wind and run-off have stripped them of topsoil."

"You probably think I'm crazy for trying to make this work," she murmured

"It won't be easy," he said slowly. "But I don't think you're crazy."

"What else could you call me for doing this?"

"Stubborn, maybe." He glanced down at Cody. "This is a great life for a kid."

"Do you… do you think I can make this work? Be completely honest with me. Please."

"You won't ever get rich, but yeah, I think you can make this place turn a profit." He nodded toward the westernmost fence line. "How long's that been down?"

She followed his gaze and groaned. She'd forgotten about the broken post that had dragged the barbed wire down. "A few weeks now. Jim was supposed to get up here to fix it, but he's been so busy down at the Grant

Ranch lately."

Gabe eyed the fence with a scowl. "That's another thing I'd do—if this were my ranch. Hire someone more reliable. That's the third thing I know of he's let you down on since I've known you."

"It's not his fault."

"How do you figure? You're paying him to help you, and he isn't."

"I'm not actually employing Jim. He works for the Grants, and Thomas—senior, of course—pays him extra to help me." She sighed. "I need to get it fixed soon, though, so I can move the cows over to this pasture."

"Well…." Gabe glanced back toward the barn. "We can either postpone our date or I'll have to finish wiring the cabin some other day. After work tomorrow and Tuesday if I have to."

"Does postpone mean we won't get to go to the pizza place?" Cody asked.

"I'm afraid so, squirt," Gabe replied.

Cody's shoulders slumped in disappointment, and Gabe pressed his lips into a line.

"I guess that answers *that* question. Looks like I'll be finishing the cabin after work."

"Gabe, you don't have to do that. He knows how to handle being told no."

"I know he does," he replied quietly. "That's why I don't want to tell him no right now. Let's head back and get what we need to fix the fence. You have a post-hole digger and a wire stretcher, right?"

"I'm pretty sure."

"We have to head back already?" Cody asked.

"If you want to go get pizza tonight," Gabe said, "yes, we do. Your mom and I need to get that fence fixed."

She hadn't realized the passage of time, but they'd already been out riding for close to two hours, and by the time they returned to the barn and unsaddled the horses, it was almost one. Since they hadn't eaten, Gabe volunteered to find and load the requisite materials and what tools he didn't have into his truck while she made sandwiches to take along. Another thirty minutes gone. Because the downed fence was on the far corner of the ranch from the cabin with only a primitive, rock-strewn, rutted trail to it, it took almost half an hour to get back to it. Two o'clock. They scarfed their sandwiches and got to work.

Please let this be an easy fix. She did *not* want to postpone their date any more than her son did. They'd been looking forward to it all week.

Tugging the leather gloves she'd remembered to grab out of her truck at the last minute before they'd left the cabin, Annemarie rolled up her sleeves. The air was still cool, but the sun was hot, beating down on her with a relentlessness that would soon have sweat dampening her skin. It had to be sixty degrees already, and after the cold and fitful snow flurries of the past week, her body wasn't used to the heat.

While Gabe pulled the tools out of the back of his truck and Cody perched on the tailgate to watch, she lifted the downed post and examined it. Its base was rotten—no doubt because it was right in the middle of a narrow ditch where water ran when it rained or the snows melted—and it probably hadn't taken much to snap what had been left. The barbed wire appeared to be intact, but she straightened the post to see. Sure enough, though they were rusty, all three strings were whole and undamaged, so they only needed to replace the post. She dropped the old one and turned toward the truck to grab the new post.

That shift in position saved her face and neck.

The top wire snapped, and it sprang back with the sudden release of tension, whipping a barb across the forearm she lifted to protect the side of her face. It snagged in her upper arm just below her shoulder, and she let out a yelp.

"Oh, Jesus, Annie!" Gabe cried, leaping to her side. "Are you all right?"

She carefully plucked the barb from her arm and released the wire. "Ow."

"Let me see."

The barb had torn a long gash from the outside of her wrist nearly to the inside of her elbow, but it appeared to be narrow and shallow. Gabe's hands were as gentle as they were strong as he inspected the cut, and the concern in his eyes was a powerful distraction from the stinging. When he delicately peeled her shirt and bra strap down over her shoulder, lifting the material away from her skin so he didn't drag it across her wound, she sucked a breath through her teeth. He briefly met her gaze with apologetic eyes, probably thinking he'd hurt her. The puncture in her shoulder burned and ached at once, but it too was relatively small.

"I don't think you'll need stitches, but we should get these cleaned up." He glanced over his shoulder at her son, who had jumped off the tailgate and inched his way closer to see if she was all right. "Cody? Would you grab the first aid kit out of my truck? It's under the passenger seat. Come sit on the tailgate, Annie."

She did as he asked, and Cody zipped around from the cab of the truck with a large, well-stocked first aid kit in hand.

"How practical of you," she mused, catching Gabe's gaze.

He held out one of his hands for her inspection, and for the first time, she noticed the numerous fine scars. As much as those capable, long-fingered hands fascinated her, she'd never paid much attention to the details, and she realized that, no matter how careful he was, minor injuries were par for the course in his line of work—both as an electrician and on the ranch.

She winced when he cleaned her wounds with antiseptic.

"Sorry," he murmured.

"For what? Taking care of me?"

One corner of his mouth twitched, but the frown returned as he concentrated. The puncture was easy enough to bandage, but the jagged cut on her forearm was so long that it took several non-stick pads to cover it. He wrapped a gauzy bandage around her entire forearm and tucked the ends under. She liked the way he let his hands linger as if he were reluctant to break contact. When he spoke, his voice was quiet.

"There you go. All patched up."

"Is Mom going to be okay?" Cody asked.

"I think so, squirt," Gabe replied. "It looked worse than it is."

"I'm lucky," Annemarie agreed. "If I'd turned away even half a second later, it would've gotten me in the face."

"Lucky indeed." Gabe tugged her shirt back into place and reached into the bed of his truck to grab the new post and post-hole digger.

Annemarie remained where she was for a few minutes, assuring Cody that she would be just fine. The sound of the post-hole digger striking the ground drew her attention to Gabe. She felt like she was watching someone dance and waiting with anticipation for the right moment to step into the swing of it with him. There was a strange and wonderful rhythm between them, and more and more as the days passed, she was anxious to embrace it fully.

Without a doubt, she'd never felt *anything* like it with Tom.

"Is Gabe gonna be my dad now?"

Her head whipped around to her son faster than the barbed wire that had attacked her. "Wh-what?" she stammered. "Where did you get an idea like that?"

"When I told Caleb about last weekend at Gabe's ranch, he said Gabe might want to be my dad like Tad wanted to be his dad."

"I don't know, Cody. Maybe."

"How come Tom doesn't want to be my dad?"

"I can't answer that, Cody. All I can say is that he doesn't know what he's missing." She wrapped her arms around him, wincing when her injuries complained. "Because you are a wonderful little boy."

"Do you think Gabe thinks I'm wonderful?"

She shifted her gaze to the electrician and smiled. "I know he does. But being a dad is a big job—even more so when one man's already turned it down—and Gabe may not want to take that on. He may just want to be our friend."

"That'd be okay, too," he said thoughtfully. Then he smiled. "But I'd rather have him as my dad."

Annemarie was torn between amusement at her son's response and the pain that he'd been robbed thus far of the happy family so many of his friends at school had. Until he'd started kindergarten in the fall, he hadn't been aware that his situation was unusual, but he certainly was now. She considered herself lucky that he hadn't quizzed her relentlessly about it like he quizzed her about everything else.

"We'll see what happens, bud. In the meantime, I'd better go help Gabe or we *will* have to postpone our pizza date."

Gabe had the hole dug by the time she reached him

despite needing to knock some rocks loose with the pick-ax. It was several feet over from where the old post had been, and when she glanced to the other side of the sandy water track, she saw that he'd dug a second hole. Smart. Replacing the single, ill-placed post with two, out-of-the-waterway posts would ensure this repair lasted longer.

"I'm going to owe you at least another week's worth of bookkeeping for this. At this rate, it'll be Christmas before I fulfill my end of our deal."

"You don't need to add this to our deal."

"Yes, I do. Because you're right. I need reliable help around here."

"We'll talk about it later."

"By later, I assume you mean so much later that you hope I'll forget about it."

He answered with a chuckle and picked up the new fence post and dropped it in the hole.

"All right, boss. What do you need me to do?"

"Hold this upright." He grabbed the shovel and started filling in around the post.

They worked well together, but it still took time to secure the two new posts, run and stretch new wire, and clean up. When the tools were loaded in the truck, Anne-marie glanced at her watch. Four o'clock. Four-thirty by the time they got back, probably five-thirty by the time they were showered and changed. And it would take forty-five minutes to get into town. Too bad they had to cross the Grant Ranch. It would've shaved fifteen minutes off the trip if they could take the Garrett Ranch road.

"One more thing on the list," she muttered. "Fix the road."

The auction was this Friday, and that was a major relief, but she'd already spent the money three times over, so she doubted there'd be any left over for road repairs. And who knew how much it would cost, anyhow? Several thousand dollars, probably, even if she only filled in the part that had washed out without worrying about having the full half mile of it graded.

"Whatever you're worrying about," Gabe interrupted, "quit. The fence is mended, and we're going to have a fun evening. No worrying allowed."

"Right you are."

Back at the cabin, they quickly stowed the tools and the materials they hadn't needed. Annemarie sent Cody to his room to change. Since Gabe had done most of the work—again—she was clean enough to forgo a shower. That should save some time.

"Clock's ticking," she said and shoved Gabe into the bathroom.

He turned around to face her. "Since you're in such a hurry, would you mind grabbing my clothes out of my truck? They're in the little duffel bag on the passenger seat."

She nodded and pulled the door closed, once again surprised by his practicality. Since his original plan for the day was to spend most of it in the attic, he must've brought a change of clothes so he wouldn't have to ride home covered in itchy insulation. Of course, he hadn't ended up crawling around the attic, and she was both glad he'd have to come out at least another day to finish wiring her cabin and annoyed that she was imposing so much on his generosity.

"Oh, towel." She trotted into her bedroom. Because the cabin had precious little storage space, her closet was the only place she had to store linens. She grabbed a clean towel and returned to the bathroom. Gabe opened the door a crack, standing in the tub and holding the sea-themed shower curtain so a blue-and-green polka-dotted starfish obscured the most sensitive part of his anatomy.

"You might need this," she said, holding the towel out to him and stubbornly refusing to let her eyes wander.

"Yeah, that might come in handy. Thanks."

Again, she closed the door and swallowed a giggle as a delightful playfulness bubbled through her. There was a naked man in her house, and the moment was appealing for reasons far beyond the spark of carnal intrigue. Temporary though it was, it held the promise of what it would be like to share her house and her son and her life with that man, to have her own family, to embrace life rather than struggle to survive the circumstances of it.

She opened the front door and immediately jerked back. Her smile disappeared. "Tom. What are you doing here?"

Cody's sire stood on her front porch with his black Stetson perched on his head and that devastating, cocky smile lifting one side of his mouth. Her stomach lurched simultaneously, and she braced her hand on the doorframe, suddenly dizzy.

"Hello, Annemarie."

"Why are you here?" she asked again.

"I came to talk to you about the Torrington auction on Friday."

What about it? she almost asked. The way he glanced behind him at Gabe's truck struck her wrong, so instead, she asked, "Isn't your phone working?"

"I was out this way checking the fence line with Jim, so it was easier to stop by. He said—"

"Does your wife know you're here?" she interrupted.

"No." Undeterred, he hooked his thumbs in his pockets and narrowed his eyes. "Jim said you've hired a driver."

"Not exactly. Gabe offered, and Jim knows that."

"Gabe." His brows dipped and then rose—too smooth to be genuine confusion. "The electrician?"

"Yes." She shouldered past him and strode out to Gabe's truck with stiff, determined steps. The duffel bag was exactly where he said it would be, so she snatched it and headed back inside, fully intending to shut the door in Tom's face if she had to.

"I can spare Jim to drive for you so you don't have to pay Mr. Collins. We hired another hand to fill in for Johnny."

"Thank you, but that won't be necessary." As an afterthought, she added, "I hope Johnny is healing well."

"Well enough, but it's sounding like he may not be

able to come back to work for me."

"What a pity."

"What's with the cold shoulder?" he asked when she brushed past him, shooting out his hand to stop the door from closing after her.

She spun on him. "The only time you've *stopped by* since Cody and I have been living out here was that first day, and then you only came because your mother and father dragged you along. And you've spent the last six-plus years making it *very* clear I was nothing more than a conquest or a... a *dalliance* to you." She cursed her trembling voice and clenched her fingers around the handles of Gabe's bag so tightly her knuckles ached. "So give up the chit chat. Why are you really here?"

"I told you. I—"

"The truth, Tom." Bitterness raged through her so forcefully that she shook with it, but she *would not* cry. "For once in your life, why don't you give it a try?"

She heard the door to the bathroom open, and the way Tom's expression turned from charming to frigid was all the answer she needed. She stepped back—not to invite Tom in but to face Gabe. He walked over from the bathroom door with a towel around his waist, rivers of water streaming down his body, and a dark look in his eyes that made her shiver. In the doorway to the left of the bathroom, Cody appeared wearing only his jeans. If Tom weren't encroaching on her sanctuary, the sight of him imitating Gabe's arms-crossed pose and looking like a shorter, scrawnier, and blonder version of him would have melted her heart.

Irritation at Tom's intrusion flared hotter, burning away the threat of tears.

"Everything all right, Annie?" Gabe asked in a carefully level voice, his eyes locked on Tom.

She turned back to Tom just in time to catch a glimpse of his sneer at Gabe's familiar name for her. As if that tiny clue made it clearer that Gabe was more than her electrician than him standing in only a towel in her living room dripping water onto the scarred pine floor. "Tom was just stopping by to say he can spare Jim to drive my cows."

"I've already made the arrangements to use my family's truck and trailer and cleared my schedule," Gabe said to Tom. "But thank you. If it's not too much trouble, please tell Jim we appreciate the offer. Would you also let him know that he doesn't need to worry about the fence? We fixed that this afternoon."

If Gabe's nickname for her had triggered annoyance, his reference to them as a couple made Tom seethe. He was too practiced, though, to let it show anywhere but in his eyes, which flashed with a possessive gleam that made Annemarie inch away from him and closer to Gabe.

"I thought you were an electrician," Tom remarked, glancing over Gabe.

"If you'll excuse us, Tom," Annemarie said through gritted teeth, "we're already running late."

"Late for what?"

"None of your—"

"Gabe's taking us out for pizza," Cody replied.

"Is he now?"

"Yep."

"You have two seconds to leave before I slam this door in your face." Because two seconds was all she had before she lost what little remained of her composure.

"Too bad you never thought to say that before now."

Disgust muffled her shriek, and it came out as a whimper as she grabbed the door and swung it hard. He jumped back as it rushed toward him, narrowly avoiding getting hit by it. The loud crack as it slammed brought a smirk of satisfaction to her face, but it did little to assuage the surging tidal wave of self-loathing and queasiness.

"Are you okay?" Gabe asked gently after a moment, grazing her shoulder with his fingertips in a show of support.

"I'm fine."

"Why don't I believe that?"

"Allow me to clarify. I'll *be* fine." Cringing, she pinched her lips between her teeth and squeezed her eyes closed. "I'm sorry, Gabe. I didn't mean to snap at you. That was rude and inconsiderate, especially after everything you've done for me, and you deserve it least of *anyone*."

"I can handle it, Annie. I'm a big boy."

She snorted. *You're definitely that.* She opened her eyes and stared at the closed door when she heard Tom's truck leaving. She'd known Gabe was taller and broader than Tom, but it wasn't until just now when they'd been standing eye to eye—or rather eye to chin—that she'd realized he had a good four or five inches and easily thirty pounds or more of muscle on Tom. She couldn't begin to explain why that reassured her. "I know you can handle it, but that's beside the point."

"I'd rather you unload on me than beat yourself up over it. Everyone needs someone sometime. Even a strong, independent woman like you."

"I don't know that I'm all that strong *or* independent, but thank you. Here." She handed him his bag. "Would you mind getting dressed in my room?"

"Uh, sure. Why?"

"I changed my mind. I *do* want a shower after all. Sorry that we're going to be even later."

"After that, I'm surprised you don't want to reschedule."

"After that, I need our date even more."

He cleared his throat. "There should be plenty of hot water left."

She inhaled deeply, held it for a count of five, and then let it out slowly. With her stomach settling and her head clearing, she became suddenly and fully aware of the man beside her, and she pivoted toward him like iron toward a magnet. Though the warm air in the cabin had stopped the rivulets, water still glittered on his skin, clinging to the lines and planes of his body. Only the sight of her son standing in the doorway of his room kept her from reaching out to brush the droplets away.

What shocked her more than her immediate, visceral reaction to Gabe's physique was that it paled in comparison to the emotional connection she felt with him. Again, she had that sense that she was watching him, getting a sense of his rhythm so she could slip right in and join him in that dance without missing a beat.

"You wanted a shower…?"

"Yeah…" she muttered, yanking her gaze away. She ensconced herself in the steamy bathroom and stripped out of her clothes, dismayed by the way her body quivered. At least it wasn't anger or disgust that had her trembling this time, though *this* reason might prove to be a bigger source of consternation. "I guess it doesn't matter if there's any hot water left."

Chapter Eight

"**G**ABRIEL COLLINS! IT'S BEEN too long since I've seen you in here."

Gabe leaned in to give the hostess a quick peck on the cheek without letting go of Annie's hand. "I've been busy. How've you been, Delia?"

"I've been good. Oh, my goodness! Who is this pretty lady and this adorable young man?" she cried, noticing his companions at last.

Jealousy flickered briefly in her eyes, but she was too good to let it stay long. Still, Gabe hoped Annemarie didn't notice.

He stepped back to introduce them. "My date, Annemarie Garrett, and her son, Cody. Annie, Cody, this is Delia Tucci. Her family owns the Buffalo Bill Pizzeria."

"Your date?" Delia asked. "Then I won't keep you. We can catch up later."

Smiling politely, he took up the rear as she led them

to a booth in a quiet corner of the busy restaurant. She took their drink order and sauntered into the kitchen to fill it. There was a time when he would've watched that sassy backside all the way until it disappeared behind the swinging doors, but tonight, whatever interest she'd held for him was absent, and he had a feeling it was a permanent change. Across the table from him, Annemarie pored over the menu with her son even though they'd all decided on a pepperoni pizza on the drive in from Garrett Ranch.

Did she have any idea how beautiful she was to him? Doubtful. She had the kind of self-deprecating humility that would prevent her from seeing herself as anything more than average at best. But she *was* beautiful. It was her eyes. In a face that was more softly pretty than strikingly exquisite, they glittered like a clear summer sky and sucked him in, exuding an innocence that aroused a strong, primal need in him to protect her. How the hell could Tom have looked into those eyes and lied to her and used her like he had?

You have two seconds to leave before I slam this door in your face.

Too bad you never thought to say that before now.

The cocky gleam in the rancher's eyes and the pale horror that splashed across Annie's face in reaction made Gabe ill. What he'd caught of their exchange had relieved some of his concerns but added fuel to others. Annemarie wouldn't ever again be deceived by Tom, and even if she harbored anything other than bitterness and anger for him—doubtful—she wouldn't let it take root. No, the complication that worried him now was Tom's desire to possess what he couldn't have.

The whole story about "sparing" Jim to drive her cattle to auction was a ploy, and a thin one at that. Gabe guessed Tom had heard rumors—perhaps from his own wife—that someone else might be interested in one of his discarded playthings. So he'd come to investigate, and undoubtedly, he'd seen plenty to confirm those rumors. *That* had the potential to land Gabe in trouble. He wouldn't tolerate Tom crossing the line from merely wanting what he couldn't have to trying to claim her.

Delia returned with their beverages and took their order—a large pepperoni pizza, of course—then left them alone. Gabe had told Annemarie earlier that bad thoughts weren't allowed tonight, and since ignoring his own edict would make him a hypocrite, he resolved to worry about Tom later and enjoy his date with Annemarie and Cody. He stood, holding out his hands to them, then led them into the game room. The pizzeria boasted skee-ball, air hockey, several arcade games, and a small, ten-horse carousel that had Cody bouncing in place in excitement. Gabe pulled a quarter out of his pocket and handed it to the attendant. Cody claimed a black horse with ornate blue, green, and silver adornments, and Gabe stood back with Annemarie to watch him ride the wooden steed around and around.

"So… Delia," she said.

"What about her?"

"She's gorgeous. And… friendly. Something

happen between you two?"

Gabe shrugged. "We went on a couple dates a few years ago."

"A few years ago? Was that before or after Leigh?"

"Right after. I wasn't ready."

"Ah. And nothing happened when you were?"

"Nope."

"Why not?"

"I met you."

Her eyes rounded when she caught his meaning. "Oh."

He tugged her hand out of her pocket and with a deliberate unhurriedness, slid his fingers between hers and brought her knuckles to his lips. His favorite shy smile brightened her face, and the way she tilted her head up and leaned in to him invited him to take it a step further. God knew he wanted to take her up on that offer and kiss until they were both breathless, but he didn't. He wanted to savor every touch, taste, and experience with her, and just as much, he refused to let the focus be the physical. He wanted much more than that.

"It'd be all right if you kiss me," she murmured.

"I will, but not yet. I fully plan to be a proper gentleman and treat you like a lady."

"You don't need to do that, Gabe. I'm not some delicate, virginal flower." She snorted. "Obviously. I have a child, for God's sake."

"I know I don't need to, but I'm going to."

"Why?" she asked. Her tone was dull, and the way

she looked away said she wasn't after an explanation but asking *why bother.*

"Because that's who I want to be." With his free hand, he tilted her face up to him again, skimming his thumb along her jaw. Unable to resist, he kissed the top of her head before folding her into his arms. A foot shorter and half his weight, she always felt small to him, but right now, there was a fragility about her, too. "But mostly because you deserve it."

With a sigh, she rested her head against his chest and tucked her arms around his waist. "If you're thinking you need to prove to me that you're different than Tom, you don't. You're about as different from him as it's possible to be... *without* trying."

"Well, that's a relief," he joked. "It's not going to change anything, though."

"I'm not used to this, so please don't be offended if I don't know how to react."

"All the more reason to bring back a little chivalry." He trailed his fingers down her spine, and she shivered. "How're your arm and shoulder?"

"Fine."

"The kind of fine that means you're not, like you used earlier, or are you *actually* fine?"

She laughed softly. "They don't hurt much anymore. And I'm okay the other way, too, now."

"Glad to hear it."

The carousel slowed and stopped, and Cody bounded over, beaming and begging his mother and Gabe to teach him how to play skee-ball. Gabe was happy to indulge him and showed him how to hold the ball, draw his arm back, and release the ball at just the right time to send it rolling rather than bouncing up the ramp to the pockets. After a few practice runs with Gabe guiding Cody's hand, he stepped back to let the boy have at it. On his first solo throw, he sunk the ball into the fifty-point pocket.

"That was a great shot, Cody!" Gabe cheered, grinning almost as broadly as the little boy.

Annemarie rested her hand on Gabe's chest to get his attention and then whispered. "I need to use the restroom. Be right back."

He caught her hand as she turned away and kissed her knuckles again, pleased when her entire face lit up with a delighted smile. Gabe hooked his thumbs in the pockets of his jeans and watched Cody play. For a five-year-old, the kid had a sharp eye and a strong arm. He hit the forty and fifty pockets more often than not and once hit the one-hundred. When he did that, leapt into the air, pumping his fist and hooting with pride. Gabe laughed and held his hand out for a high-five. Cody slapped his hand hard enough to make it sting, and he made a show of shaking the pain off.

A few other kids milled around the arcade area, but Gabe paid them little attention. He glanced over his shoulder to check on their table to make sure Delia hadn't brought out their pizza yet.

"Give it back, TJ!" Cody yelled.

He jerked his head back. An older boy with dark hair had joined Cody and held one of the skee balls high over the little boy's head with a callous sneer Gabe had seen somewhere but couldn't pinpoint. He was ten or eleven, maybe twelve—plenty old enough to know better than to taunt a kid half his age.

"Make me, slimeball."

Gabe plucked the ball from the kid's hand, and the boy whirled on him, full of bluster for about half a second before he realized it wasn't another kid who'd snatched his stolen item. His eyes sprang wide as he craned his neck to look up at Gabe.

"Leave," Gabe said. "Now."

The kid affected a scowl, but the uncertainty in his eyes contradicted the bravado of it. "You can't make me."

Gabe leaned down until he was at eye-level with the kid. "You sure you want to test that theory?"

The kid backed up, his eyes round again. "You c-can't. My dad'll be pissed you talked to me like this, and you don't want to mess with him. He's—"

"First, watch your mouth. Second, I don't give a donkey's backside about who your father is. Don't let me catch you harassing Cody again. Now, git!"

The boy curled his lip but stalked away toward the front of the restaurant. Gabe straightened and handed the ball back to Cody. "Here you go, squirt. Let's see if you can hit that one-hundred pocket again."

Cody stared at the ball but didn't make a move to return to his game.

"All right. Who was that kid?"

"My brother," he mumbled.

Brother? How could…? Tom's son with his wife. Of course. "You mean your half-brother."

He nodded.

"Why does that not surprise me?" Gabe muttered. "Just like his prick of a father."

He squatted in front of the little boy, forcing Cody to look at him. Tears shimmered in the boy's blue eyes and his lower lip wobbled, but beneath the pain of rejection, Gabe saw determination. He opened his arms, and Cody didn't hesitate to throw himself into them. Gabe hugged him tightly, and within seconds, hot tears seeped through the thin material of his T-shirt.

"Don't let him get to you," he murmured.

"Why is he always so mean to me?"

"Because he's a spoiled brat."

"Mom says I'm spoiled. Does that mean I'm gonna be mean like TJ?"

"Absolutely not. You're spoiled with love, and love makes people nice and kind."

"Is that why you're so nice? Because your family spoiled you with love like my mom spoils me with love?"

"You bet that's why."

Cody sighed raggedly and laid his head on Gabe's shoulder. "Good, because I want to be like you. I don't want to be like TJ."

If there was a greater compliment in the world, Gabe couldn't think of it. "I get the feeling you're going to be better than all of us, squirt," he whispered.

Sensing someone watching him, he glanced up. Annemarie stood a few feet away with her lips pressed between her teeth and something in her eyes he couldn't name, but it hit him in the chest like the kick from a horse.

He opened his mouth to fill her in, but she held her hand up.

"I can guess what happened. I spotted Tom and Sandy in a booth near ours on my way back. What'd TJ say this time?"

"Not much. He took the ball from Cody, held it out of his reach… and then I put an end to that."

"Thank you," Annie murmured. "I saw Delia heading to our table with our pizza just a moment ago."

Gabe tried to stand, but Cody wouldn't let go, so he picked the boy up with a steadying arm hooked around his waist and carried him to their table. When they passed by Tom and Sandy's table, TJ let out a crow of laughter.

"Wook it!" he piped. "Wittle baby Cody's cwying. Cwy me a wiver, wittle baby."

"Ignore him, Cody," Gabe whispered and did the same himself.

"That's not nice, TJ," said the little girl just a couple years older than Cody—Tom and Sandy's daughter, no doubt—sitting beside TJ. "Gramps'll tan your backside when he hears you're being mean to Cody again."

Gabe's lips twitched and he sat down at his and Annemarie's table. So Mom and Dad were fine with their son's behavior, but Grandpa Thomas wouldn't be if he heard about it. More and more, Gabe liked Thomas Sr. Too bad his only son hadn't followed his example.

Cody unpeeled his arms from Gabe's neck and slouched in the booth next to him to wait for his mother to flop a slice of pizza on his plate. He glared over the two booths between their table and the Grants' at his half-brother. Annemarie sat across from Gabe and her son with her back to her ex-lover and his family with a notice-able determination to ignore them. Gabe was inclined to do the same, but he kept an eye on Tom.

"This pizza is fantastic," Annemarie purred. "No wonder this is your favorite restaurant. Why have I never been in here before?"

"Because eating out is a frivolous waste of money?" Gabe took a bite of his first slice. "It's good, but not as good as yours."

"You're a liar, but thank you."

"I'm not lying. I like yours better." He leaned back with one arm propped casually on the back of the booth and did his best to ignore the Grants and enjoy his meal.

It wasn't easy.

Numerous times, the rancher glanced their way with what Gabe could only describe as a covetous gleam in his eyes. His wife appeared to be oblivious to his distraction. Or maybe she noticed and didn't know how else to deal with it other than to pretend it wasn't happening. Either way, it was sad, and Gabe felt sorry for her. Maybe his previous conversation with her had left a foul taste in his mouth, but she *was* honoring her vows and standing by her husband even when he couldn't be troubled to do the same, and Gabe admired the courage it took to stay when she had every right to leave.

After they finished their pizza, they ventured into the game room for a little while and let Cody ride the carousel again. Gabe was in no hurry to end their date, but the proximity of Tom and his wife and obnoxious son had soured the mood some. Before, he'd been distracted by shielding Cody from TJ's taunts and then by observing Tom, but now that he wasn't, it occurred to him that it was highly unlikely Tom choosing the same restaurant Gabe had was a coincidence.

Sandy strolled into the game room with TJ and her daughter—Andrea, he learned. After a brief glance at Gabe and Annemarie, the woman was careful not to look their way again. Gabe shook his head. *Sad*, he thought again. *One life to live, and she's squandering it with a man who doesn't give a shit about disrespecting her every time he lets his dick do the thinking.*

"It's getting late," he remarked to Annemarie as the carousel wound down. "Are you ready to call it a night?"

"No," she sighed, "but we should. Cody has school tomorrow."

She didn't mention Tom, but he sensed that she was as ready to get away from the man as he was, so they wrangled an unhappy Cody and left the game room. Gabe headed to the register to pay while Annemarie checked their table to make sure they hadn't left anything behind. Tom lounged at a table near the door, chatting with someone he knew and sipping a beer, but his eyes tracked between Gabe and Annemarie.

"How was everything?" Delia asked, drawing Gabe's attention.

"Great, as always. Thanks, Delia."

"Always a pleasure, Gabriel."

She took his cash, made the change, and he told her to keep it. She wiggled her brows suggestively and leaned over the counter, giving him a full view of the ample breasts nearly spilling out of her low-cut top. Not so long ago, he would've considered taking her up on her offer. Now, it required no effort to keep his eyes on her face.

"I was hoping I'd finally get that third date you promised me," she said quietly, "but it's looking like I never will. It's serious, huh?"

"It's too early to know yet."

His eyes sought Annemarie and took in every line of her body as she sat on the bench of their booth and reached under the table to retrieve the stuffed horse Cody had lost under it and forgotten in the excitement of the evening. Delia was curvier, sassier, and some might say more beautiful, but to Gabe, Annemarie was the more attractive of the two.

"Oh God, it's definitely serious. If you're looking at her like that this early in the relationship, you're a goner."

"Maybe it's true. Everyone seems to think so."

"Who's 'everyone'?"

"Her son's grandfather, my entire family, and now you."

"Hey, as long as she makes you happy, that's what matters, right? But you'll have to forgive me if I hate her."

"Don't hate her. She's got enough to deal with."

"Ugh," Delia groaned, but it disintegrated into laughter. "Get out of my restaurant, you big ol' sap."

He chuckled and walked away. Moments later, his smile faded.

Tom sauntered by Annemarie on his way back to his table, and he leaned down to whisper something in her ear. She snapped upright and for a moment Gabe thought she might slap him. He lengthened his stride.

"If I needed to know what a real man is," she bit out loud enough for the closest tables to hear, "believe me, Tom, you would be the last person I'd look at for an example. Let's go, Cody."

She gripped her son's hand, and when she reached Gabe, she took his, too, and pulled his arm around her shoulders in what he suspected was a deliberate message to Tom. He wasn't about to complain, but the way her body vibrated with tension ignited his temper, and he almost turned around to confront the rancher. But it wasn't his job to fight her battles for her, and she was the kind of woman to resent it if he tried, so he only tightened his arm around her to let her know he supported her. He wouldn't say anything.

For now.

He held the door open for her and Cody and walked them to her truck. At Cody's request, he helped the little boy get buckled in, then gave him a big hug.

"You be a good boy for your mama. See you tomorrow, squirt."

"But tomorrow's Monday."

"I'll be out to the ranch after work to finish the wiring since I didn't get to it today."

"Oh. See you tomorrow, then."

Gabe kissed the top of the kid's head, then walked around to the driver's side. Annemarie leaned against the door, waiting for him with her head tilted and expectant smile lifting one corner of her mouth. God damn, he wanted to kiss her. He wanted to do a lot more than that, but with her son sitting just a few feet away and watching them intently, he tightened the reins on his urges and settled for slipping his hand along her jaw. With his fingers curled around the side of her neck, he brushed his thumb over her cheek and drew her toward him. It wasn't fair to tease her, but he lowered his head like he was going to press his lips to hers, shifting his head to the side at the last second to kiss her cheek instead. Her grunt of disappointment was oddly satisfying.

"How long are you going to make me wait until you kiss me properly?" she asked huskily, staring into his eyes with an intoxicating fire burning in their blue depths.

"Don't know. I'm kinda winging this." He pulled her against him, wrapping his arms around her and resting his cheek on top of her head, and let out a sigh of relief as the tension from their encounter with Tom ebbed at last. "We need to do this again. Soon. But next time, I'll try to pick a restaurant where we hopefully won't be interrupted."

"That *did* cast a bit of a shadow over our evening," she agreed. "But I still had a wonderful time, and I know Cody did, too."

He gave her one last squeeze before releasing her so she could get in her truck. She rolled the window down and started the engine.

"Goodnight, Annie. Drive safe."

"I'll call you when we get home so you don't spend all night worrying."

He hadn't wanted to ask, unsure if she was ready yet to have him worrying about her, so he was glad he didn't need to. Chuckling, he remarked, "I never used to be so transparent."

"Transparent isn't a bad thing to be," she replied. "Makes you easy to trust. Goodnight, Gabe."

"See you tomorrow."

Nodding, she put her truck in reverse and backed out of her spot. He stepped over to his truck and, with his hand on the door handle, watched until her taillights disappeared around the block. Exhaling, he slid in behind the steering wheel and started the engine. As he drove home to his house on the southeastern edge of Cody, he laughed.

Delia was right. He was a goner.

────── *Chapter Nine* ──────

ANNEMARIE SAT ON THE EDGE of one of the dining room chairs chewing on her bottom lip while she watched the dim, wavering glow coming from the open trap door to the basement—the only light in her pitch-black house. She'd put Cody to bed two hours ago, and it hadn't been easy. He'd wanted to stay up to see the lights come on when Gabe turned the power back on, as if they would look any different simply because they were running on new, up-to-code wiring. His weariness had won out in the end, and after Gabe had helped her tuck him in, she had been relieved when he drifted off within minutes. They had a long day in the truck ahead of them tomorrow, and Cody wasn't fond of snoozing on the road, too afraid he might miss something exciting.

Suddenly, light flooded the dining room from the new wrought-iron chandelier Gabe had installed only an hour ago, blinding her dark-accustomed eyes. Moments later, she heard the door on the shiny new breaker panel close.

Gabe climbed out of the musty basement grinning. "That's it. You're officially running on your brand-spankin'-new wiring."

"Completely?"

"One hundred percent. I still have some holes to patch for you, which'll have to wait until we get back from Torrington, but otherwise, you're good to go."

"No more tripped breakers, melted outlets, or bulbs burning out after a week?"

"Nope. Go ahead and try it. Run the microwave and turn the oven on."

"At the same time?"

He chuckled. "Yes, at the same time."

She did, and the breaker didn't trip. Five minutes she waited for it to happen, but it didn't, and she almost squealed her delight. She threw her arms around Gabe's neck, laughing when he locked his arms around her waist and hoisted her off her feet. "Thank you!"

"You're welcome."

"I'm going to be doing your books for weeks yet to pay you back for this."

"Mmm. I'd tell you we're even, but I'm looking forward to having an excuse to come see you."

She buried her face against the curve of his neck and let out a tiny squeak as relief and joy and desire and a dozen other wonderful emotions consumed her.

Realizing his skin was slightly damp and gritty, she leaned back in his arms. He hadn't set her down yet. "You probably want a hot shower right about now, and here I am keeping you from it."

"A shower would be great," he said. "But this is nice, too. Unless you're trying to tell me I stink."

"No… not really." She couldn't quite describe it, but *stink* wasn't the right word. The mustiness of her basement clung to him, but beneath that was a subtle, not unpleasant scent. He smelled… male. "But we do have an early wake-up call, and I'm sure you're exhausted. Between your other jobs and finishing up here tonight, you must've put in close to eighteen hours today."

"Pretty—" He yawned. "—close."

"Go take your shower."

"Yes, ma'am."

While Gabe was in the bathroom, Annemarie made a quick bedtime snack for them, turned off the lights in the dining room and kitchen, and changed into her pajamas, then sat on the couch with her feet tucked under her to watch the flames dance behind the glass door of the wood stove. She'd been too afraid to try lighting a fire in it, certain a bird or some other critter had made a nest in the stovepipe, but Gabe had cleaned both out yesterday, and she added it to the long list of things she was grateful to him for. He had done so much for her in the short time she'd known him that she could keep his books for the rest of his career and never come close to paying him back. It wasn't any single task or even the sum of them all.

It was the peace of mind. It was the hope that she might actually be able to make this life work.

For the first time since a positive pregnancy test had shattered all her carefully organized plans for her future and forced her down a road she hadn't seen coming, she believed she might find real happiness again.

Gabe stepped out of the bathroom wearing flannel pajama pants of a sky-blue and black plaid that brought out the contrast of his dark hair and gorgeous blue eyes. She was disappointed that he also wore a plain white T-shirt. She'd been hoping for a repeat of Sunday afternoon so she could have a chance to fully appreciate him without Tom's intrusion to distract her.

An absurd thought struck her, but it became less off-the-wall when she recalled the day she'd met him and how he'd asked her to turn around while he stripped out of his stained T-shirt and changed into his button-up work shirt.

"Gabriel Collins, you aren't shy… are you?"

"Maybe a little."

"But… why?"

He shrugged and grabbed his sleeping bag, pillow, and the rolled-up memory foam. "I'm going to blame my brothers."

She helped him unroll the narrow foam in front of the couch. "Did they tease you?"

"Mercilessly. They thought it was funny how long it took me to shed the baby fat."

"You were a chunk? I don't believe it."

"Well, I was until about twelve or so, and then the growth spurts started, and I couldn't add weight and muscle fast enough. Guess I never outgrew the self-consciousness."

She tried to picture it but couldn't. Maybe she'd ask his mother for pictures the next time she visited the family ranch. "I'm afraid of what Cody's going to go through when he hits that stage because he's already such a slender kid."

"Maybe he'll get lucky and take the slow and steady route. How tall do you think he'll be?"

"I'm guessing he'll reach an inch or two over six feet."

He glanced at her with his brows lifted and a teasing glint in his eyes. "You think he'll be that tall, huh?"

She stuck her tongue out at him. "The boys in my family get all the height. Dad is six-one, and Robert is six-two, while I barely managed to reach five-five."

"Poor you."

"The only time you'll hear me complain might be when I need something on the top shelf."

He sat on the couch beside her to lay his sleeping bag out on the foam pad, pausing for a moment with his elbows braced on his knees and barely enough energy left to lift his head. After scrubbing his hands over his face and through his damp hair, he finished getting his bed ready but made no move to get into it. She rubbed her hand across his back, and he turned his head toward her, smiling tiredly.

"That feels good," he mumbled.

"Why don't you take your shirt off and lie down, and I'll give you a proper back rub."

"We've been on one date and you're already trying to get me out of my clothes?"

"Sorry to burst your bubble, but I've already seen you pretty much naked with nothing more than a cartoon starfish to preserve your modesty. And you didn't seem to have a problem strutting out of the bathroom when Tom showed up."

"First of all, I didn't strut. Secondly, that was different."

"How so?"

"I had to make sure you were all right. The distress in your voice...." He shook his head, frowning. "I don't like it when you're upset. It does strange things to me."

Annemarie didn't know how to respond to that, so she smoothed her hand over his back and shoulders again and stared into the fire.

"Mind if I grab a glass of water?" he asked.

"Help yourself."

Hands on his knees, he pushed himself off the couch, and her gaze followed him into the kitchen. Would she ever get tired of watching him? Highly unlikely. Glancing over his bed for the night as she sat beside it to wait for him, she asked, "Wouldn't a blow-up mattress have been more comfortable?"

"The only ones I've ever tried to sleep on weren't long enough, and I spent the night either scrunched up or with my feet hanging over the end," he replied, striding into the kitchen. "Didn't get much sleep. Believe me, shorty, the foam is *way* more comfortable. Try it."

"Shorty? Gee, thanks." She stretched out on his makeshift bed. With the sleeping bag laid over it, it was more comfortable than her springy old mattress. "Okay, you're right. It's better than my bed. Wanna trade? Or, better yet, can I join you down here?"

"Tempting."

"But you're not going to let me."

"I need to get some sleep, Annie, so I don't run us off the road tomorrow."

She sat up and stuck her bottom lip out in a mock pout, and he nearly choked on his water. He set the empty glass in the sink and wandered back into the living room, dragging his T-shirt over his head with an adorable reluctance. It was possible that his remark about his brothers teasing him might have been exaggerated, but he *was* shy about his body.

Foolish man.

"Would you quit looking at me like that?" he muttered.

"Why? You're incredibly sexy, Gabe, and you should be proud of that. I imagine it took a lot of hard work to get that way and even more to maintain it."

With a grunt, he lowered himself to the floor and slid into his sleeping bag. She twirled her finger in the air and pointed to his pillow. He lay on his stomach, crossed his arms, and rested his head on them, eying her. She leaned over him, sliding her hands over the tense muscles of his back, and within seconds, his eyes drifted closed and he began to relax.

Tom hadn't ever let her touch him like this, without the assumption that sex would follow, and she realized now that it had prevented a genuine sense of togetherness.

She started to chastise herself for letting him intrude, but the comparison helped her disconnect him from sensuality, and she needed that. As she stroked her hands over Gabe's back, shoulders, and arms, delighting in the contours of muscle and the way they slackened beneath her persistent kneading, she admitted that being able to touch him knowing it *wouldn't* lead to sex was freeing. It introduced a different level of intimacy that had been entirely missing with Tom.

"How's that?" she whispered.

"Mmm. Marvelous," he slurred.

Suddenly, she remembered something she needed to tell him, but she hesitated, disinclined to drag him back to full consciousness. She sighed. It would be better to get it out now before he was more asleep than awake. "I forgot to tell you. Jim'll be here at three-thirty to help you load the cows."

"He doesn't need to do that." His brows furrowed, and he opened one eye. "You and I can manage."

"Trust me. You'll be glad to have him helping you instead of me. And this way I'll be able to get all our bags loaded and hopefully get Cody to go back to sleep in the truck."

"You don't give yourself nearly enough credit, Annie."

Because he'd try to convince her otherwise if she disagreed, she said, "Probably not. Close your eyes."

He was exhausted enough to obey. With a sigh, the tension that had momentarily returned to his body eased again.

She continued her ministrations and let the heat of his skin and the play of golden firelight and cool shadow steal her focus until there wasn't anything left in her head but him. His breathing slowed and deepened, and when she whispered his name, he didn't respond. Tilting her head, she ran her fingers through his hair and watched him sleep for a while.

She'd been wrong to think Tom might have been her first love. He was her first *something* but not her first love. She didn't know if Gabe would be, but the strange wonder that filled her hinted that he might be. To think that she was just now, at almost twenty-five, discovering that she'd never fallen in love was silly.

Or maybe it wasn't. Maybe she wasn't as sullied as she'd claimed when Gabe had told her on their date that he wanted to treat her like a lady. There might be some innocence left in her that hadn't crashed and burned in the sharp turn her life had taken.

Clinging to that thought, she pressed her lips to Gabe's cheek, and tiptoed into her bedroom, leaving the door open. She had no need for privacy from the man who had already done so much to repair her heart.

Chapter Ten

A SHORT FIVE HOURS later at 3:00 AM sharp, Gabe groaned and reached for his battery-powered alarm clock, fumbling until he found the button on top that would make the obnoxious chirping stop. He rolled onto his stomach and propped up on his elbows with his forehead resting on his arms for a moment, wishing he could rewind to right before he'd fallen asleep. He allowed himself several minutes to recall the soothing touch of Annemarie's hands. He never would've imagined that her hands, so fine and soft, could be so strong and confident. The unexpected massage had been a wonderful, much appreciated end to a long day.

With another low groan, he forced his mind elsewhere. Thinking like that wasn't a good idea right now. Not with the woman at the center of his attention likely waking up. And not after the way she'd looked at him last night.

Besides, he had less than half an hour until Jim showed up to help him load cattle.

A curious energy built as he lay there, and the promise of spending the next five days with her and Cody—not just a handful of hours, but every waking minute—spurred him to get up. He dragged himself out of his sleeping bag and tiptoed across the dark house to the bathroom, closing the door before he turned on the light.

He caught sight of his reflection in the mirror and ran his hand over the rough stubble. He needed a shave, but they were on a tight schedule. It'd have to wait until they got settled at the hotel this afternoon.

It took him less than ten minutes to complete his morning routine—minus the shave—but since he'd given himself a few minutes to wake up, he was running behind schedule.

He wasn't the only one. When he stepped out the bathroom, the house was still dark, and there was no movement from Annie's room. He grabbed his T-shirt from the couch cushion where she'd left it neatly folded and started to pull it on, then tossed it over his shoulder instead. She seemed to enjoy the view, so who was he to deny her?

He knocked on her door, mildly surprised she'd left it open.

"Is it three already?" she mumbled.

"Quarter after."

"Frick. Would you turn on the light?"

He found the switch just inside the door with no

trouble; he ought to know where it was, considering that he'd put it there. Light flooded the room, and she blinked against its sudden brightness for a few seconds before reaching for her alarm clock. From across the room, he couldn't read the small clock—identical to his—but it didn't look like the second hand was moving.

"Battery's dead. Good thing you set yours," she muttered, swinging her legs out of bed. Turning to him, her face split in a grin. "Well, hello there. You're not dressed."

He raked his hand through his hair and lowered his gaze. "I was getting to that when I realized you weren't up yet."

She slid out of bed and sidled over to him, gazing up at him with a smile teasing her lips. "Were you this shy with Leigh and the other women you've been with?"

"Yes, but to let you in on a little secret, I haven't been with that many women."

"How many?"

He crossed his arms over his chest, defensive.

"It's none of my business…. But I want to know you, because I apparently didn't know the last man I was with."

Bitterness crept into her voice, and his heart ached for her. Momentarily, he forgot his own discomfort, wishing he could some how spare her from that persisting pain. She had every reason to have trust issues, and after Leigh, he could relate too well to the damage that could do, how it could make even a simple friendship a source of anxiety.

If someone who was supposed to love them could hurt them, anyone could. He wanted her to trust him, to trust her in return, and the surest way to do that was to be open and honest. Even about the things he'd rather keep hidden and safe.

"The first was Leigh," he murmured, stuffing his hands in the pockets of his pajama pants. "The next was my only other serious girlfriend, Jen. Then Leigh again. And only one since who was more of a friend with occasional benefits than a girlfriend."

"Three? That's it?"

"Not including the handful of dates that ended at the front door, yep, that's it."

"The friend-with-benefits—what was her name?"

"Terri."

Her brows shot up. "Terri my vet? You know, I wondered that day Angel was born."

"It was over a long time before I met you." Heat crawled up his neck, and he shifted his weight. "She was looking for a no-strings-attached arrangement after her divorce, and well, I guess that was what I needed then, too."

"Hey, you don't have to explain it to me. I understand what it is to need human contact." Annie flashed a grin. "She's got good taste in men. But she's gotta be, what, eight, ten years older than you."

"I'm eight years older than you." A fact he had a tendency to forget but which was currently quite apparent. She wore a thread-bare white tank top with the brown bronc-rider emblem of the University of Wyoming and a pair of soft, fitted shorts that made her look more like a college freshman than the mother of a six-year-old boy. In the cool air, her nipples were taut, and he quickly averted his gaze before part of his own anatomy decided to salute them. It was too damned early, and he wasn't awake enough yet to reign in the leaping and bucking desire that had been building since they'd first met and was more than ready to break out of the gate.

He turned away and started toward his bag with the thought that now would be a very good time to get dressed, but she curled her fingers around his and tugged.

"Just two for me. Jed, a boy I dated off and on in high school. It wasn't anything serious, just teenaged curiosity. And Tom. He did such a good job of ruining me that I haven't had the courage to take a chance again." She clasped his face and stood on her toes to press a kiss to his cheek. "Until you."

Abruptly, she released him and strode from the room. He stared after her. Talk about a weighty start to the morning.

He grabbed his bag and dressed in her bedroom while she was in the bathroom and was about to roll up his sleeping bag and foam when she joined him in the living room.

"I can take care of that. Jim should be here any minute, and while you boys are loading cows, I'll fix us some breakfast burritos to take with us."

"That would be wonderful."

Headlights flashed across the dark living room—

the only lights they'd turned on were the one in Annie's bedroom, the bathroom, and the dim one over the kitchen sink in an attempt not to wake Cody. A soft knock sounded on the door moments later. Three-thirty on the nose. Gabe answered the door while Annemarie busied herself assembling their bags and piling them on the couch.

He wasn't sure what he'd expected Jim to look like, but the slight, wiry man who looked a lot like a small version of Sam Elliot—right down to the bushy horseshoe mustache—standing on the other side of Annemarie's door wasn't it. The ranch hand was barely taller than Annie and had gentle eyes that contrasted his otherwise stern countenance. The man extended his hand, and Gabe shook it.

"Jim Hanson."

He even sounded a bit like the actor.

"Gabe Collins."

"You apprenticed under Gus Cherry, didn't you. And your family has a spread out Meeteetse way, up the Greybull River somewhere. Gus was a good friend of mine back in the day, and I remember him mentioning an apprentice he thought showed a lot of promise. You're a master electrician now?"

"Yes, sir."

"Guess he was right." He leaned in the door and greeted Annemarie with a smile. "Morning, darlin'."

"Good morning, Jim. Thank you for getting up so early to help."

"Least I could do." To Gabe, the cowhand asked, "Ready to get this done?"

Nodding, Gabe stepped out into the chilly, black morning. The stars were veiled and there was a damp bite to the air that promised snow. The forecast didn't call for any in western Wyoming, but there was a chance he'd run into some around Casper and eastward toward Torrington, and that wasn't supposed to amount to more than a dusting.

The truck he'd borrowed from his parents—a class six that his family referred to as their "mini semi"—was parked down on the bench with the trailer backed up to the loading chute and ready to be loaded, so he climbed into the passenger seat of Jim's old ranch truck. The headlights bounced over the terrain as the truck lurched on the uneven trail. Like everything else on Garrett Ranch, the main "road" that connected the barn, corrals, chute, cabin, and pastures had fallen into disrepair from years without use or maintenance.

"Tom made a pretty damned clear statement giving her this land, didn't he," he muttered.

He hadn't meant for Jim to hear, but the ranch hand responded.

"Yes, he did. Makes me so damned angry that he'd treat such a sweet girl as Annemarie like he does that I've almost quit my job at the Grant Ranch a dozen times in the last year. But I got bills to pay, and not too many folks'll hire a busted old hand like me." Jim glanced at Gabe. "I imagine you don't think too highly of me, the number of times you've had to pick up the slack around here for me, but the other reason I ain't quit is Annemarie. If I quit, she won't have no one to help her out. Maybe I ain't the hand I used to be and maybe Tom's an asshole who likes to make sure I ain't got much left to give her, but I care about her. Thomas Sr. does, too."

"I understand he's the one who pays you to help Annie."

The cowhand nodded. "I wish he'd do more."

"Why doesn't he? He's still the power in that family, isn't he?"

"I think he's still hoping Tom will come around on his own and do the right thing by Annemarie and that boy."

Gabe snorted. There was a better chance of hell freezing over, and Jim's bark of humorless laughter said he thought the same.

"You're right. I haven't thought too kindly of you," Gabe admitted, "and for that I apologize. The fact that you're here to help her at three in the morning says a lot. I assume you won't get paid for this."

"No, sir, I won't."

"When we get back, I'll cut you a check. Just don't tell Annie about it. I won't take no for an answer."

"You don't need to do that. I owe her."

"Maybe you do, but like you said, you have bills to pay."

Jim regarded him with narrowed eyes, then let out a guffaw. "*You're* the man who's got Tom all in a tizzy.

Shoulda guessed. He was in a foul mood Monday morning, saying something about Annemarie hooking up with a man who only wanted her ranch. He tried to make it sound like he was concerned about her, but I wasn't born yesterday. He's jealous as hell."

"Wants what he can't have," Gabe remarked.

"Damned right. You'd best watch your back around him, young fella. He ain't used to not getting his way."

Gabe wanted to ask what he should watch out for as dread coiled in his gut, but they'd arrived at the loading chute, so he said only, "Thanks for the heads up."

Thomas Sr. had helped Gabe cut the cattle heading to auction from her small herd yesterday afternoon before Annie and Cody had arrived home from work and school and sequestered them in the pen attached to the loading chute. In theory, that should've made his and Jim's job easy this morning, but after a night in the pen, the fourteen animals—ten bred heifers and four yearling bulls—wanted back out into the pasture. Between the floodlights on the trailer and the headlights of Jim's truck, they had plenty of light to work by. Piece of cake.

Within five minutes, Gabe was glad for the cowhand's experience. The confines of the pen didn't stop the heifers from trying to dart past him and Jim, but they were able to contain the animals and move them slowly closer to the chute. Neither of them needed to be told what to do, and that made a big difference.

Once the first six were loaded, the rest began to follow along with minimal fuss. Gabe was just about to let out a sigh of relief when the final yearling bull's front left hoof punched a hole in the weathered deck of the chute. He yanked it free, hopping and bucking in fright. Gabe saw his hind legs come up just in time to drag Jim out of the way of the sharp hooves. Unfazed, the cowhand slapped the bull's rump with his cowboy hat, and the animal shot forward into the trailer.

"Don't know what you cows are being so damned ornery about," Jim growled, closing and locking the trailer doors. "Ain't a one of you that's going to the slaughterhouse any time soon. Probably end up someplace a lot greener than this."

Gabe added the loading chute to his list of things to find a way to convince Annie to let him fix, and started his final check of the truck and trailer. He double-checked it, and checked it again, and Jim did the same. Satisfied that the rig was ready for the road, they walked around to the cab.

Jim glanced up at the inky sky and exhaled. His breath was a plume of silver in the headlights. "Miss this?"

"More than a little. I love what I do for a living, but I do get to missing the ranch sometimes."

"It's a special kind of life. Ain't an easy one, but I ain't never wanted anything else."

Gabe nodded in agreement, climbed in behind the wheel of the truck, and drove slowly to the cabin. Jim followed behind in his pickup. Half an hour was all it had taken them to get the cattle loaded and the rig checked. It could've taken a lot longer.

Leaving the truck running, Gabe returned to the cabin with Jim walking behind him. He knocked lightly on the door before opening it, but he needn't have worried about startling Annie.

"Come in for a minute, Jim. I've got some coffee on."

He'd thought he was sufficiently awake now, but the promise of a steaming hot cup of coffee dragged a purr out of him.

"You're an angel, Annemarie," Jim replied, putting Gabe's exact thought into words.

They followed her into the kitchen, leaning against the counter to wait while she poured the coffee. To Jim's, she added a teaspoon of sugar and a splash of half-and-half. After she handed the mug to the cowhand, she turned to Gabe and frowned.

"I don't know how you take yours or if you even drink coffee," she said, perplexed. "But I feel like I should."

"I don't drink it often. Mostly on early mornings like this one. Black is fine, but a little cream would be nice, if it's not too much trouble."

She poured just enough half-and-half in Gabe's mug to turn the coffee opaque. "How's that?"

He took a sip and closed his eyes to savor the rich flavor. "Perfect. Thank you."

They enjoyed their coffee in silence until Annemarie finished hers and washed out her cup. Setting it on the dishtowel laid out on the counter to dry, she said. "You boys got done fast."

Gabe shrugged. "Jim's a great hand."

"See? I told you you'd be glad to have him helping."

"Yes, you did, and you were right."

"That's something you'd never hear Tom say." Jim drained his coffee and set the mug in the sink, then clapped Gabe on the back. "This one's worth hangin' on to, darlin'."

She met Gabe's gaze and smiled. "Yes, he is."

"I'll get out of your hair so you can get on the road. Safe travels."

Gabe grabbed the cooler of snacks and followed Jim out. He opened the rear driver-side door of his parents' truck and settled the cooler on the floor between the driver seat and the back bench so Annie would be able to reach it from the passenger seat. Then he closed the door and walked over to Jim's pickup, reaching in the open window to shake the man's hand. "Pleasure meeting you, sir."

"Pleasure's mine. I look forward to seein' more of you around here in the future."

Jim could've meant that he'd have more time to help Annie out now that calving, branding, and moving cattle to spring pastures was winding down at the Grant Ranch, but Gabe doubted it.

"I'll pay you a visit when we get back."

"You don't have to pay me, you know."

"Depends on how you define 'have to,' don't you think?"

Jim let out a sniff of laughter. "I s'pose it does. I

appreciate it."

Gabe watched the cowhand's taillights shrink into the night with his thumbs hooked in his pockets. He was glad to be proven wrong about the man, and knowing that someone else had Annemarie's best interests at heart was a relief, too. He inhaled, drawing the cold air deep into his lungs, and grabbed Cody's booster seat out of Annemarie's truck. Anticipation of the road trip sang through him as he settled the booster seat in the center of the back seat. He figured they could pile their bags and his sleeping bag and foam roll on one side of the bench with a pillow so Cody could have something comfortable to lean on but still be buckled in.

Annemarie stepped outside with her hands full with his bag and hers. Her mouth fell open. "I thought you said we were taking your parents' smaller truck."

"Minnie *is* the smaller truck."

"What's the *bigger* truck, then?"

"Bertha. She's a class eight—a full-size semi."

"Minnie and Bertha. That's cute."

"Yeah," he agreed. He took the bags from her and stacked them on the bench. "My nephew Cole came up with the nicknames."

"Cole… he's one of Abe and Cindy's sons, right?"

"Correct. Well remembered."

She opened the passenger side door and inspected the interior of the cab. "This is really nice. It's brand new, isn't it? Or close to new."

"Mom and Dad bought it last summer. These

bucket seats are so much more comfortable than the ones in Bertha. She's getting up there in years and miles."

They went back into the house and Gabe finished loading the truck while she finished their breakfast burritos. Since they were ahead of schedule, they ate in the kitchen and after, Gabe helped her wash and dry the few dishes.

"We about ready to go?" he asked, surveying the cabin.

"Yep. I just have to get Cody and do my final check of the house to make sure everything's turned off."

"Why don't I get Cody so you can do your check?"

"You've got a deal."

He tiptoed into the boy's room, and scooped him up—blanket, pillow, and all—with one arm behind Cody's shoulders and the other behind his knees. The kid murmured but didn't wake up. Annemarie had left both the cabin's front door and the truck's rear door open, so he didn't need help getting Cody into the truck, leaving Annemarie free to inspect the house. It was almost like they'd worked it all out in advance.

Like a team.

He buckled the sleeping boy into his booster seat. He propped the pillow against the pile of bags and bedding and gently leaned Cody against it, then tucked the blanket around him. Reverently, he smoothed his hand over the little boy's silky, sandy-colored hair.

There was nowhere else he'd rather be and nothing he'd rather be doing right now.

Annie left the house, locked the door behind her, and joined him at the cab. She tucked her arm around his waist and, after glancing at her son, she gazed up at Gabe with a faint, poignant smile. "He didn't wake up?"

"Nope."

"That's amazing. Last time I had to get him in the car at this time in the morning, he woke up, and I had to deal with a cranky boy all the way to Casper."

"He doesn't like road trips?"

"He loves them. Hence why he wouldn't go back to sleep." She shifted around him, sliding her other arm around his waist and locking her hands together behind his back, and rested her cheek on his chest. "Thank you. For all of this."

He wanted to tell her that it was no trouble, that she deserved what help he could give her and so much more, but the words refused to cooperate, so he folded his arms around her and held her for almost a full minute. Then he let her go, reluctant to end the moment but anxious to put the taillights to Tom and Garrett Ranch and see what would happen when they were away from all the things that stressed Annie and dampened her spirit. "Shall we get this show on the road?"

"Yes, let's."

They climbed into the cab and strapped in, and Gabe shifted the truck into gear, glancing at Annemarie.

She beamed at him. "This is kind of exciting, isn't it?"

"It is," he agreed.

They chatted as the truck rumbled over the gravel road through the Grant Ranch, but despite the coffee, Annemarie struggled to stay awake. Gradually, their conversation dwindled until Gabe finally asked what time she'd gone to sleep.

"It was after midnight," she replied, yawning.

"Why don't you try to get some more sleep?"

"I don't think I'll have to try very hard."

Chuckling, he reached across the cab and gave her hand a squeeze. She didn't make it even halfway to Cody before she drifted off, leaving Gabe alone with his thoughts. There weren't many besides the attention he gave to the truck and trailer, and most of those existed in the background. He turned the radio on low, amused when the song that came on was the one that had topped the country charts all last month—John Michael Montgomery's slow, deeply felt love song "I Swear". He sang quietly along, surprised that he knew it so well since he'd never paid much attention to it. The lyrics resonated in a way they hadn't before, and that probably made him a complete sap, but he didn't care.

"You have a beautiful voice," Annemarie mumbled.

"I thought you were asleep."

"Mmm. Almost."

"I'll stop."

"Please don't."

By the song's end, she was asleep. For real this time, and Gabe refrained from singing along with the radio while he drove through town, as much because he didn't want to wake her again as because navigating the roads of Cody took more of his focus. With sunrise still an hour and a half away, once he left the town behind, there was nothing but two lanes of dark, empty highway in front of him. It was soothing, and Gabe let the absolute peace of the open road saturate him.

He loved his job and, most days, he even enjoyed the freedom of single life, but he'd been nagged by a sense of incompleteness, like he was always waiting for something. For what, he hadn't realized.

He glanced at Annie, took in her beautiful, sleep-relaxed face and the way she sat curled toward him with one knee hooked on the armrest and her hands beneath her cheek. Then he shifted his eyes to the rearview mirror at her adorable son half-sprawled in that deep, oblivious-to-the-world sleep of every kid and puppy he'd ever met.

He knew now what had been missing.

Chapter Eleven

THREE HOURS AFTER LEAVING the Torrington auction, the high of picking up a check from the office for almost half again more than Annemarie had hoped for jumped another notch. Parked behind her parents' black suburban in the looped gravel driveway in front of their doublewide modular on the northern shore of Alcova Reservoir was a familiar red Suburban. She let out a squeal.

"Cody! Uncle Robert and Aunt Julie are here, too!"

"What? They are?"

"Yeah, look. Looks like you'll get to meet my brother and his family, too, Gabe."

"He's not going to pull the protective older brother routine on me, is he?" Gabe joked.

"I don't know if he even has one. None of the guys I dated in high school were ever serious enough for him to go big brother on them, and he's never met Tom.

Besides, I'm pretty sure you could take him."

"Even if I could, I'd have to let him win as a point of deference."

"Meh. It won't come to that, anyhow. He's a softy."

"So says the little sister. Brothers are supposed to be softies to their sisters." Gabe stopped the truck. "Why don't you and Cody head inside while I get this rig turned around?"

He didn't have to offer twice. She unbuckled her seat belt, helped Cody out of his, and leapt out of the truck. Her family had undoubtedly heard the big diesel engine, and they now gathered on the covered deck—her mother and father, brother, sister-in-law and the twin terrors, her three-year-old niece and nephew, Erin and Elijah. The toddlers let out shrieks of joy when they spotted Cody, and her son was just as happy to see them, though with all the wisdom and poise of his five and a half years, he was much better at hiding it.

Her mother didn't wait for them to reach the porch. She trotted down the stairs and met her daughter in the middle of the yard with arms wide. Her father joined them, wrapping his arms around them both.

"Welcome home, sweetheart," he greeted.

With her arms around her parents' waists, she followed her son to the porch where her brother and his wife waited. Annemarie hugged Julianne first, then her niece and nephew together, and finally her brother because she knew that would take longer.

"This is such an amazing surprise, Robert," she

murmured, standing on her toes so she could wrap her arms around his neck. "I've missed you so much."

"Missed you, too." Without letting her go, he leaned back to inspect her. "You look fantastic, sis."

"You do, too."

"No, I mean it. You have this…. I don't want to say glow, because that sounds tacky, but that's what it is. I can't remember the last time I saw it."

"Life has been pretty good to me lately."

His gaze briefly sidetracked over her shoulder. "So I've heard. How'd the auction go today?"

"Great. I made way more than I would've at the Cody auction, so I suppose it's a good thing Jim had to drive cows for the Grants."

"Sounds like it. I'm happy for you, sis. This'll help you out a lot."

"Yes, it will. I might've made enough to punch an irrigation well and run some pipe."

"That's wonderful."

Suddenly, the rumble of the truck's engine stopped, plunging them into silence. With a hand curled around her brother's arm, she stepped to the side in time to see Gabe jump down out of the cab. She thought he'd come right over, but instead, he opened the rear door and dragged their bags out of the back. Slinging two of them over his shoulder, he closed the door with his free hand and turned toward them.

She was struck again—for the ten-thousandth time—by his smooth, long-legged gait. So unhurried and fluid.

Beside her, Robert let out a low whistle, and when she tore her gaze away to reprimand him for being a smart-alec, his eyes were on her, not Gabe, and there was no teasing light in them. "Can't say I've *ever* seen you look at a man like that."

"You never saw the way I looked at Tom."

"No, but I did," Judy said quietly. "You looked at him like the starry-eyed, gullible girl you were."

"Oh? And how do I look at Gabe? Because I *feel* pretty starry-eyed."

"You look at him like a woman who knows exactly what she wants and what she deserves."

Gabe was close enough now that he'd be able to hear their conversation, so Annemarie didn't ask her mother to explain. She started to introduce him to her family, but Cody beat her to it.

"Everyone, this is Gabe. Gabe, this is our family."

Laughing, Annemarie elaborated. "This handsome devil is my brother, Robert, and standing on his other side is his gorgeous and ever-patient wife, Julianne. She likes to go by Julie most of the time. Standing with Cody are their twins, Elijah and Erin, and over here, this beautiful woman and ornery old cuss are my parents, Judy and Bill."

Gabe shook each offered hand in turn, then asked playfully, "Is this everyone?"

"Yes." She snorted. "I can't help it if it takes all three generations of my family to equal just your genera-tion of your family."

"Seriously?" Robert asked. "Just how many siblings do you have?"

"Six older brothers and one younger sister."

"How was that growing up? Because I had a hard enough time keeping up with just one sister."

Annemarie elbowed him.

"See?"

Gabe chuckled. "It was interesting. Never a dull moment."

"I'll bet not."

"Come on in," Judy said, ushering everyone inside. "Let's get you situated in your room. You can gawk over Gabe's big family later, Robert."

"Yes'm."

She had figured she and Cody would sleep in her old room and Gabe would take Robert's old room, but with her brother and his family here, that wasn't going to work. Would he set aside his prohibition and sleep with her? Cody wouldn't mind sleeping on the floor. He'd probably think it was a treat. The thought of spending the night with Gabe wrapped around her was definitely appealing, but she doubted he'd go for it. Besides, he had his overnight bed in the truck. Undoubtedly, he'd take the noble route and sleep on that out in the living room. The disappointment attached to that thought was thick.

Sure enough, as soon as he'd set their bags in her old room, he headed back out to the truck. She sighed.

"What is there left to get?" Judy asked, gesturing to their bags. "Isn't this everything?"

"He went out to grab his bed roll."

"I thought you'd be sharing the bed. I even got the blow-up out for Cody." Her mother eyed her. "You expect me to believe you two haven't already had relations?"

"We haven't even kissed."

"Why the heck not? If I were you, I'd've been all over him by now."

"Mom!"

"What?" Judy asked with wide eyes.

The innocent routine might've worked if a grin of pure mischief weren't curving her lips and making her eyes sparkle.

"Gabe's not letting us get carried away. For one, he is surprisingly shy. And… he says he wants to treat me how a gentleman should treat a lady." Annemarie shrugged as her mother's mouth fell open. "I like it most of the time. There's no pressure. With Tom, there was nothing *but* pressure."

Judy walked over to the room's single window, which faced the driveway, to study Gabe. "If I knew nothing else about your man, what you just told me would be enough. He's the real deal, babe."

"I hope so."

"You hope he's the real deal or you hope your relationship is—as in ends with the two of you rocking in the porch swing together when you're old and gray?"

"The old and gray part. I know Gabe's the real deal. He's proven that so many times now that I'm starting to lose count." Suddenly, she smiled. "I don't think his parents would let him be anything but. You'd love them, Mom."

"Judging by what I've seen and heard of their son so far, I suspect you're right. Anyhow, I'd best get dinner started. I'd've had it waiting for you, but I wasn't sure how long it would take to get through the end-of-auction business."

"Can I help?"

"No. You've already had a long day, so just sit back and relax… and try to keep your brother and your father from interrogating poor Gabe too relentlessly."

"Mmm. I'm sure he'd appreciate that."

Judy left to start dinner, and Gabe returned moments later to drop his bedding off in Annemarie's room. He didn't say anything about where he planned to unroll it, only took her hand and led her into the kitchen to ask her mother how they could help. With a wink at her daughter, Judy promptly chased them out to the lakeside deck where Bill, Robert, Julie, and the kids were enjoying cold beverages. Cody had lemonade. His cousins were enjoying chocolate milk, and Julie sipped an iced tea. Bill and Robert were ignoring their beers in favor of playing with the children. Annemarie gave Gabe less than a minute before he joined the men and kids.

He didn't disappoint, and Cody immediately tackled him.

"Gabe, can I get you a beer?" Robert offered.

"I think I'll hold off for a while, but I'd take an iced tea, if it's not too much trouble."

"Why hold off?" Bill asked. "We're not going any-where else tonight."

"Actually," Gabe replied, "I have a plan for after dinner, if Annemarie's up for it."

"Depends on what the plan is," she answered.

"I'll let you know in a bit." His face split in a grin of pure mischief. "In the meantime, have a seat. You're making me tired, standing there."

She perched primly on one of the cushioned chairs at the table and poured herself some iced tea when her father was done pouring a glass for Gabe.

What a gorgeous evening. The sun was nearly touching the hills on the western shores of Alcova Lake and a faint breeze stirred the water just enough to make it glitter with golden light. The air temperature was down-right balmy, feeling more like June than late March. The snow that had made their trip east a sloppy mess had long since disappeared, and a pocket of warmth had settled over the region. She leaned back in her chair, tipped her head back, and closed her eyes. Life was good.

"Annemarie tells us you're an electrician," Bill said, climbing into a chair across the table from her for a breather. "And that you grew up on a ranch."

"Yes, sir," Gabe replied.

"Didn't feel like ranching?"

"Didn't have much choice. Our spread isn't big enough to support all the kids and their families, so I had to find something else to do with myself." Gabe braced his hands behind him and stretched his legs out in front of him. Cody flopped beside him, leaning against him and pretending to be worn out when the twins tried to grab his hands and drag him back into play. Gabe smiled fondly at their antics. "We had a family friend who was a master electrician—Gus Cherry—and he offered to take me on as an apprentice. I enjoy it."

"And you own your own business?"

"Yes, sir."

"How much would you charge to wire in a couple lights out here?"

"Dad," Annemarie groaned, "he's not here to—"

"Not much," Gabe answered. "Why don't you show me what you're looking at?"

When all three men got up to go discuss Bill's ideas, Annemarie rolled her eyes.

"Well, since the men are talking shop, shall we talk men?" Julie inquired.

With a mock reluctance, Annemarie asked, "What do you want to talk about?"

"Anything. It's been a while since I felt that brand-new love, so indulge me."

"Um, it's great. He rewired my house essentially for free—the amount of bookkeeping I'm doing in exchange doesn't even come close to balancing it out. And he's helped out quite a bit with the ranching, too."

"And Cody obviously *adores* him," Julie added quietly, nodding her head toward the men. "Looks like the feeling is mutual."

Annemarie followed her sister-in-law's gaze. Cody

had snuck after the men and currently gripped Gabe's hand as he listened intently to what his new electrician friend was telling his grandfather and uncle. How many times had she watched them together with her heart leaping? Too many to count, but this was somehow different. It wasn't new anymore. It was comfortingly familiar the way Gabe held Cody's hand as if it were so natural to him that he hadn't spared it even a second's thought.

Gabe was the piece that completed the jigsaw puzzle of her family.

How was it they hadn't even *kissed* yet?

"And *damn*, woman," Julie remarked with a wink. "There's a whole lotta man there to keep you warm at night. He's gotta be six-five-ish."

"About that, yeah."

"Mmm, mmm, mmm. He is a superb representation of his gender."

"You better not let my brother hear you say that."

"He couldn't care less. I don't have eyes for anyone but him, and the butthead knows it." Loud enough for her husband to hear, she added, "Don't ya, honey?"

"Don't I what?" Robert asked.

"Know that you spoiled me for any other man."

"You'd better believe it."

"See?" Julie asked Annemarie.

Laughing, Annemarie held up her hands. "Okay, okay. I believe you."

Judy came out of the house with an armload of paper plates, silverware, and napkins. "Dinner's about ready, if you girls would kindly set these out."

"Already?" Annemarie asked.

"I put the lasagna together this morning, so all I had to do was put it in the oven as soon as you three arrived."

You three. Annemarie almost purred at the thought.

"Where'd the boys go?"

"Uh, they were just…. Oh, this is ridiculous."

In her distraction, Bill, Robert, Gabe, and Cody had disappeared. Excusing herself, she left the table to track them down with a promise that she'd help set the table when she returned.

She found the menfolk out of sight from the deck on the flagstone path down to the lakeshore. She didn't have to hear the conversation to know what her father was asking of Gabe; he'd been talking about adding lights along the path for years now.

"I thought you asked about porch lights," she said.

"I did, but while I have an electrician here," Bill replied, "I thought I'd ask his opinion."

"Well, dinner's done."

"We'll be up in a minute."

Annemarie folded her arms over her chest and tapped her foot. Robert took the hint and headed toward the deck, gripping her shoulder as he passed her.

"Good luck getting Gabe away from Dad while you're here," he remarked.

"Yeah, thanks. Go help your wife set the table."

"Rawr. Kitty's got claws."

She smacked his shoulder as he trotted away

chuckling. Clearing her throat noisily, she turned point-edly to her father and Gabe. They looked at her with matching looks of surprise-edged amusement. "Not when it's too dark to keep plotting. Now. You can talk about all your grand lighting schemes over dinner."

"Yes, ma'am," Gabe replied, taking Cody's hand again. "Guess we'd better listen to your mom if we want any dessert."

Did they have to be so cute? When Gabe met her gaze with a twinkle in his eye, she knew he saw right through her, and it only made him that much more irre-sistible. As he reached her, he held his free hand out and hooked her around the waist, pulling her along with him behind her father.

"So, what's this plan you have for later in the even-ing?" she asked.

"Patience."

They crested the steps up to the deck, and Annema-rie sent Cody on ahead, then turned to Gabe.

"You seem to have a lot of faith in my patience, first asking me to wait to even kiss you and again now."

"I wanted us to take our time because I want to do this right. Because you deserve it."

"And what do *you* deserve, Gabe?"

"I hope I deserve your heart."

That took the wind right out of her sails and at the same time propelled her to new speeds.

"As to my idea for tonight…."

He took her hand, lifted it over her head, and

twirled her.

"Dancing?"

"Mmm-hmm. I mentioned it to Robert to see if he'd be willing to watch Cody for us."

Us. There it was again, an offhand remark binding them. As if she weren't already in danger of melting to the deck in a puddle of quivering giddiness and…. Dare she think it?

Love. I'm falling in love with him.

Another voice, smug, said, *About time you admitted it.*

"And your dad suggested he and your mom watch all three kids," he continued, eyeing her with his smile fading into uncertainty. "It seems Robert and Julianne could use a little adult time, too."

He waited for her response, but she was incapable of giving one. She could only stare at him in wonder. After a moment, he started talking again, rambling as hopefulness tinted that endearing uncertainty with warmth.

"As long as you don't mind them joining us. I figured you might appreciate spending the time with your brother. Robert says he knows of a bar in Casper that usually has a live band on Friday nights. What do you think, Annie? I know we've had a long day already, but—"

She wasn't sure which of them was more surprised when she clasped his face, stood on her toes, and planted her lips firmly against his. At first, he was too stunned to kiss her back, but then he took her face in his hands and pulled her body against his with such hunger that it snatched her breath away and made her dizzy. It was like he couldn't hold back, couldn't resist her.

Dear lord, she'd never been kissed like this. *Never.*

Hoots and whistles from the table barely made an impression on her; there was no room in her mind for anything but Gabe and the way his lips felt and how her body fit against his.

"Hey, you two!" Julianne called. "Knock it off or get a room!"

Gabe relinquished her mouth for a moment, then pressed a softer kiss to her lips before resting his brow against hers, reluctant to let her go. When he brushed his thumb over her cheek, she sighed. Finally, he straightened and started toward the table, his hand still linked with hers.

No one mentioned the kiss when they joined everyone at the table, but Annemarie blushed anyhow. As soon as everyone had a plate of lasagna, garlic bread, and salad, her father said grace.

"I guess you can't say you haven't kissed anymore," Judy remarked.

"You're saying…." Julianne glanced from her mother-in-law to Annemarie. "That was your first kiss? Get out!"

Annemarie caught Gabe's eyes for just a moment before he lowered his gaze to his plate and took a bite. His face and neck were adorably red. He was usually so easygoing and confident that the moments like this, when his shyness rose to the surface, hypnotized her.

"This is delicious, Judy," he said quietly. "Thank you."

Conversation was sparse as they enjoyed their meal and the soft spring sunset that blossomed over the lake. Somewhere out on the water, a pair of loons started calling back and forth, their voices echoing across the lake, long and hauntingly beautiful. Annemarie closed her eyes and smiled.

"Oh, listen!" Judy sighed. "I love when the loons stop by. It seems like they do less and less as the years go by."

"We had a pair that used to nest on our upper pond when I was a kid," he said thoughtfully. "They stopped coming, until last year."

"You think it's the same pair? I guess they can live quite a while. Something like thirty years?"

"Could be. I'd like to think so."

He stood and started gathering plates, but Judy quickly put an end to that.

"Oh no you don't. You've already helped enough today for my daughter. Sit and relax."

"Actually… Robert and I have a proposition. Bill said he and you wouldn't mind watching Cody, Elijah, and Erin for the evening so Robert and I can take Julianne and Annie out dancing."

"You got it. What do you think, Cody? You want to hang out with Grandma and Grandpa for the evening?"

"But… can't I go with you and Mom, Gabe?"

"Not tonight, kiddo. Your mom needs some grown-up time."

Cody pouted, casting a betrayed look at Annemarie.

She opened her mouth to chastise him, but Gabe silenced her with a look that said he wasn't going to let her be the bad guy.

"I'll tell you what. Tomorrow, you and your mom and I will do something together. Maybe go fishing, or whatever you want to do. Let your mom have tonight and you can have all day tomorrow. How's that sound?"

"I thought you were gonna put up Grandpa's lights tomorrow."

"Your grandpa's waited quite a while to have those lights installed, so I'm sure he wouldn't mind waiting another day. I can get it done before we leave for home on Sunday. Deal?"

The little boy held on to his pout for a few moments longer, but then he gave in and sighed. "Promise?"

"I promise." Gabe opened his arms for a hug, and Cody didn't hesitate to accept the invitation. "We're all yours tomorrow."

Judy gripped Annemarie's knee under the table to get her attention. When she looked at her mother, Judy gave her one of those brows-lifted, bright-eyed, not-quite-smiling looks of approval. Annemarie caught her bottom lip between her teeth, but that did nothing to stop the grin from taking over her face.

"All right, if you all are going into Casper," Bill said, "you'd best get going. The kiddos can help Mama and I wash dishes."

"By *help* you mean paint the kitchen with bubbles, right?" Robert inquired.

"Yep. And we'll have a blast doing it, too. Won't we, kiddos?"

His question was met with exuberant cheers and a roll of the eyes from his wife. Annemarie stood and gave her son a hug and a kiss. "You be good for Grandma and Grandpa, all right? And have fun making a mess of the kitchen. Love you."

He nodded solemnly. "Love you, too."

"We won't be too late," Gabe said.

"Nonsense," Judy replied. "Take your time and have fun. But someone had better be the designated driver. I've already done my kid raising, thank you."

Gabe raised his hand. "It was my idea, so I guess that means I get to be the DD."

"I second that," Robert said.

"Motion passed," Julie added.

"Good." Gabe held out his hand for the keys to their suburban. Robert didn't hesitate to hand them over.

Annemarie tucked her hands around Gabe's arm and grinning up at him. "I can be your sober navigator."

"You don't need to be. Have a drink or three. Relax."

"I don't want a drink or three. I want to remember every detail of tonight."

He surprised her by lowering his mouth to hers in a light kiss. "As you wish, ma'am."

————*Chapter Twelve*————

"**I** KNOW I SHOULDN'T FEEL guilty for excluding Cody," Gabe remarked, leaning back against the high top table, "because Annie needs this. But I do."

"Yes, she does, and no you shouldn't," Robert agreed, raising his beer in an impromptu toast. After Gabe clinked his glass of Coke to the bottle, Robert continued, waxing philosophical. "She missed out on all the fun 'cause she had Cody so young. Didn't get to let loose and party and do all the stupid, insanely fun crap Julie and I and I'll bet even you got to do."

"Even me?"

"Yeah, even you. You're Mr. Responsible now, but I'll bet you were a hellion back in the day."

"I didn't get much chance. My brothers ruined it for me. When it was finally my turn to be a stupid teenager, my parents had already seen it all, and I didn't have a chance in hell of getting away with anything."

"You poor bastard."

Gabe chuckled. "I *did* total my first pickup jumping ditches on the ranch, though." He took a sip of his Coke and let his gaze wander back to Annemarie. Her smile outshone the moon as she line-danced with her sister-in-law and several other women to the Charlie Daniels Band "The Devil Went Down to Georgia." No, it wasn't line dancing. Clogging. That was the term. "Annie and Julie seem to be having a marvelous time."

"Yes, indeed. Fun to watch aren't they?"

"Mmm-hmm."

"Also, I still can't believe she lets you call her Annie. She'd kick my ass if I did. And I probably deserve it, 'cause I called her that when we were kids and I was teasing her. How'd you talk her into it?"

"It slipped out one day. And then it kept slipping out."

"Huh."

They lapsed into silence, sipping their drinks while the women danced. The band had declared this a song for ladies only, and the result had every man in the place watching intently, including Gabe. He'd never seen Annie so open and carefree, and the effect it had on him was powerful. He hadn't had a drop of alcohol, but he was dizzy. He needed a distraction, and fast.

"Since we spent most of the evening talking about your dad's lights, I never got a chance to ask what everyone does for a living. I think Annie mentioned that your mother is a teacher and your father does something for the city."

Robert nodded. "High school math. Dad works for Casper's city planning department, and I am a city engineer for Laramie. Julie's a kindergarten teacher."

"A lot of math in the family. No wonder Annie's such a good accountant. Pretty amazing she finished school."

"Yes, it is. Don't you dare tell her this, but my little sister is my hero. She's twice as strong as me, for sure. I don't think I could do half of what she's done."

"She's an amazing woman," Gabe murmured. *So much for a distraction.* His gaze sidetracked to her again. It was impossible to keep his eyes off her, and it was only the distance between them that made it possible to keep his hands to himself.

"Why the hell we talking about my family's jobs?" Robert asked suddenly. "The devil's long gone from ol' Georgia, so you should be out on the dance floor with my sister or reenacting that kiss."

He wasn't going to address the second question. Not when *that kiss* was still branded on his lips two hours later. Not when the memory of it demanded a repeat... and a whole lot more. "I care about her, and I want to know her. Knowing her family is part of that."

"There'll be plenty of time for that later." Robert gripped his shoulder. "Apparently my sister isn't the only one who needs to let loose a little tonight. C'mon. We've spent enough time warming these stools. Time to go set the dance floor on fire. Yo, Julie!"

Gabe watched Robert saunter across the crowded dance floor to his wife with the rolling steps of someone half-inebriated. Julie was steadier than her husband, but he doubted that would last much longer. Fine by him. With three-year-old twins at home, they needed this chance to unwind as much or more than he and Annie did.

Annemarie joined him at the table and drained the rest of his Coke before draping herself around him. She wasn't panting, exactly, but the exertion of the dance had her breaths coming and going in a fast rhythm that had his pulse racing to catch up.

"It's been a long time since I've had this much fun," she said breathlessly.

"Me, too."

"Sorry my brother and sister-in-law are already half-drunk."

"Why? They're having a good time. You up for another dance, or would you rather sit this song out?"

"I think I'll sit this one out, but you're on for the next one."

She tipped his glass back to drink the tiny pool of ice that had melted in the last minute, so he flagged a waiter. They sat in silence, enjoying the band's cover of Tim McGraw's "Indian Outlaw" and Robert's and Julie's not-entirely steady but entertaining dance moves. More than once as she watched her brother and his wife, Annie let out a quiet laugh. Shortly before the song ended, she returned her attention to Gabe with the excitement of the day giving way to a gentle affection.

"Thank you for this," she said. "Not just for taking me out so I could remember that I'm more than Cody's mom or a broke wannabe rancher but also for making it so I could enjoy some time with my brother."

"You two are pretty close. Closer, I think, than even Lilah and me."

She nodded. "He's my best friend in the world. Growing up out on Alcova got pretty lonely sometimes, and we only had each other for company."

"I guess that explains how you can deal with being by yourself out at your ranch."

"That's a little harder than I let on." She pursed her lips and studied him with narrowed eyes. "Can I ask you something?"

"Sure."

"Why have you been so insistent on taking our relationship so slow?"

"I told you. I want—"

"I know what you told me, and I appreciate the sentiment, but we're getting to a point that I'm beginning to think there's something else. I get that you're way more self-conscious than you need to be... but even about kissing? I don't think that's it, either. Not after the way you kissed me back tonight before dinner. So what is it? Are you afraid I'll turn out to be like Leigh, that I'm only—"

He grabbed her by the chin and dragged her mouth to his, kissing her fiercely to stem the flow of doubt. After half a second's hesitation, she reacted in kind, sliding off her stool and slipping willingly into his waiting arms. She tasted sweet in a way that had nothing to do with the Coke, and he gave his desire a little more rein, crushing her to him and demanding more. When she gave it, he nearly lost it. Damn, the woman could kiss.

Taking her face in his hands, he nipped at her lip and whispered less than an inch from her mouth, "Don't ever again liken yourself to that bitch. You are *not* like Leigh."

"Do you really believe that? Because I've been taking advantage of you just like she did."

"I'm serious, Annie. You aren't taking advantage of me. If anything, it's the other way around. Maybe I'm so willing to help you around the ranch because I miss it. Even as much as I love what I do for a living, I miss that life. And—"

He bit back the words. What would she think if he admitted that she and her son had proven beyond a doubt that he was tired of being alone? Tired of being asked by his family when he was planning to settle down—not because the probes annoyed him but because they reminded him that he *hadn't* found the woman he wanted to make a family with. Because the one he'd thought was that woman had burned him so badly that he'd lost faith in his own judgment.

"And what?" she pressed.

"And I didn't know how much I was beginning to want a family of my own until I met you and Cody. I didn't let myself think about it, but you and your beautiful son… you've made it impossible to ignore."

"But…?"

"Leigh screwed me up pretty good. It wasn't about the money, as terrifying as it was trying to figure out how I was going to pay it all back without going under. But I think you know that."

She nodded. "I suspect she's the bigger reason for your self-consciousness, too, much more so than your brothers. All she wanted was your paycheck—the least important thing about you."

She pressed a tender kiss to his lips, deepening it after a moment and combing her fingers through his hair. Delightful tingles soothed away the surge of despair, and he pulled her onto his lap. She draped an arm around his shoulders and continued to brush her fingers through his hair.

"What I can't fathom is how she could be so blind. If she would've just opened her eyes for a second…."

He opened his eyes again, and she leaned back, searching his face with a thoughtful frown.

"Selfishly, I'm glad she couldn't see what I do. You're an amazingly generous, kind, sexy, compassionate man, Gabriel Collins." She kissed him lightly. "And if she'd realized that, you never would have given me a second thought because you would've had a wife to go home to."

"In that case… I'm glad she didn't see what you do."

He didn't give her the chance to analyze that, sweeping her into a slow dance as the band took up a familiar song he had the feeling would forever remind him of Annie.

My Annie. How right Thomas Sr. had been.

She fell easily into step with him—of the two of them, she was undoubtedly the better dancer.

"Oh!" she breathed. "That's the song you were singing when we left Cody!"

"Yes, it is."

"Would you… sing it for me again?"

He tilted his head and looked down at her with a self-deprecating twist of his lips. "Really? You want me to sing? In front of all these people?"

"As if they could hear you over the band. Please? You have a beautiful voice."

He suspected he'd have a hard time ever saying no to her. With those big blue eyes that still somehow managed to exude innocence despite her hardships, she was irresistible, and everything in him yearned to do whatever it took to make her happy. Once upon a time, he'd felt that way about Leigh, but the second time around, something had changed, and it hadn't been nearly so difficult to draw a line with her. Hell, the crack that had finally shattered the spell of their relationship had been his refusal to let her live with him rent-free. He couldn't imagine ever giving Annie that ultimatum, and not only because he knew how hard she worked and how much she struggled despite it.

She was what he hadn't known to look for. Honest. Loyal. Determined. Compassionate.

I love you, Annie.

He didn't dare say it. Not yet. Neither of them was ready for it, true though it might be. And he was in no more hurry to pressure her emotionally than he was to pressure her physically. He wouldn't do to her what Tom had, what Leigh had done to him. He could've had a future with Jen if Leigh hadn't shown up on his front step with a heart-wrenching story she'd known would ensnare him. Now, with Annemarie's slender body swaying in time to the music with his and the brilliant glow of love in his heart, he was glad Jen hadn't worked out, either—for the first time since she had walked away, rightly unwilling to put up with Leigh's blatant advances.

He sang along with the band, quietly so no one else could hear. Not because his usual self-consciousness demanded it but because he didn't want to share the moment with anyone but her.

When the song ended, he kissed her, giving in to the desire and affection consuming him. It was like she had opened the gate with that first kiss, and now that the horse was sprinting down the track, he had no hope of holding back.

The band struck up a lively tune of their own composition, and Gabe frowned, mourning the end of the romantic moment.

"Up for another dance?" he asked.

"Actually, as much fun as I'm having, I'm ready to

go home," she replied. "I just want to sit someplace quiet with you."

He studied her for a moment with a brow and one corner of his mouth lifted. "Is that all?"

"Okay, being away from Cody is freaking me out a little. This is the longest I've been away from him other than when he's in school. And we should probably cut my brother off before he gets to the point that he'll puke in the car. He and alcohol and moving vehicles don't mix too well past a certain point."

"Ah. In that case, let's get out of here."

Neither Robert nor Julie put up much of a fight; it appeared that even through the haze of alcohol, they weren't any more comfortable being away from their twins than Annie was being away from Cody. While Gabe couldn't personally relate to their parental worries, he still felt guilty about excluding Annemarie's son, so he hooked his arm around Robert to help Annie's inebriated brother out to the Suburban.

A fine rain had begun to fall, cold but refreshing after the heat of the bar. It glittered in Annie's fine hair beneath the blue-white parking lot lights, and for a moment, Gabe was too mesmerized to climb in behind the wheel.

"What?" she asked, noticing his preoccupation.

"You're beautiful. I don't know that I've ever told you that before, but you are."

They slid into the vehicle, and Gabe grabbed her hand to press a kiss to her knuckles before he started the engine and pulled out into the dark night.

The married couple passed out just a few miles outside of Casper and snored the entire way back to the Garretts' house. Gabe and Annemarie didn't talk other than to crack jokes at her brother's expense, but after a while, they fell silent, content to enjoy each other's presence and the quiet patter of rain on the windshield and the sluicing of water on the road.

Back home, they managed to get Robert and Julie into their room without waking the rest of the house. Annemarie's parents had put the twins and Cody to sleep out in the living room on a blow-up mattress. Undoubtedly, it was a big, exciting deal to them—a campout indoors—but Gabe glanced between them and Annemarie's room and shifted his weight. He *had* planned to sleep in the living room on his bedroll, but with the kids out here… would Annie try to convince him otherwise?

"Why don't we sit outside for a while?" she invited.

"It's still raining."

"So? Didn't you see the porch swing? It's under cover for nights like this."

"No, I guess I didn't see it."

"Come sit with me for a bit. Unless you'd rather just go to bed. It *has* been a long day."

"It has," he agreed, "but I don't think I could sleep just yet."

The swing in question was suspended from the partial roof over the deck that he'd been too busy thinking about lights earlier to notice. She sat close beside him, nearly in his lap, with his arm tucked around her and her head resting on his chest, and he kept the swing moving in a slow, relaxing rhythm. The rain continued unabated, filling the quiet of the night with a soft drumming on the metal roof over the swing, and Gabe let his eyes slide closed.

"Thank you for tonight," she murmured. "I needed that. And this."

He expected the kiss. He didn't expect her to pivot in his lap until she was straddling him, but there she was with her body pressed against his and her knees resting beside his hips. He'd been close to dozing off a moment ago, but he was thoroughly awake again now with his body humming in readiness.

Old habits momentarily quarreled with raging desire, and then he wondered, *Why?* No one else was awake, and she had no hesitation. Wasn't the idea behind taking it slow to make sure she was comfortable and unrushed?

As soon as that thought entered his mind, it and every other one fled, chased away by her seeking hands. She slid hands chilled by the cool, damp night under his coat and shirt, and the way she purred as the warmth of his body soothed away the cold hit him with a shot of pure need. He gripped her hips and rocked his pelvis up, and she let out a gasp.

"You're serious?" she asked breathlessly.

"About making love in your parents' house with them and your son and niece and nephew and brother and sister-in-law only a thin wall away?" He captured her bottom lip between his teeth and tugged. "No."

She sat back on his thighs and regarded him with a comical pout that somehow remained achingly adorable. He let out a groan. Her pout snapped into a triumphant grin. Sassy devil.

"Neither of is ready for that step just yet."

She wiggled her brows and then her hips in a most distracting way. "I beg to differ."

"That's not what I meant." He sighed. Gently, he brushed her hair back from her face and tucked it behind her ears. "I don't want to chance repeating history."

Understanding washed across her face, and he nearly laughed, supposing it was a compliment that she'd been so caught up in the moment that all rational thought and planning had abandoned her.

"See? We're not ready." He rocked forward onto his feet, lifting her with his hands under her rump. Instinctively, she wrapped her arms and legs around him. "And anyhow, when we are ready—as much fun as sneaking around can be—I'd rather take my time without worrying about being interrupted. In the meantime… it's time for bed."

"Bed?"

"Yeah, you know that soft, springy thing you sleep on?"

"I know what a bed is."

Chuckling, he carried her inside, closing the door quietly behind them and stepping carefully across the living room so he didn't disturb the sleeping kids.

"I assume I can't talk you into forgoing your oh-so-comfortable foam pad and joining me on the horrible bed." She gestured to her son sleeping out in the living room. "Even though my parents apparently expect us to share the god-awful thing."

"I could be persuaded."

"Oh, really? How might I persuade you?"

He tossed her unceremoniously on the bed and shut the door with a barely perceptible snick, then locked it. She eyed him with a startling combination of uncertainty and curiosity. Despite her eagerness only moments ago, she wasn't so sure of herself now that she'd had a few moments to think it through. Further proof that he was right.

"Take your shirt and pants off and lie on your stomach," he murmured.

"How is that going to persuade you?"

"Just do it."

She peeled off her layers, slowly and tantalizingly, but her wide eyes made him think it was shyness rather than any intentional attempt to seduce him, and that had an interesting effect on him. It made this easier—both resisting the gnawing hunger and ignoring the little voice in the back of his mind telling him that he wasn't strong enough or handsome enough or whatever enough for her—because he wasn't the only one who knew what it was to be found lacking by a partner. Money in his case and sex in hers. That's all he and Annie had been to Leigh and Tom.

But there was so much more to both of them, and

it was freeing to know there was someone who saw it.

When she lay on the bed with her head pillowed on her forearms, he stripped out of his shirt and sat on the bed beside her. His gaze snagged on the long cut on her forearm and the puncture wound from the barbed wire. Both were healing nicely with no trace of infection, but he winced. He'd never been bothered by the sight of blood, but seeing her in pain had damned near brought him to his knees. It was only the knowledge that cleaning and bandaging the cuts would alleviate some of that pain that had made it possible for him to subvert that strange intensity.

He shifted his gaze elsewhere, skimming his hands over her back. Lightly at first, then with increasing pressure. He followed his hands with his lips, trailing kisses from the small of her back up her spine to the nape of her neck. She twisted her body to kiss him, taking his hand and dragging it over her breast. Giving him permission—no, encouraging him—to touch her. She writhed beneath his caresses, and when he lowered his head to press a kiss between her breasts, she arched her back and let out a soft moan.

Boldly, he reached behind her back and unhooked her bra. Casting it aside, he cupped one breast in his hand, idly skimming his thumb over her taut nipple while he kissed and nuzzled her neck. She dug her fingers into his back, and he shuddered. Stroking his hand up her neck, he claimed her mouth again.

"Gabe…."

He turned his attention to her other breast and the other side of her neck. He wanted nothing more than to flick his tongue over her nipples, but that would be a very, very bad idea right now. His grip on his control was weak enough as it was.

"Gabriel."

"Hmm?"

"I thought you said we weren't going to do this."

"I said we weren't going to make love. I didn't say we couldn't have a little fun."

"Much more fun and I'm going to lose it. I'm serious, Gabe. Either take it down a notch or take it all the way."

With a reluctant sigh, he touched his lips to hers and sat up. "For the record, you started it."

"I did not!"

"Yes, you did. When you rolled over. I was just trying to give you a nice back rub like the one you gave me the other night, and you—"

"Okay, you're right. I started it. Have you been persuaded?"

"To do what?"

"Stay right here in bed with me."

"Technically, we're *on* the bed."

She stuck her tongue out at him, and he chuckled. "Add adorable to beautiful."

"Uh-huh." She crawled off the bed and snatched her pajamas out of her bag.

"Now who's being shy?"

"This isn't me being shy. This is me taking preventative measures."

"I'm not going to jump you in the middle of the night."

"I'm not worried about *you*."

Grinning, he changed out of his jeans into his pajama pants, unlocked the door and opened it a hair, and crawled under the blankets with Annemarie. She snuggled against his side with her arm tucked around his waist, and he closed his eyes, savoring the warmth of her body against his and the softness of her skin. He kissed the top of her head, inhaling the gentle scents of woman and rain that clung to her silky hair.

"That was… unexpected and delightful," she murmured. "What changed?"

"What do you mean?"

"You didn't hold back tonight. Not much, anyhow."

"I don't know." He lifted the arm that wasn't pinned beneath her head and threaded his fingers with hers. "Get some sleep."

He *did* know. From now on, no more holding back. He'd let this play out how it would without second-guessing her, himself, or what was between them.

He trusted it.

He trusted *her*.

—— *Chapter Thirteen* ——

WITH THEIR BAGS all packed in "Minnie", Annemarie did a final sweep of her parents' house for anything she might've missed. When she didn't find anything, she joined her mother at the snack bar, leaning against it to watch Gabe and Robert make complete fools of themselves with Cody and the twins in the monstrous fort they'd built in the living room yesterday.

Friday night's rain had changed to snow overnight, and over the course of Saturday, the weather system had deposited a sloppy two inches of slushy white all over. Fishing and every other outdoor activity Cody had on his list had been scratched off, much to his disappointment, but just when Annemarie had opened her mouth to scold him for being obstinate, Gabe had stepped in with the fort idea.

If the squeals of laughter were anything to judge by,

it was a resounding hit.

Cody and Gabe were having so much fun that Annemarie had packed their bags and loaded the truck while they played. Now, as the day headed into early afternoon, it was time to start for home. It would take them three hours or so to get to Collins Ranch to drop off Minnie and pick up Gabe's truck, and then another hour and a half before they arrived home, and that wasn't factoring in any time they were sure to spend with Gabe's parents.

She couldn't seem to bring herself to put an end to their fun just yet, though. They were just too cute. Thinking back to Cody's out-of-the-blue question about whether or not Gabe wanted to be his daddy, she caught her lip between her teeth. Her little boy was too quickly growing into a big boy, and there were things he'd need a man to teach him. The more time she spent with Gabe, the more impossible it became to picture anyone else being the role model she wanted for her son. Her father and brother were, of course, wonderful influences on him, but he saw them only a few times a year. There were also Thomas Sr. and Jim, but Tom tainted those relationships.

"You about ready to head out?" her mother asked. "It's getting late."

Nodding, Annemarie turned to hug her. "I'm so glad we were all able to get together this weekend. It was wonderful."

"Yes, it was. I'm glad we got to meet Gabe, too. I hope he sticks around. For a long time."

"Me, too." With a sigh, she finally headed into the

living room. "All right kiddies, it's that time."

"Ah, Mom!" Cody whined.

"Cody," Gabe warned. "Remember what I said?"

"When it's time to go, it's time to go."

"That's right. And it's time to go. Come on, squirt. Let's pack away our fort."

"Oh, don't worry about that," Judy said. "You need to get going. No telling what the roads will be like. And anyhow, Robert and Julie aren't leaving just yet. I imagine Elijah and Erin would like to play in the fort a while longer."

Gabe nodded in acquiescence. "Yes, ma'am."

"Annemarie?"

"Hmm?"

"Your dad and I were thinking we might come out your way next weekend. There's no school on Friday, and Bill already has the day off because we thought maybe we'd take a weekend away, so we could drive up Friday and be there by the time you get off work. Then drive back Sunday. I know it's short notice, but would that work for you?"

"Absolutely!" Annemarie hugged her mother tightly.

"Maybe we could take Cody one of those nights?"

Judy glanced conspicuously between her daughter and Gabe. Annemarie shifted her gaze to him, but his expression was neutral. Carefully so.

"Um, why don't we talk about that later?" she replied.

"Talk about what later?" Bill asked, returning from the garage with more fort-building supplies—a pair of folding sawhorses.

"About us taking Cody one of the nights we're visiting Annemarie so she and Gabe can have a little more one on one time."

"Sure. We'd love to."

Annemarie rolled her eyes. "And where do you expect us to sleep?"

"We thought we'd hotel it this time," Bill replied.

"Or you and I can stay at my place," Gabe suggested. "You still haven't seen it, you know."

She opened her mouth, then snapped it shut. No, she hadn't. "I guess that's because you're always out at the ranch saving our backsides. That actually sounds like a wonderful idea." Suddenly, she laughed. "I can't believe my *parents* are trying to set me up."

Judy gave her hand a squeeze. "We understand how difficult it can be to put yourself first sometimes, and we at least had each other. Of course, you've had a lot more help lately." She embraced Gabe and whispered, "Thank you for taking care of our girl."

"It's my pleasure." Gabe replied just as quietly. Straightening, he said more loudly, "I guess we'll see you in a few days."

"We'll be there with bells on."

And then, before Annemarie knew it, she, Gabe, and Cody were buckled into Minnie and pulling onto Lakeshore Drive with her parents and brother standing on their porch waving, too far away to make out anything but the vaguest details of them. She stared at their house until Gabe drove around a curve that blocked it from her sight, then tipped her head back and smiled. Not a trace of the usual reluctance to leave plagued her. For once, she was looking forward to going home. It wasn't that she was in a hurry to escape her family; quite the contrary.

She was at peace.

Occasionally, she watched Gabe as he drove. He handled the truck and trailer with the relaxed confidence with which he seemed to tackle every task, and after a while, she kicked off her shoes and propped her feet on the dash. In the backseat, Cody was thoroughly engrossed with the new coloring book Robert and Julie had surprised him with this morning.

Her lips curved, and she sighed happily, enjoying the ride and the company even more.

She could picture them doing this every year, hauling cattle to auction in Torrington and staying the weekend with her parents.

"Did you mean it?" she asked abruptly. "What you said at the bar Friday night?"

"I tend to mean everything I say," Gabe replied, glancing at her. "But which part, specifically?"

She chewed her lip. Did she really have the guts to ask? "About wanting a family."

He spared her a longer look. Then, turning his eyes back to the road, he nodded. "Yes, I did."

"So… it shouldn't scare you that I was just thinking

we should do this every year."

"Why would that scare me? Sounds like a fun tradition to me."

"Well, it's thinking about us in the long term."

"Is that a problem?"

Here she'd been thinking he might balk at the idea of a long-term relationship, but *she* was the one suddenly turning shy about it. Again, he glanced at her.

"Because I thought long term was on the table. Tell me now if it isn't."

She jerked back and dropped her feet to the floor at the sudden sharpness in his voice, gazing at him with eyes wide. "N-no. I mean, yes, it's on the table." She folded her hands in her lap and stared at them. "I'm sorry. I'm no good at this. I've never actually had a real relationship. I don't know what the rules are or what to expect."

"As far as I can tell, there aren't any. You just go with it." He let out a long sigh. "And don't apologize. I'm the one who should be sorry. I was thinking about Leigh, and that's the surest way to put me in a surly mood."

"What were you thinking about?"

"How stupid I was to think I could've married her—that I believed I loved her enough to spend my life with her."

"You were young."

"The first time, but what about the second? I let a good woman walk away when Leigh came back, and I thought that was confirmation that I loved her. Why would I let Jen leave if I didn't love Leigh more?"

"You loved Jen?"

"Not as much as I should have. She was a sweetheart. Kind. Loyal. Giving. Like you."

"Why did she walk away?"

"I bet you can imagine why."

In fact, she could. From what she knew of Leigh, the woman was as tenacious as a starving dog after a steak. And what better way to chase another woman away from the prize than to make her believe the prize was already Leigh's? "She hit on you in front of Jen."

Gabe snorted. "That's a mild way of putting it. First time I saw her again, I was holding hands with Jen—obviously with her—and Leigh walked right up and kissed me. I tried to brush it off, to explain that she'd just been excited to see me, but me introducing Jen as my girlfriend didn't stop her from hugging me or hanging on me in front of Jen, and as you might imagine, Jen got tired of it."

"But you told her to stop, didn't you?"

"Of course I did. It wasn't enough, and I knew it because I knew Leigh. But I felt responsible for her. Habit. And she knew all the buttons to push. She knew how to play me so I wouldn't turn her away." He shook his head. "Amazing what you learn when you think you know it all."

Annemarie didn't like the hard set of his jaw or the disgust curling his lip because it wasn't directed where it should be, at Leigh. It was directed inward. She opened her mouth to tell him to forgive himself, that everyone made mistakes, but he spoke first, glancing at her.

"You want to know what I've learned most recently?"

"Sure."

"I learned that even in high school, when things were the best they ever were with Leigh, it was nothing compared to this." He slowed to a stop at an intersection, and he turned his eyes on her again, holding her gaze. "I'm in this for keeps, Annie. I'm not saying we'll make it, but I want us to and I want to find out if we will. How's *that* for thinking about us in the long term?"

It was probably the wrong reaction, but she laughed. Then she unbuckled her seatbelt and stretched across the wide cab to kiss his cheek. As she buckled herself back in, she said, "We're driving on the same road, and that is wonderfully reassuring. So… this coming weekend."

"What about it?"

"You're not getting off the hook like you did Friday night. And last night."

He chuckled. "Yes, ma'am."

Annemarie focused her attention on the road, knitting her hands together over her stomach and propping her feet on the dash again. She sucked her lips between her teeth, trying to hide the smug grin and failing miserably, but Gabe's attention was on the road, so at least he didn't see it. Wiggling her toes, she reclined her seat and hummed along with the radio—that same song Gabe had sung on their early morning departure from Cody and at the bar Friday night was on. She didn't dislike country music, but she'd never listened to it much. That was likely to change. That song and every one that came on the radio after it suited Gabe and would forever make her think of him. And thinking of him was something she didn't think she'd ever tire of.

The ride home was pleasant. Fun even, with her son and Gabe engaging in a lively game of I Spy once Cody had decided to save what was left of his coloring book for a worktable more stable than his lap. Annemarie chimed in occasionally when they wouldn't let her back out, but she was content to listen to them.

The flat gray ceiling of clouds disintegrated as they headed west, and by the time they entered the Wind River Canyon south of Thermopolis, the sun broke through. Annemarie stared at the towering walls of the canyon, watched the river swirling around the giant boulders in its path, and enjoyed the ceaseless, throaty purr of the truck's diesel engine and the hum of the highway beneath the tires. She held her breath when they passed through the short tunnels carved through the stone and let it out with a soft laugh.

They stopped in Thermopolis to say hello to Gabe's brother Michael and ended up staying for dinner. Though she'd only met Michael and his family once, they treated her and Cody like old friends. She had become so used to being alone out at Garrett Ranch that she found herself soaking up their love.

"We're very sorry to eat and run," Annemarie said to Michael as she embraced his wife on the front porch.

"But dinner was delicious. Thank you so much."

"You're most welcome," Karen replied. "Does my heart good to see you again, Annemarie. And Cody, too. I hope this means we'll be seeing more of you both…?"

"I hope so, too."

"Oh, I think we'll be seeing a *lot* more of her," Michael said. "That's at least the twelfth time in the last thirty minutes I've heard either her or my brother refer to themselves as 'we'."

"We're working on it," Gabe remarked.

"Thirteen. And work is great and all, but if you have to work too hard, that's not a good sign."

Annemarie gazed up at Gabe only to find him smiling down at her. "It's the easiest work I've done in a long time. Your brother's an incredible man, Michael."

"Shh! Don't let him hear that, or all those years of whoopin' up on him and trying to prove otherwise will be for naught."

Gabe rolled his eyes and took Cody's hand. Annemarie turned back to Michael and Karen. "We could've grabbed something from McDonald's, but I'm so glad we didn't have to. Thank you again."

Karen dismissed that with a wave of her hand. "You're family, and family doesn't make do with fast food when we have a fully functional kitchen."

Annemarie hugged her again. "Thank you for that, too."

"You'd best get on the road," Michael said. "Mom won't be happy if she doesn't get to spend more than a minute with you three."

"Right you are. See you soon."

"Count on it."

A little over an hour later, with a stunning array of tattered, gold-tinged clouds above them, they pulled up in front of the Collinses' barn. Gabe's dark blue Chevy pickup—not the white work truck she was accustomed to—was parked across the broad yard beside the main ranch house. At the sight of it, a pang of disappointment shot through her. Their trip was almost over, and as happy as she was to get home and sleep in her own bed, she was definitely *not* excited about sleeping in it alone, nor was she quite ready for her uninterrupted time with Gabe to end.

"You and Cody head inside while I unhook the trailer and load our gear in my truck," Gabe said after he'd backed the trailer around to the side of the barn.

"We can help."

"All right. You want to back me in to the bay there after I get the trailer unhooked?"

"Sure."

He made quick work of unhooking the trailer, and she hopped out to guide him into the garage bay on the same side of the barn. Not that he needed it. She marveled at his skill, wishing she had half his confidence. When she mentioned it as they transferred their bags to his pickup, he laughed it off.

"It's that eight years I have on you."

"I seriously doubt that, Gabe. You can wire a house,

drive a semi—or an almost-semi—fix a fence, and deliver a foal like it's nothing. What can I do? I'm a half decent cook and maybe I'm an okay accountant. I'm still learning."

"Exactly. You're still in the learning-new-skills stage whereas I'm finally at the stage of mastering skills I've already picked up. I'm telling you. Eight years makes a helluva difference." He settled the last of their bags in the bed of his pickup and snatched her hand, bringing her knuckles to his lips with a devilish grin. "Also, you're an amazing cook, and if I didn't think you were a talented accountant, I wouldn't be planning to hire you as mine when your end of our bargain has been fulfilled."

She blinked at him. "You're going to hire me as your accountant? Even after Leigh?"

"You're not Leigh."

Gabe let go of her hand and waved Cody over, then hoisted her son to his shoulders. It reminded her forcefully of her first trip here, and she couldn't help but mark how much had changed in the weeks since. It was here that he'd first asked her out, and it was strange to think that they hadn't officially been a couple on that trip when it felt now like they'd been together for ages.

Ruth greeted them at the kitchen door with a warm smile and strong hugs as she beckoned them inside. "You're just in time."

"For what?" Gabe asked.

"Blackberry pie. The store finally had some blackberries in stock, so I had to make one. You can stay long enough for a slice, can't you?"

Annemarie glanced up at Gabe.

He shrugged. "I'm not the one with a kid to get in bed and ready for school in the morning."

"Not yet," she murmured too quietly for anyone else to hear. Grinning, she added. "But I'm hopeful."

"Is that your way of asking me to stay over tonight, or are you referring to something a little farther down the road?"

"Both."

His parents heard that and exchanged matching grins of amusement. Annemarie's face warmed, and she ducked her gaze.

"I guess we have time," she said shyly, "if it's not too much trouble."

"It's no trouble at all, honey," Ruth replied. "I'll dish us some pie and ice cream."

Annemarie perched on a stool at the island with Cody between her and Gabe. She'd expected to see Sam and Isaiah and their families, but John informed her that they still hadn't returned from camping yet. She was surprisingly disappointed; she'd been looking forward to the noise and busyness of the big family. How funny, since she'd been a little overwhelmed by them at first on her last visit.

"A little noise is nice once in a while, isn't it," Gabe observed.

She nodded. Ruth set a slice of pie with a scoop of vanilla ice cream—both homemade if she had to guess—

in front of her, and she was soon too awestruck by the dessert to respond to Gabe's insightful remark. She purred when she slipped the first, tartly-sweet bite into her mouth.

"Good?" Ruth asked, smiling.

"Amazing. I think I'm going to be spending a lot of time in this kitchen with you. I'd love to learn how to bake like this and make homemade ice cream."

"You're on as long as you teach me how you make that pizza Gabe keeps telling me about."

"You've got a deal."

As she enjoyed her pie and ice cream, Annemarie decided this was something else she'd love to add to their tradition—stopping at Michael and Karen's on the way home from Torrington and then at the Collinses' ranch. Between his family and hers—okay, mostly his—they could take any highway in Wyoming and not be too far from someone they knew. What an amazing, wonderful thing.

"I guess Grandpa is right," she mused aloud. "Wyoming really is one great big small town."

"That it is," Gabe replied. "Did you know that Ezra took a girl from Kemmerer to his prom?"

"Isn't it like a six-hour-drive from there to Cody?"

"Closer to five in good weather, which it wasn't. I think it took her and her parents almost eight hours. South Pass was nasty, and there were a couple wrecks. They stayed out at the ranch."

"How'd they meet?"

"Same way a lot of kids do," Ruth replied. "School sporting events. In their case, they met at a wrestling tournament. She was her team's manager."

"He wrestled?" Annemarie asked. She turned to Gabe. "Did you play any sports?"

He shrugged, his mouth full.

"He played football and wrestled," John said. "Took state in wrestling three years in a row, sophomore through senior year."

She glanced over him. "Why am I not surprised?"

Again, he shrugged.

"What about you, Annemarie?" Ruth inquired. "Any sports? Cheerleading?"

"Volleyball. We never won state, though. Came close once my junior year—we lost in the championship."

"So you know how Wyoming high school sports are. For some towns, they're the only real entertainment."

She nodded. "I do to some extent, but I don't think the bigger schools like Casper get quite as much interaction as the smaller schools do."

"Not as much need, I suppose," John mused.

After living out at the ranch for close to half a year, she was beginning to truly understand that need. She'd thought she'd understood it living out on Alcova Lake for much of her childhood, but with Casper only a forty-minute drive away—a shorter trip than those between most towns in Wyoming—she'd had easy access to friends, shopping, and entertainment. Cody had all kinds of touristy attractions with its proximity to Yellowstone, but it was quite a bit smaller than Casper and comparatively remote.

"Needing people isn't such a bad thing," she murmured. "If I hadn't needed an electrician, I wouldn't have met your son."

"Amen to that," Ruth said, raising her cup of coffee in a toast. "Cody, honey, would you like some more pie? If it's all right with your mama."

"Please, Mom?"

Annemarie glanced at his plate and realized with a start that he'd cleared it already, finishing well ahead of the adults. "I swear Karen and Michael fed him and he ate like a horse. Guess this means we'll be going clothes shopping again soon."

Laughing, Ruth slid another slice of pie onto Cody's plate. "That's what kids do. They grow."

Annemarie poked Gabe's arm. "I bet you know that better than most, what with your crew of giants."

"Hardy har har," Gabe replied, rolling his eyes. He held his plate out for another scoop of ice cream. "Thanks, Mom."

"You two seem considerably more, um, serious."

Gabe caught her eye, smiled, and nodded to his mother.

"How serious?"

"I guess we'll see," he replied, "but I think we're both hopeful."

"What about Cody?"

The boy snapped his head up. "Huh?" he asked

around a mouthful of pie. Abruptly he covered his mouth. "Sorry."

"Oh, I'm pretty sure he's on board," Annemarie said.

"You've talked about it with him?" Gabe asked, brows lifted.

"Sort of. He brought it up. Anyhow… that's a conversation we may all need to sit down and have before too much longer."

He nodded in agreement, and Cody glanced between them with one of those smiles that was half confused and half hopeful. He wasn't quite sure what was going on, but he had a good idea.

"*That* serious, huh?" Ruth beamed and clapped. "Oh, I love this. About time, Gabriel."

"I take that to mean you approve. You know, he's such a gentleman that I feel like I should ask for your permission to date him. He already has my family's rather enthusiastic approval." Annemarie laughed. "In fact, my parents are so happy about it, they're coming out this weekend and taking Cody for a night, and they weren't shy about saying why."

Gabe nearly choked on his last bite of pie.

His father slapped him on the back, which only made it worse. He coughed until his eyes watered and finally managed to subdue it enough to take a drink from the glass of water Ruth brought him.

"You bet your sweet, beautiful heart we approve," Ruth said. "After what he went through both times with

Leigh, I've been waiting for him to find someone like you. If everyone's done… boys, get out of my kitchen. Annemarie, come talk with me."

"I can do the dishes," Gabe said, standing with his plate in hand. "Go relax, Mom."

"Go sit," Annemarie said at the same time as Ruth said it, snatching his plate.

Gabe threw up his hands. "Yes, ma'am. Come on, Cody."

As soon as the menfolk were out of earshot in the living room, Ruth started clearing the table. Annemarie jumped over to the sink and had already started filling it with soapy water when Ruth pointed out the dishwasher. She laughed at herself.

"Habit," she said and continued hand-washing the plates. If nothing else, it'd give her more time to talk with Ruth.

"You know, if you two ever want some alone time, we have an empty cabin here on the ranch, and I'd love to watch Cody for you."

"I may take you up on that. You're really sure you're okay with me dating your son?"

"Why wouldn't I be?"

"Because some days I feel like I'm taking advantage of him just like Leigh did. I know he says I'm not, but… that's how I feel."

"How you feel and how he feels are two different things, and how he feels about it is what matters because he's the party being used… or not." Ruth set the plate she was drying down and tossed the towel over her shoulder. "Look at me, Annemarie."

Grudgingly, she met the older woman's gaze.

"If he had charged you for the wiring job and never done any of the other things that make you feel like you're taking advantage of him, would you still want to be with him?"

"Of course I would."

"Well, there's your answer."

Nodding, Annemarie went back to washing the dishes. "Am I ever going to stop feeling like that?"

"I suspect if you did, that'd be the end of it. John and I have been married almost forty-seven years now, and there are still times I feel like I'm not giving him enough in return for everything he does for me. Wanting to do as much—more even—for your partner as they do for you, that's called love, honey."

Love.

She tasted the word, savored it. It was more familiar now than the first few times she'd tested it, and she knew Ruth was right.

"Hey, Annie?" Gabe asked, strolling into the kitchen.

"Hmm?" she asked. Not trusting herself to look at him right now, she kept her gaze trained on what few dishes were left to wash.

"We should probably get back on the road. Cody's not going to make it much longer."

"We're almost done." She glanced at him as she set

the second to last plate in the dish drainer. "Oh."

Gabe had Cody propped on his hip with her son's head resting on his shoulder. Cody's limbs were completely limp, and his eyes were closed—he was out cold.

"I think he's already done," she mused.

Shifting his head back to look at the boy, Gabe let out a huff of laughter. He smoothed his free hand over Cody's hair, and his smile gentled from amusement to paternal fondness. "That was quick. I guess I'd better get him settled in the truck. Meet you outside in a few?"

Annemarie nodded and set the last plate in the rack, then started fishing the forks out of the bottom of the sink, smiling and shaking her head as she watched her boys out the window.

My boys. Why not? If things kept going the way they were, Gabe would be hers just as much as Cody was, and vice versa.

I hope we make it, he'd said.

There was only one response to that that felt right. *I hope we do, too.*

—— *Chapter Fourteen* ——

"Y OU'RE ALL SET, JOANIE," Gabe announced when he strode into the lobby of Terri's animal hospital. "Go ahead and test it."

The silver-haired receptionist flipped the switch on the front desk, and the track lighting he'd installed flooded the area with crisp light. She turned a big smile on him. "You are a worker of wonders, Gabe. I really appreciate you squeezing us in today."

"My pleasure, Joanie."

Gabe grabbed the broom and swept up his mess while the woman admired the new lighting.

"Oh, yes. This is much better. I'm sure Terri'll be happy and relieved, too. I've been on her for months about getting more light up here."

He hauled his tools out to his truck and returned with Terri's invoice. Joanie handed him the check Terri had written out ahead of time. He thanked her, waved, and headed out to his truck. He'd finished a couple hours earlier today than he'd planned, so he stopped by his house to change out of his work clothes and then drove to Annemarie's office with some bookkeeping for her. She might not think she was doing him much of a favor, but not having to worry about his books had—as he'd suspected when he'd made the offer—freed up quite a bit of time and even more brainpower.

He parked beside a familiar truck in front of McCoy Accountants. Joanie had said Terri was out on a call, so what was she doing here? This might be interesting.

When he located Annie's open door, it became immediately clear why Terri was here; she and Annie were discussing payroll. He knocked lightly, and both women jerked their heads up.

"I see you took my suggestion, Terri," he remarked. "I thought you were out on a ranch call."

"I was. I finished early, so I figured it would be a good time to meet my new accountant." She looked him up and down. "Looks like I'm not the only one who finished early today. You can't be done with my side job already."

"I am. The guy who wired your place did a great job. Made that little fix a piece of cake for me. Almost like he knew you were going to change your mind."

"He's modest, too."

Holding his hands out to the side with palms up, he shrugged. "What can I say? I'm good at what I do."

"That's for damned sure. Thanks a million, Sparky. Joanie paid you, right?"

He nodded. Shifting his attention to Annie, he asked, "What time do you get off?"

"I was supposed to be off in ten, but I have some tax returns I need to finish up from this morning. I haven't had a chance to get back to them all day." She tilted her head and adorably caught her lip between her teeth. "Um… I have a huge favor to ask. Would you mind picking Cody up from school and heading out to my place? My parents should be there by four, and I forgot to leave the key out for them."

"Sure."

"Thanks." She dug her keys out of her purse, slid the house key off the ring, and handed it to him. "His booster seat is in my truck—it's unlocked—and I'll call the school to let them know."

He leaned over her desk to give her a quick peck on the lips, then strode out of the office. He sensed Terri following him out, so he held the door for her. She flashed him a smile as she slipped past him, and he couldn't be sure, but he thought it held an air of regret.

"I really appreciate you squeezing me in," she said when they reached their trucks. She leaned against the front fender of hers.

"You're welcome." Taking in her expression—eyes narrowed and lips pursed—he shifted his weight. "Something on your mind?"

"Yeah, I guess so. You and Annemarie Garrett."

"What about us?"

"Us," she murmured. "And you're picking her kid up from school. Guess that means the rumors are true. Damn. I was hoping you might be up for a little fooling around one of these days, but it looks like that door's been closed tight."

"I think so."

She lowered her gaze and drew patterns in the dirt of a pothole with the toe of her boot. It was so unlike her that he sighed and acknowledged the pang of remorse. There was nothing more between them than friendship and—once upon a time—a mutual need for physical companionship.

Maybe not so once-upon-a-time for her.

He hooked his thumbs in his pockets. "I'm sorry, Terri."

She met his gaze again at last. "Don't be. She deserves a good man."

His lips twitched. "Thanks. I thought you were still seeing Jonathan."

"That went south right about the time you started wiring Annemarie's house."

"Sorry to hear that."

"Why? I'm not."

That was more like the Terri he knew, and he let out a breath.

"You tell her about us yet?"

He nodded. "Before we left for Torrington."

"It's a done deal for sure, then." She let out a laugh.

"She knows we've slept together, and there wasn't a trace of jealousy or possessiveness about her the whole time she and I were talking. You're hers, and she's absolutely secure in that."

"She's pretty understanding."

"She's that and one of the sweetest people I've ever met, but women are just as territorial as men, Sparky. She's understanding because she knows there's no chance of an interloper trespassing on her turf. Makes the situation crystal clear to me, especially when I consider who her son's father is."

"You know?"

"It wasn't too hard to figure it out. And old Jim Hanson confirmed it for me one day last year. Around town, it's still just a rumor, but I'd love to see it become common knowledge. Tom and Sandy could both stand to be brought down a peg or two."

"As long as it didn't come back on Annie and Cody, I agree."

"If I ever find a man I trust as much as she trusts you...." Terri shook her head and let out a snort.

"God help the world," Gabe finished for her. "Because you two will set it on fire."

Laughing, she embraced him and then strode around to the driver-side door of her truck. "I best let you go. Don't want you to be late picking up your future stepson." She winked. "See ya 'round, Sparky."

Gabe grabbed Cody's booster seat out of Annie's truck, climbed into his, and drove to the school with

Terri's final words echoing in his mind. It wasn't Terri's insinuation that he and Annie would end up married that sat wrong. It was the *step* in front of son. That implied Cody had had a father in his life, but Tom had not once attempted to fill that role. There would be no *stepping* into another man's position in Cody's life.

He pulled into a parking spot near the office of Cody's school and strode inside. He knew the secretary—she'd been at her post since he'd started school, and she'd been his mother's best friend since kindergarten—and when he rang the bell on the counter, she glanced up from her work and greeted him with a smile.

"Gabriel, what are you doing here?" she asked.

"I'm here to pick up Cody Garrett. But you already know that."

"Does your mother know you're picking up your girlfriend's son from school?"

"I'm sure she will soon without me having to tell her," he quipped. "Just as I'm sure you're not nearly as surprised to see me as you sound."

"You're right. I'm not. Ruth was over the moon about you and Ms. Garrett when I talked to her last night." The woman winked and picked up the phone. "Mrs. Jensen, would you send Cody to the office? Gabe is here to pick him up. Yes, *that* Gabe. Thank you."

He rolled his eyes. "She doesn't have to send him down right now. He glanced at the clock. "There's still ten minutes left."

"Oh, they're cleaning up and getting ready to go,

anyhow. I'm pretty sure this is more important."

"The curse and the blessing of small towns," he murmured. "Tell my mother hello when you talk to her tonight. Because I know you will."

He walked over to the entrance to the kindergarten hall to wait for Cody, not in the mood to discuss the details of his private life with his mother's gossip-prone best friend. Quelling his nerves about tonight seemed like a much better use of his time, though he couldn't begin to explain why he was nervous. Or maybe he wasn't. Maybe it was excitement and anticipation. It had been so long since he'd felt it—and never so acutely—that he couldn't be sure.

"Gabe!" Cody yelled and sprinted down the hall, launching himself at Gabe.

"Hiya, squirt. Aren't you supposed to *walk* in the halls?"

"Sorry." Leaning back in Gabe's arms, Cody glanced around the lobby. "Where's Mom?"

"She has to work a little late tonight, so you and I are going to go home to meet your Grandma and Grandpa. Are you excited to spend the night with them?"

"Uh-huh. Last night when I talked to them, they said we could build a fort in the living room like we did last weekend and camp out!"

"I'm jealous! I love camping."

"Can we go camping this summer? Not in the living room but real camping?"

"You bet." He hooked one arm around Cody's

waist and waved to the secretary as he headed out the door.

Just outside, Gabe set Cody on his feet, and they raced out to his pickup. Cody talked the entire way to the turn-off toward the Grant Ranch about everything he'd learned at school, where he thought it would be fun to go camping this summer, how much he'd love to go back out to Collins Ranch, and a hundred other topics. If Gabe weren't used to the rapid-fire subject changes from his nieces and nephews he might've gotten lost, but fortunately, he was able to keep up even when his mind drifted to his plans for the evenings. Or rather, his lack of plans. He figured Annie might appreciate a little spontaneity. With a young child at home and few friends or family nearby she could ask to watch Cody, it was something she didn't often get to try.

Undoubtedly, they'd end up in bed together—she was staying the night at his place, after all—and he was prepared for *that* and ready for it, but that didn't mean they couldn't let things happen how they would. Natural, spontaneous, fun. No pressure.

"Hey, it's Jim," Cody remarked. "I think he wants to talk to us."

Sure enough, the ranch hand stood in the open door of a tractor, arms waving. He climbed down and trotted across the uneven, freshly tilled earth toward the gate of the field, and Gabe slowed his truck to a stop and rolled down the window. He leaned out with his wrist resting casually on the windowsill.

"Afternoon, Jim," he greeted.

"You're just the man I'm looking for," Jim returned. "Tom wants to talk to you."

Gabe's brows shot up. He could think of at least one reason Tom might want to talk to him, and it wasn't a conversation he wanted to have. Ever. It wouldn't end well. "Oh? About what?"

"He finally convinced Thomas to build that new bunkhouse, and he wants to get a quote from you on the cost to wire it."

"Uh-huh. Is he getting quotes from Halverson or Gentry?"

"Hell if I know." Jim held up his hands. "I'm just the messenger. He's up in the arena, if you have a minute or ten."

Even if Tom was serious about hiring him and this wasn't some ploy to chase him off and even if the money was damned good, it was unlikely he'd ever be able to work for the man. It was bad enough having to cross Grant Ranch to get to Garrett Ranch. He should just say no right now. And yet, he was curious. "I have a few, but not many. Annie's parents are due shortly, and I need to be there when they arrive."

"I doubt it'll take more than five minutes. Ten tops."

"Can you spare a couple minutes to run interference?"

"Unfortunately not. I'm already behind schedule. Thomas is up there, though." Jim snorted. "'Course, he's as likely to start trouble with Tom as he is to stop it. Might be more of a hindrance than a help."

With a sigh, Gabe shifted his truck into gear and waved farewell to Jim as he turned toward the massive arena. He drummed his thumbs on the steering wheel as he drove the quarter mile into the heart of the Grant Ranch compound, more and more certain the closer he came that this was a stupid idea. Damn his curiosity.

Funny how his first trip by the compound had filled him with such longing for ranch life when now it filled him with dread.

He glanced at Cody, who sat silently in his booster seat staring ahead with wide eyes. Suddenly, his face lit up.

"Gramps is here!" He rolled down his window and called out to his grandfather.

Thomas's face brightened with the same joy, and Gabe parked his truck beside the old rancher.

"Afternoon, Gabe." Thomas leaned in the passenger-side window. "Cody, my boy, how was school?"

"Great!"

Gabe slid out of his pickup right as Tom stepped out of the arena, blinking against the brilliant spring sunlight. The tight-lipped, narrowed-eyed expression on the other man's face instantly set Gabe on alert.

"We're working the Belgians with the show wagon. Do you want to watch for a minute while Gabe talks with Tom?" Thomas asked Cody. He turned his eyes on Gabe. "If that's all right with you, of course."

"I'd rather he be with you than around Tom."

"I figured as much."

"You're not making me feel any better about his intentions."

Thomas shrugged and took Cody's hand to lead the boy into the arena. Gabe watched them disappear inside before he marched over to Tom.

"Jim flagged me down," he said. Best to get right down to business. "Said you might have some electrical work."

"Yes," Tom replied.

He reached into his pickup and pulled out what Gabe assumed was a house plan. He unrolled the paper across the hood of his truck, and Gabe's guess was confirmed. Two bedrooms, one bath with laundry, and an open kitchen-living-dining area. It was bigger than his first house.

"This is a *bunkhouse*?" Gabe couldn't help asking.

"Or a guest house. Dad thinks we should get into the hospitality business, add a little dude ranching to the operation. We're not decided on that yet, but even if we don't go for it, we could always use the extra housing for the ranch hands. Jim and Cam are pretty cramped in their bunkhouse."

While Tom talked, Gabe inspected the plans, plotting the circuits in his head along with the best placement for lights, outlets, and switches. By the time Tom had finished his narrative, Gabe had a ballpark figure of what he'd charge for the job. Then he added a couple thousand to cover the annoyance of working for the man. It'd make his quote higher than either of his competitors, but that was the point. He didn't want the job.

"Is there anything special you want?" he asked. He rolled up the floor plan and handed it to Tom, who waved it away.

"You hold on to that. It's a copy. And no. Standard oven and range, fridge, dishwasher, microwave in the kitchen. Nothing fancy for the washer and dryer. I'll leave the placement of lights and outlets and all that to your judgment. How quick do you think you can have a quote put together for me?"

"Monday morning."

"Not working weekends anymore?"

Gabe met the man's gaze head on, and the meaning behind the words was as clear as the sky above. "Not as an electrician."

"I see." Tom folded his arms across his chest, and his semi-polite expression shifted into a dark scowl. "Stay away from Annemarie, Collins."

Walk away. Now. "What does it matter to you?"

"I don't want to see her get hurt."

Gabe gave a bark of laughter. "You are so full of shit it's no wonder your eyes are brown. Compared to how badly you hurt her, I could be the biggest asshole in the world and not come anywhere near what you did."

"I mean it, Collins. Stay away from her. And stay away from my son."

"TJ? No problem there. The kid's a bona fide brat."

"I meant Cody."

"If he weren't such an afterthought to you, I might consider your input, but at this point, Cody is more my son than yours. That makes them *both* mine to protect. Not yours." He hurled the floor plan through the open window of Tom's shiny new pickup. "As long as their well-being is my concern, Collins Electrical will never work for Grant Ranch. And in case you're wondering how long that might be, quite possibly the rest of my life."

"Over my dead body."

Gabe gripped the handle of the arena door. "Don't tempt me."

"You don't have the balls."

Rolling his eyes, Gabe yanked the door open.

"You're proving me right, Collins."

"No, I'm refusing to lower myself to your level. Cody deserves a better example to follow, and you are not worth spoiling that."

He stepped inside, bringing the conversation to an abrupt end when he jerked the door closed behind him. Thomas leaned against the metal gate separating the arena floor from the entryway, and Cody perched on the rails. One of the Grants' other hands—Jim's bunkmate, Cam, he thought—had a quartet of Belgian draft horses pulling a glossy red and white buckboard-style wagon around the arena at a trot. Their chestnut coats and flaxen manes and tails, recently groomed for a show, shimmered in the shafts of sunlight pouring through the skylights.

There was enough resemblance between Cody and Thomas that Gabe didn't need the confirmation of a paternity test to know that Tom was indeed Cody's father and Thomas his grandfather. At the moment, though, that resemblance was a source of satisfaction rather than consternation. When he was with Cody, Thomas's entire countenance changed. Gone was the stubborn, cantankerous old rancher, and in his place was a doting grandfather. Gabe much preferred the latter and wished Tom had inherited more of it. Hell, *any* of it.

"Come on, Cody," he announced. Despite his delight in this quiet moment between grandfather and grandson, his voice still held the edge from his chat with Tom. "It's time to go."

Thomas took one look at Gabe's expression and swore. "What'd he do?"

"Was he ever serious about hiring me to wire the new guesthouse, or was that just an excuse to try to pick a fight with me?"

"Yes he was, but I assume that isn't going to happen now."

"No, it isn't. Not this job and not any future job you might've wanted me to do. I will not work for Grant Ranch until either that son of a bitch is dead or he owns up to the hell he's put Annie through. I know he's your son, and I'm sorry to speak so crassly about him, but he's earned it." He gave Cody's shoulder a squeeze. "Sorry for the language, squirt."

"There's no way I can change your mind?"

"I'm sorry, but there isn't."

Thomas sighed. "I was afraid of that. I didn't want

to have to hire Halverson or Gentry. Never had much use for either of them."

"It's still your ranch, isn't it? Why are you letting him damage its reputation like this?" Gabe shook his head, remembering what Jim had told him that morning they'd loaded cows together. "Never mind. I guess I already know the answer to that."

"I don't know how I still have hope for him," Thomas said quietly.

"I do. He's your son."

"That's where Ginny and I went wrong. He's the only child we were able to have, and we let that get in the way." Thomas's face lifted momentarily in a humorless smile. His expression warmed some as he ruffled Cody's hair and turned his gaze on Gabe. "I'd tell you not to make the same mistake with this one, but I already know you won't. Please tell the Garretts I say hello."

"Will do."

Gabe waited for Cody to give his grandfather a hug, then took his hand and led him out of the arena. He half expected Tom to be right outside waiting to sucker punch him, but there was no sign of Cody's sire. Gabe let out a breath and helped Cody into his booster seat. As he drove down toward the main ranch road, he concentrated on his breathing, consciously subverting the fury still licking through him. He was proud of himself for not letting Tom get to him even as much as Sandy had all those weeks ago, especially now that he had far more reason to be angry.

"Well, that was a waste of time, wasn't it?" he

remarked. "I hope you had fun watching Cam work the Belgians."

"Yeah. It's so neat how he does it."

"You think you'd want to train horses someday?"

"Maybe. But I want to be an electrician like you more."

Gabe turned to Cody with a smile. "I can't imagine a greater compliment, Cody. Thank you."

The cloud of dust curling into the air behind the tractor caught Gabe's attention, and the last of his anger fizzled. A devious plan took shape, and he grinned. Instead of turning toward Garrett Ranch, he stopped by the field where Jim was plowing. He told Cody to wait in the truck for a minute and jogged over to the tractor. Jim opened the door and leaned out.

"How much would it take to convince you to come work for Annie full time?" Gabe asked.

"Well, about as much as I make working for the Grants, I suppose."

"Why don't you and I get together on your next day off and talk about it?"

"I'm off Monday. First thing in the morning good for you?"

"Perfect. See you then if not before."

Part one started. He trotted back to his truck and smiled at Cody. "Mind if we take another detour before we head home?"

"Where to?"

"You said the Garrett Ranch road—the one out

that'll take you directly out to the highway—washed out, right?"

"Yeah."

"We're going to go see how much it'll take to fix it."

"Mom already called about it after it happened, and she said it's *way* too expensive."

"I have a way around that. But first, I need to see how bad it is."

"Gabe?"

"Hmm?"

"Do you love my mom?"

He glanced sharply at the kid, startled though he probably shouldn't be. He started to say he wasn't sure yet, but it was a lie. "Yes, I do."

"And… me, too?"

"You bet I love you, too."

"Does that mean you'd want to be my dad if you marry my mom?"

"Absolutely. You're a great kid, Cody. One any man would be proud to call his son."

"Tom isn't."

"That's because Tom is an idiot. I know that's not nice to say, but if he can't see how wonderful you are, it's his loss, and I'll be happy to pick up the slack. But that's all up to your mom. *She* may not want to marry *me*. And there's the question of whether or not *you* want me to marry her."

Cody nodded shyly. "You make her happy. And then we'd all be a family for real. Like Caleb and his mom and his new dad Tad."

"I hope so, and yes we would."

Satisfied with the way the conversation had gone, Cody turned his attention to their detour and tried to pry information out of him all the way to the boundary of Garrett Ranch, but Gabe wasn't about to give anything up. The little boy would undoubtedly try his best to keep the secret, but he was young enough that it might slip out anyhow, and this was one part of his plan Gabe didn't want Annie to have any idea about until he was ready to reveal it. He didn't think being skinned alive would be a pleasant experience, and if she found out ahead of time that he was spending more money on her—not exactly true, in this case—he was certain she'd give it a try.

He passed the turn to the cabin, continuing along the track toward the highway. As Cody had said, the road was completely washed out about halfway between the cabin and the highway where—if he had to guess—a flash flood had turned the tiny trickle coursing down the gully into a force of erosion the too-small culvert hadn't been able to handle. Rushing water had carved a canyon that went from three feet deep on one side of the road to six feet deep on the other and pushed the culvert out of its original position. Road construction wasn't his area of expertise, but it looked to him like this trickle was prone to flash floods. Debris in varying stages of decay littered the narrow gully, and the shoulders of the road bore the traces of long-dried runoff. A bridge would probably be the most effective fix, though not the cheapest. So long as there was no more damage to the road elsewhere, the favor he was owed should cover the repair.

"All right, squirt. We'd best get back to the house before your grandparents show up. If they haven't already."

As it turned out, Bill and Judy Garrett were just stepping out of their Suburban when Gabe and Cody reached the cabin. After asking where Annie was, neither of them seemed at all surprised that Gabe had picked Cody up from school. But they wouldn't let him shrug it off when he tried.

"It may not seem like a big deal to you," Judy remarked as Gabe unlocked the door and let everyone in. "But it is. For her to have someone she trusts with her son…. That's an incredible burden lifted."

Bill asked Cody to help him bring in their bags from the Suburban, and while the little boy was busy, Gabe turned to Judy.

"Speaking of burdens," he said, "there's another one I need to take care of. If you'll excuse me, I need to call in a favor."

She eyed him with one brow lifted and her lips quirked but didn't ask for details.

Gabe picked up the cordless and dialed his friend's shop.

"Tomlinson Construction, this is Darren."

"Darren, it's Gabe."

"Hey, man. What can I do for you?"

"I'm calling in that favor you owe me."

"About damned time. What do you need?"

"A bridge, I think. Not a big one, just enough to span a creek that's usually less than a foot wide but seems prone to flooding."

"No problem. Where?"

"The road to Garrett Ranch."

— *Chapter Fifteen* —

GABE'S PICKUP AND HER parents' Suburban were parked in front of her house, but the cabin was empty. She didn't need too many guesses to figure out where they were, and she took the opportunity to change out of her work clothes and into something that was sure to shock them all—a form-fitting black dress with a hem a few inches above her knees that she'd picked up this week in anticipation of tonight. She freshened up her makeup, shook out her hair and brushed it until it gleamed, decided to leave it down, and stood back to inspect her reflection in the tall, narrow mirror on the back of the bathroom door.

It had been so long since she'd dressed up that the woman gazing back at her looked like a stranger. The neckline was low enough that she ought to put on a necklace, but she had just the one her parents had given her to commemorate Cody's birth—an asymmetrical white-gold heart with five tiny rubies set into one side. Its chain was so delicate that she'd hardly worn it, too afraid it might break and she'd lose it. But tonight was a special occasion, and it was a way to bring Cody with her. Gabe would appreciate that sentiment.

A coy smile transformed her face, and for the first time, she thought she caught a glimpse of what Gabe found beautiful about her. Cody was her heart, and that Gabe both understood and embraced that was more than she'd allowed herself to hope she'd find in a man.

It's time.

She slipped her feet into a pair of comfortable tennis shoes and grabbed her black strappy heels—the only dressy shoes she owned—and laughed at the thought that the additional couple inches they'd give her wouldn't make her even noticeably closer to Gabe in height. She took the shoes and the overnight bag she'd packed last night out to Gabe's truck then trotted down the road to the barn.

She slipped discreetly inside, and the sound of cherished voices greeted her as her family and Gabe discussed Angel's somewhat miraculous arrival to the world. When her eyes adjusted, she spied her parents leaning against the gate of the stall where Gabe had helped Diamond Dot deliver her colt. Cody perched almost exactly where he'd sat that day, and Gabe was once again in the stall, stroking his hand down the paint mare's neck. Angel nosed his free hand, demanding attention. Annemarie had to bite back a laugh so she didn't alert them to her presence. She wasn't quite ready to join them yet.

It felt like a lifetime ago since she had first met Gabe right here in this barn. He had become such a treasured fixture in her routine that it was difficult to recall what her life had been like without him in it. She had transformed into a new version of herself, one entwined with him, and even those many memories she'd made before she'd met him were viewed now through the eyes of this new Annemarie, with altered lenses.

She liked the new her. This Annemarie wasn't scared and heartbroken. She was confident and hopeful.

She hadn't made a sound or moved another inch, and yet Gabe lifted his gaze and met hers with a tender smile that quickly morphed into awestruck surprise as he took in the whole of her. She didn't need the lopsided grin to know that he liked what he saw; his eyes said more than enough.

The jolt of familiar desire and connection zapped her, and her lips lifted to match. She couldn't say if it was that first kiss that had shattered the last wall between them or if it was their Torrington road trip in general, but they were in sync now. That metaphorical dance she'd pictured them inching closer into? She wasn't waiting and watching for the moment to slip into his arms anymore. She was fully there, moving with him through complex and dizzying steps.

"You are all *so* predictable," she remarked at last, sauntering to the stall.

"Oh, Mom," Cody sighed. "Wow. You're…. Gabe,

what's the G word that means really, really pretty?"

"Gorgeous."

"Yeah. You're gorgeous, Mom."

"Yes, she is," Gabe murmured.

"Oh, sweetheart!" her mother cheered, hugging her tightly. "You look stunning. And you're wearing your necklace. The one your dad and I bought you when Cody was born."

She nodded, watching Gabe, who couldn't tear his eyes away. At the moment, he was focused on her pendant, and when he met her gaze a moment later, his smile had softened. Without being told, he understood why she'd chosen to wear it, and gratitude for this incredible man swamped her.

"Mind if we stop by my place so I can change into something a little nicer so I'm not so completely underdressed?" he asked.

"I don't care about that. You're just fine as you are."

"I won't have my lady's ravishing beauty sullied by this wastrel's rags."

The playfully gallant turn of phrase caught her by surprise, and she laughed. "As you wish, good sir. Mom, Dad, Cody… have fun tonight."

"We'll try not to destroy the house," Bill quipped.

"Oh, go ahead and destroy it. Just have a good time doing it."

Annemarie snatched Gabe's hand and dragged him out of the stall. She hugged her son, reminded him to be good for his grandparents, and rushed through thanking her parents and bidding them goodnight so she wasn't tempted to linger. This would be her first night away from her son, and as much as she was looking forward to her time with Gabe, she hoped desperately that the separation anxiety wouldn't ruin it.

On the ride into town, she tried to avoid the topic of missing her son by talking about anything *but* that, and it only made her more anxious. Finally, Gabe broached the subject, and she found that talking about it helped. A lot. So did admitting to the guilt she felt for being relieved to have the large chunk of time to be an adult and focus on herself. When he observed that taking care of herself for a few hours would probably allow her to take care of her son with a renewed energy, she let out a sigh and consciously let go of her guilt.

Gabe's house was located in a quiet neighborhood on the southwest side of Cody, an early 1900s home with a finished room in the attic, she guessed, gazing up at the tall, narrow window upstairs. It had been remodeled in recent years, and instead of the plain white, horizontal siding she would've expected, it was sided with vertical rough-sawn planks. The trim around the roofline, door, and windows was stained a dark blue that allowed the wood's grain to show through. Gabe parked in the long driveway that ended at the surprisingly large, newer garage in the back right corner of the oversized lot. Two quaking aspens flanked the walkway up to the enclosed front porch.

She recognized the house right next door as Terri's. The veterinarian was out in her yard weeding the flowerbed around one of the two towering spruce trees, and when Annemarie stepped out of Gabe's truck—now wearing her strappy heels—she let out a whistle.

"You clean up nice, Garrett," the vet called. "Hot date tonight, huh?"

"I hope so, but I'm not sure what the plan is yet."

"We're being spontaneous," Gabe explained.

"You? Spontaneous? Since when, Sparky?"

"Since now."

"Welcome to the wild side."

"Thanks," he chuckled and held the door for Annemarie.

The porch was adorned with a glass-topped wicker coffee table and a pair of matching wicker chairs that looked quite comfortable with their overstuffed cushions. An empty coffee mug sat on the table beside a well-worn paperback, and she guessed he spent a fair amount of his free time out here. She craned her neck to see what book he was reading. Larry McMurtry's *Lonesome Dove*—a fitting choice for a man born and bred for the cowboy way of life.

Gabe unlocked the door into the house and stepped aside so she could enter.

The interior had undergone a major remodel as well. It didn't have the closed-off floor plan she had expected. Instead, the living room and dining room were open, separated from the kitchen by only an island. The stairs to the attic sat right in the middle of the house with the kitchen to the right and what appeared to be an office to the left. Sliding, glass-paneled doors separated it from the living area but didn't give quite the same closed-off feeling solid doors would have. The downstairs bathroom was tucked away under the stairs and was larger than she expected, opening into some of the space she'd thought was all part of the office. At the rear of the house was a large bedroom, and the master suite took up the entire attic, he informed her, complete with its own bathroom that featured a Jacuzzi tub.

The walls were painted a warm reddish sand color that would make the place feel warm even on the coldest winter day, and the trim was all weathered barn wood. A wreath of rusted barbed wire hung on one wall in the living room, horseshoe lamps and art, and other artifacts from a ranch—Gabe's family's or someone else's, she didn't know—were scattered throughout the house, but there were very few personal touches. She spotted a few family photos, and there was a shelving unit full of books and photos and knickknacks, but otherwise, it looked more like a show house than a residence.

She leaned in to inspect a larger photo in the center of the bookshelf. It was of Gabe, his parents, and all seven of his siblings. She picked him out easily because he was the youngest boy, but he had changed a *lot* since the photo was taken. He wasn't, as she'd teasingly remarked, a chunk, but next to his strapping older brothers—the eldest of whom were already fully grown men in the photo— the lingering baby softness made him an obvious target for harassment. Turning away from the photo, she slipped her hand into Gabe's and leaned her head on his shoulder as she let her gaze roam around the rest of the house again.

"This is a beautiful home," she murmured. "I can't believe it's a rental."

"My landlord and I did the remodel three years ago."

"His style or yours?"

"Mine. Why?"

"It suits you. And yet… it barely looks lived in."

He shrugged. "I work a lot."

"Was this the house you lived in when Leigh….?"

"No, it's the one we were going to move into. My other place was an old singlewide trailer out of town, and I was perfectly happy there, but she wasn't keen about moving into it. I was saving up to buy my own land, so I didn't want to be spending a bunch of money on rent, which is why I told her she needed to chip in if we were going to move into this place. You already know how that conversation went."

"Then why'd you move in here?"

"Call it a sacrifice for something I couldn't see then that I'd never have with her."

"What, marriage?"

"More than that." He hooked his thumbs in his pockets and glanced around the space. "I'm proud of the work I've done on this place, but it'll never be home. Crazy as it sounds, your little cabin is more welcoming to me than this place. It's cozier."

"Funny. Until you started spending time out there,

that's the last thing I would've called it. But now… you're right." She turned to him and slid her hands around his waist, hooking them behind his back. Smiling up at him, she murmured, "I imagine if Cody and I were here, this place would be much less empty."

"It would indeed."

He lowered his mouth to hers with his hands cupping her face, and she leaned into him.

"It's beginning to feel a lot more like home already," he whispered. "Come on upstairs, and we'll finish the tour before I get changed."

Her pulse quickened as she followed him up the steep, narrow stairs. At the top was a sitting area that took up the back third of the attic. French doors stained to match the barn wood throughout the house opened out onto a balcony barely big enough to fit two chairs, and four-foot walls shielded either side of the staircase while giving the room an open feel. Annemarie turned toward the front of the house and noted the wall that separated the sitting room from the bedroom. She followed Gabe, almost giggling when he had to tip his head sharply to the left so he didn't knock it on the slanted ceiling to the right of the stairs. She had no trouble walking entirely upright.

"How many times have you hit your head?" she asked, unable to resist.

"A few. Here's the master suite."

They'd passed the separating wall, and Annemarie first noticed the log bed that dominated the bedroom. The bathroom sat in the corner to her left, a triangle with the two acute angles cut off and a walk-in closet behind the left wall of the bedroom. The Jacuzzi tub sat directly across from the sliding doors, which matched the ones to the office downstairs but had frosted glass instead of clear. To the right of the tub was a stunning, glass-enclosed shower tiled with slate. The toilet was tucked off to the left, and between that and the tub was a beautiful sink and vanity with a slate counter and a barn wood stand. As she would expect in a house remodeled by an electrician, there was plenty of light throughout—canned lights above, wall sconces beside the vanity and shower, and a row of round bulbs above the big mirror.

"This is gorgeous, Gabe," she breathed. "Did you really design it all?"

"Most of it."

"I am seriously impressed."

She backed out of the bathroom and faced the bed again. It stood beneath the window, neatly made and covered with an heirloom quilt with horses and the same warm earth colors and cool blues and grays of the barn wood and slate. She suspected that had inspired the entire remodel, and when she asked, he confirmed it.

"It was my Aunt Naomi's wedding present for my parents—she made it herself."

"It's beautiful." She walked over to the bed and skimmed her hand over the quilt, admiring the elegant stitching and the swirled pattern of the quilting. "How did you end up with it? Seems like something they would want to keep."

"Supposedly it didn't match the décor they picked when they remodeled the main house, but I think Mom's still a little miffed that Aunt Naomi was more concerned about it getting ruined than she was about Mom being in the midst of giving birth."

She jerked her head around to him. "Wait. Who was born at home?"

He raised a hand with a guilty smile. "Guess I was a little overeager to meet the world."

"Cody was, too," she said, snuggling into his side. "Not quite as eager as you were—I *did* make it to the hospital—but he came two weeks before his due date, and I was only in labor for four hours. My doctor kept telling me to wait, that'd it probably take quite a while since he was my first, and I finally told Mom she needed to drive me in to Casper. My water broke in the lobby of the hospital, and Cody was born half an hour later."

"You were out at your parents' house?"

"Yep. On summer break from college."

"Have I ever told you how much it amazes me that you stuck it out and finished school? That can't have been easy."

She shook her head and swiveled to face him. "It wasn't, but it was something I had to do. I didn't want to quit and resent my son for it."

"Don't ever doubt your strength again, Annemarie." His voice was gentle, as were his fingers when he brushed them over her cheeks.

"Yes, sir."

She stood on her toes to kiss him, fiddling with the top buttons of his shirt. He didn't seem to notice until she had them all undone and slid her hands between that shirt and the T-shirt beneath, slyly working it over his shoulders.

"What are you doing?" he asked.

"You wanted to be spontaneous, so let's be spontaneous."

"We'll be late for dinner."

"Do we have reservations someplace?"

"No."

"Then how can we be late?"

He rolled his shoulders as she tugged the shirt down his arms to make the process easier.

"You're not going to stop me?"

"Not this time. I know everything about us that I need to."

He claimed her mouth with a fierce desire that sent her pulse skyrocketing. There would be no holding back, no stopping this time, and the promise of sating the ravenous hunger consumed her.

"What do you know?" she asked hoarsely.

"I know your strength and your spirit." He trailed kisses down the side of her neck and over her shoulder, drawing a shiver from her. "I know your heart. In a few minutes, I'll know your body, too."

"What else do you know?"

He kissed her mouth again before he answered, splaying his hands across her back and holding her close with a reverence that left her breathless.

"That I trust you."

He raked his teeth over her neck, and she shuddered. Goose bumps tingled across her skin, and she leaned into him.

"Also that I love you."

Relief. It permeated her with wonderful intensity. She'd suspected as much, and he hadn't been shy about letting her know she was valuable to him, but to hear confirmation….

She buried her face against his chest and sagged in his arms.

"Maybe some would say it's too early to know, but I know my heart as well as I know yours—I know its weaknesses and hopes—and it's had plenty of experience with false love to know that this isn't. It's real. And I don't care how long it takes for you to arrive at the same conclusion, I'll wait."

She dragged his mouth to hers, silencing him with a kiss.

"I'm already there. I know it's real because every time you talk about Leigh, I hurt for you. I know because of that country song I ask you to sing every time it's on the radio. You're not just singing someone else's words. You mean them. Even more than that, I know because when you say I'm strong, I believe you. You *make* me feel strong. And I know because you are the kind of man I want my son to grow into." She folded her hands behind his neck and leaned back in his arms, laughing softly. "In case you didn't get the message from all that, I love you, too."

"I picked up on that," he chuckled.

"It feels really, really good to say that. Finally."

"Yes, it does." He lifted her pendant gently with his fingers and studied it with a tender smile. "Do you want to take this off before we get carried away? I'd hate for something to happen to it."

She nodded, and he reached behind her neck to unclasp the necklace, then handed it to her. She set it on top of his dresser and returned to him, sliding her hands up his stomach and chest and over his shoulders before burying them in his hair, suddenly annoyed by the thin fabric of his T-shirt. She wanted to feel warm, naked skin beneath her palms, to explore the lines of his body with her lips. She wanted to claim him. She tugged the hem of his T-shirt free from his jeans, and he bent over so she could pull it over his head.

They kicked off their shoes, and after sighing at the loss of those couple extra inches, Annemarie focused on the beauty of the man in front of her. It was absurd that he could be so shy about his body. He didn't have the chiseled six-pack those romance-cover cowboys had, but he was undeniably toned. She suspected he worked out to hone the edges, but most of it was probably the product of his highly physical job and enviable genetics.

"If I can't doubt my strength anymore," she whispered, nipping at his jaw, "you're not allowed to question how beautiful you are, either."

"Not a word I've ever associated with myself," he said, inhaling sharply, "but when you say it, I believe it."

"Good."

He unzipped her dress, and she let it fall to the floor. Her bra and panties followed quickly and then his jeans and boxers and socks. He lifted her off the floor and settled her on the bed with a tenderness she'd never known before him, and when he slid his hands up her body before settling onto the bed beside her, she forgot about wanting to explore all the lines of him. She forgot everything but the heat of skin against skin and the taste of his mouth as he kissed her.

This wasn't about physical satisfaction, although she'd definitely find that, too. It was about making the final connection between them. She couldn't wait. She'd have plenty of time later to play.

He was ready, anyhow, so she squirmed closer to him, nudging her hip under him. When he unexpectedly latched onto her breast with his mouth, heat exploded. She gasped and arched against him. Strong hands stroked down and back up her body, and heat turned into an ache. She dug her fingers into the meat of his shoulder, pulling him on top of her, and sought his mouth as she gripped his hips with her thighs. The move pressed his arousal between her legs, and instinct took over as she rocked her hips against him.

"Not yet, sweetheart."

"Yes, yet. Now."

"As appealing as the idea of having a baby with you

is, let's take this one step at a time, all right? Marriage first, love."

"Wha…?"

"No, that wasn't a proposal. Not yet."

The sensations pounding through her left her dizzy. Did he just say *marriage* and *proposal?* Giddiness crashed through her. To stem it, she clasped his face and kissed him fiercely. She wiggled her hips and grinned when he swore under his breath.

"Hold on a minute, would ya, Annie?"

Propped above her on one arm, he reached into the drawer of his nightstand, and she took the opportunity to run her hands over his chest, tracing the contours of muscle, ribs, and collarbone so lightly with her fingertips that his skin prickled with goose bumps. He briefly dangled a condom box above her before he dove after her neck and thrust his arousal against her, tempting and teasing her. She inhaled sharply at the promise of what was to come.

"Forgetting something?" he whispered in her ear.

She nodded and daringly caressed him before the thin layer of latex became a barrier between them, delighting in the feel of silken skin against her fingertips. When she snatched the condom from him and sheathed him herself, he groaned. She glanced up to see him tip his head back and clench his jaw, and she grinned smugly.

"Mine," she purred, angling her hips toward him again.

"One hundred percent."

"Good, because I'm yours, and it's time to prove

it."

He claimed her mouth as he settled over her and pushed slowly inside her. She quivered and angled her hips to take him deeper. He filled her marvelously, and she sighed, contented and relieved to be joined with him.

Finally.

He let her set the pace, and with a confidence that surprised her, she did. Even in a position of submission, she felt powerful and in control. He was hers to drive wild. There was passion and primal instinct, but there was also tenderness and reverence, and she could say without a doubt that she'd never experienced anything like it. Sweat beaded on their skin, but he showed no signs of wanting to pick up the pace and she was too mesmerized by the tightening and loosening of the muscles of his back as she dragged her hands up and down his body to hurry it. When she slid her hands down his sides and dug her fingers into his buttocks, he shuddered.

"I can't hold on much longer," he uttered. "Sorry, Annie."

"Then go for it."

He took command, and in seconds, she was panting as they raced toward climax. She matched his pace, whimpering as the orgasm hovered just out of reach for agonizing minutes. Just when she was about to scream in frustration, Gabe took her to the edge, and they plunged over it together. Her body jerked with the force of it, and Gabe hung his head, his body trembling as he fought for breath, but he held himself above her for minutes more, still joined with her.

When he finally pulled away and lowered himself onto the bed beside her, skimming his fingers over her arm and gazing adoringly at her with his head propped in his palm, her pulse and breathing had slowed enough that she no longer feared her heart would pound right out of her chest.

"That was faster than I was hoping for," he murmured.

"Do you hear me complaining?"

"No."

"And you won't. But I fully expect you to put your stamina to the test later tonight." She wiggled her brows. "All night."

"Is that a challenge, Ms. Garrett?"

"Yes, it is. Are you up to it?"

He grinned wickedly. "I guess you're going to find out."

In contrast to the heat of their lovemaking, the air was cool, and her skin chilled as sweat dried. She reached for a blanket only to realize they'd made love on top of the bed. With a quirk of her lips, she smoothed her hand over the horse quilt and started laughing. Gabe propped himself up on one arm and eyed her with one brow lifted.

"Let's not tell your Aunt Naomi about this."

His head fell back, and he laughed. The rich, deep sound of it was heaven. Still chuckling, he flopped back into the pillows and gathered her into his arms.

"I could stay here, just like this, all night," he

murmured.

"Mmm. So could I. But I'm hungry."

"Join me for a shower?"

"You bet your sexy ass."

He jerked his head back and stared at her. "I think that's the first time I've ever heard you swear."

Grinning, she said, "I don't unless I have a good reason to."

"And my ass is reason enough?"

"Well, not just that but every… other… glorious… inch… of you." She punctuated each word with a kiss—first on his lips, then his neck, his shoulder, and finally his chest right over his heart. She lifted her head, resting her hand where her lips had been, and gazed into his eyes as his heart beat faster beneath her palm. "Especially this. This is my favorite part of you."

She laid her head on his chest with her hand beneath her cheek and sighed.

"What's wrong?" he asked.

"I'm afraid you're getting the short end of our relationship again, just like you got the short end of our deal."

"How do you figure?"

"What have I given you in return for everything you've done for me?"

"A lot. You've shown me it's safe to love again. You've invited me to be a part of your life and your son's life, given me a family to call my own for however long this lasts… and I'm hoping it lasts a very long time."

Let's take this one step at a time, he'd said. *Marriage first, love.*

Were they headed that direction? She curled herself around him and let herself imagine having this—and him—for the rest of her life.

What a life that would be.

"Can you accept that I love you and that seeing you smile is all the payment I'll ever need?"

She nodded.

"Good," he said as his stomach growled. "Because you aren't the only one who's hungry. We have all night to talk and make love, so right now, let's shower and go find something to eat."

—Chapter Sixteen—

GABE SPRAWLED ON HIS BED with his legs dangling over the side, distracted by Annie as she blow-dried her hair and reapplied her minimal makeup. He'd only made it as far as tugging on a pair of brand-new Wrangler jeans. He hadn't even gotten around to zipping and buttoning them, too enthralled by the woman at his bathroom sink clad only in lacy black panties and matching bra. The feminine curves of her hips and back, the elegant shoulders and neck, the soft, pale skin, and the cascade of silky light brown hair…. She was the most beautiful thing he'd ever seen.

Her sexy little black dress hung on the bathroom door, and the steam from their shower had done a decent job of smoothing out the wrinkles that had gathered from being piled on the floor. His gaze shifted to it, and he sighed. He should get up and finish getting dressed. She'd turned their shower into a sensual free-for-all, and he hadn't been able to resist pinning her to the slate-tiled wall and making love to her again. By the time they'd finally scrubbed each other down, the water had turned icy. Now they were in danger of being so late that they wouldn't be able to make it out to the Stagecoach Steakhouse and Saloon on Buffalo Bill Reservoir in time to catch the end of the dinner service. He briefly contemplated taking her to Buffalo Bill's Pizzeria but dismissed it. He wanted to take her somewhere nice—someplace she wasn't likely to have been before.

She met his gaze in the mirror and smiled. "You going to get dressed, or what?"

"I'm going with 'or what'. You sure you don't want me to wear my suit?"

"Positive. The Stagecoach is Western-themed, isn't it?"

He nodded.

"Well, one of us should look the part."

Finally, he sat up, but it took him a few moments more to push to his feet. He wandered over to the walk-in closet—his clothes took up depressingly little of the space—and located his two Western dress shirts.

"Which one? Red or blue?"

Annie leaned out of the bathroom. "Definitely blue."

"You sure? Red one's fancier."

"Blue."

"Yes, ma'am."

The shirt fit a little tighter across the shoulders than

the shirt he'd worn earlier, so he dragged a plain white tank out of his dresser, then shrugged into the cornflower blue, navy, and white plaid shirt, methodically joined all the snaps, and tucked it into his jeans, all the while watching his lover. It took every ounce of willpower to tear his eyes away long enough to hunt down his cowboy boots and the belt with the steer-wrestling trophy buckle.

At her whistle, he jerked his head up. While he'd been preoccupied, she'd slipped into her dress and now sauntered across the room to him.

"You clean up nice, Mr. Collins. Do you have a cowboy hat to complete the ensemble?"

"I don't, actually."

"A cowboy who doesn't own a cowboy hat?"

"Technically, I'm an electrician."

She tugged playfully on his belt buckle. "Then where did this come from?"

"Won it."

"Doing what?"

"Steer wrestling."

"I didn't know you rodeoed."

"Just the once. Ezra was bragging that he was the best steer wrestler of us all, so we put it to the test at the local rodeo when I was a junior in high school. He wouldn't settle for proving it on the ranch."

"And you won it?"

"Yep."

"I bet he was mad."

"Naturally, but that's Ezra. Highly competitive.

Probably why he and I haven't always gotten along."

"I picked up on that at the ranch that first weekend. Even so, what your family has—that support system, the roots—that's what I want for Cody."

"It's a good life. Hectic sometimes, but I wouldn't trade it."

She turned her back to him. "Would you mind zipping me up?"

He did as she asked, letting his fingers linger against the nape of her neck. He lowered his head to kiss her shoulder. The he lifted her necklace off his dresser and fastened it around her neck. "Are you about ready?"

"Just need to put on my shoes."

Night was falling outside when Gabe locked his front door behind them, and a smudge of clear lavender was all that remained of day. Above, the first stars had already appeared, twinkling brightly in the cloudless sky. On the drive out to Buffalo Bill Reservoir, they didn't talk, content to enjoy the simplicity of each other's company and the beauty of the evening. The air was so sharply clear that the dark outlines of the mountains looked like they'd been cut with a scalpel. He'd seen so many nights like this in his lifetime but couldn't recall one that had left him with the same overwhelming awe.

The difference was the woman sitting beside him. As exquisite as her svelte body was in that fitted dress, the light in her eyes was the most breathtaking part about her.

Love. Beautiful, amazing, saturating love.

After he parked his truck in the back nine of the

steakhouse's parking lot, he walked around to the passenger side and opened the door for her, offering a hand to help her out. He slid his hand around the back of her neck, caressing her cheek with his thumb, and kissed her, then held his arm out to her. She slipped her hand around it, and together, they headed toward the restaurant.

It was almost eight, but the place was still busy, and near the doors Gabe spied a familiar pickup. "Son of a bitch."

"What?"

He inclined his head toward the truck. "That's Tom's, isn't it?"

"God damn it. Yes, it is."

"I think I liked it better when you were swearing about my ass," he muttered. "You want to go someplace else?"

"Where are we going to go this late? By the time we get back into town, most of the restaurants will be getting ready to close. If we sit outside, maybe we won't run into him."

They entered cautiously, but Tom and his wife weren't anywhere within view of the hostess's desk, so they asked for a table out on the deck.

"Are you sure?" the hostess—an older woman—asked. "It's getting pretty cold out. We've already had four tables come inside."

"We're sure," Annie replied. "Thank you, though."

They followed the woman out onto the deck, and she brought them to a table facing the lake apart from the few other diners stubborn enough to endure the descending cool of night. The heater gave off plenty of heat for Gabe, but even with her coat covering her upper body and thighs, Annie's lower legs were still exposed. He asked if she'd be warm enough.

"I'm fine," she replied. She met his gaze and grinned with a suggestive twitch of her eyebrows. "And if I get cold, I'm sure you can warm me right up."

"We'd best save that for later, darlin'."

The poor hostess nearly choked trying to swallow a laugh, and Gabe apologized.

"Don't worry about it. Reminds me of my husband and me when we first got married." She set their menus in front of them and poured water. "God rest his soul, he was a wonderful man. I hope you two have as much happiness in your marriage as we had in ours."

He started to say that they weren't married but shrugged it off and reached across the table to take Annie's hand. He brushed his thumb over her knuckles. "I think we will."

Her eyes rounded, but he didn't offer any clarification or explanation.

"What can I get you folks to drink?"

"Coffee, I think," Annemarie replied.

"Coffee would be great. Thank you."

After the hostess left, Gabe scooted his chair back and faced it toward the lake and the fading twilight, then patted his leg. Annie didn't have to be asked twice. She settled onto his lap with both legs over his, and he folded his arms around her.

"Better?" he asked when she rested her head on his shoulder and sighed.

"Mmm-hmm. What a beautiful night."

He nodded in agreement, hoping it stayed that way. They didn't talk and only smiled in acknowledgement when the hostess returned with coffee and informed them that their waitress would be right out. Without moving Annie, Gabe picked up his coffee and wrapped his hands around the warm mug, staring unseeing at the steam that curled from it.

"Gabe?"

"Hmm?"

"A few minutes ago when the hostess said she hoped our marriage would be as happy as hers, why didn't you tell her we weren't married?"

"I almost did."

"But…?"

"I thought it might be fun to try the idea on, see how it fits."

"And does it?"

"So far, I'd say it's a very comfortable fit."

Their waitress arrived, cutting off any response Annie might have made. Maybe it was better that way. He might be comfortable with the idea of marrying her—exhilarated by it, now that he'd had a few hours since that comment to Tom this afternoon had slipped out—but he wasn't the only one who needed to be sure it was right.

The waitress took their orders and left again as the

hostess seated a family of three at a table nearby. Gabe didn't pay them much attention other than to note that the little boy was Cody's age. He turned his gaze back to the lake and sipped his coffee, perfectly content to hold Annie as the temperature dropped.

"Annemarie, is that you?" the woman from the nearby table asked, weaving through the chairs to their table.

Annie sat up abruptly. "Jamie, hi. Uh, Gabe, this is Jamie Tanner—formerly Jamie Hollis. Her son, Caleb, is Cody's best friend at school. Jamie, this is Gabe Collins."

Jamie shook the hand Gabe extended. "It's a pleasure to finally meet the man Cody hasn't stopped talking about for weeks now."

"Nice to meet you, too. Cody says Caleb is pretty excited about his new dad."

"He's thrilled, and Tad sure made it easy on me. He adores Caleb. Never thought I'd find someone like that."

"I know the feeling," Annie murmured, turning her face to Gabe. "I'm hoping this one is as serious about filling that position as he's been talking tonight."

Jamie sat at their table, leaning forward with glee sparking in her dark eyes. "Ooo, details, details, you two!"

"If you'll excuse me, I need to use the restroom." Annemarie stood so he could get up, and he pressed a kiss to her neck. "Before you waste a bunch of time trying to decide if I am serious or not, yes I am."

He strode away beaming smugly and left them gaping after him. The route to the restrooms took him past the bar, and he spotted Tom sitting at it with several companions, three of whom he recognized as occasional clients of his. He made it past without any of them catching sight of him.

On the way back, he wasn't so lucky.

"Gabe! Come on over here for a second," one of the men called—Matthew Mason, owner of the cozy bed and breakfast Gabe had wired a theater surround sound system for the day he'd first met Annie. "I was just telling Tom here about that theater system. Told him he'd be a fool not to hire you for that new bunkhouse."

"I appreciate the compliment," Gabe replied, crossing his arms over his chest. He shook his head when Mathew offered to buy him a beer. "We've talked about the bunkhouse, but unfortunately, I'm unavailable for the job."

Tom met his gaze, and though he contained his contempt well, it showed through in the hard set of his jaw and the cold gleam in his dark eyes. He excused himself to use the restroom, and Mathew and the other men in their group stared after him.

"That was a little chilly," Mathew observed. Turning to Gabe, he asked, "What do you mean, 'unavailable'?"

"I won't work for him."

"Why ever not? Seems to me like that could be a good paying job."

"It would, but some things aren't worth the money."

Mathew held up his hands. "Message received. But

speaking of jobs, I have a couple more for you, if you have a minute while Tom's in the bathroom."

Gabe perched on the stool Tom had vacated, waving away the bartender and keeping an eye on the restrooms while he listened to Mathew's plans for festive lighting for the new gazebo he and his wife wanted to build. It seemed like the conversation went on and on, and Tom hadn't yet returned. Minutes ticked by, and the muscles in Gabe's neck and shoulders tensed. How long did Tom need to take a piss?

Finally, Gabe couldn't stand it and politely left Mathew, promising to draw up a quote for him on Monday for the gazebo lights. He spotted the Tanners at the salad bar and quickened his pace as dread settled into his belly like a ball of ice. Annie alone on the deck and Tom MIA.... He was jogging by the time he shoved open the doors to the deck.

Tom's voice greeted him the second he stepped outside, and he froze for a moment, dumbstruck by the man's brazen arrogance. He stepped quietly, following their voices.

"You know I'm the right choice."

"Right choice? There's *no* choice between being your whore or his wife."

"Funny, I don't see a ring on your finger. *You* may have forgotten what I can do to that sweet body, but *I* haven't."

"I suggest you do because it won't happen again. Ever."

There was a pause, and Gabe glanced around. His and Annie's table was abandoned. Where were they?

"Ah," Tom said. "You have his smell on you. You smelled much better with mine on you."

"Let go of me, Tom."

Her voice trembled and Gabe lunged forward, heart hammering against his ribs. She let out a strangled shriek. He sprinted around the corner and finally found them by the railing beyond the Tanners' still-empty table. Tom had caught her wrists in his hands and backed her against the railing. Terror widened her eyes as she tried to jerk her arms free, unable to break Tom's hold, and she screamed when he tried to kiss her.

Gabe didn't bother hiding his approach. He needed to get to Annie *now*. He gripped Tom's shoulder, yanked the man around, and decked him. Tom stumbled back into a table, sending the chairs around it crashing to the side. Without turning his back to the man, Gabe sidestepped to Annie and grasped her hand tightly. She slid her arms around him, shaking, and he clenched his jaw to tighten the rein on his temper.

Tom probed the inside of his bottom lip with his tongue, then pressed his fingers to it. They came away bloody.

"For the rest of my life. Remember that conversation, Grant?" Gabe asked. With deliberate movements, he turned to Annie, brushed her hair back from her face and kissed the top of her head before drawing her closer. "Regardless of whether or not there's a ring on her finger yet, she's mine to protect. Are you all right?"

She nodded, but tears welled in her eyes and she pinched her lips between her teeth. With a supportive hand resting against the small of her back, he guided her into the restaurant to the hostess's desk.

"We need to pay our check," he said curtly. "And can you let our waitress know that we'll need our dinner in to-go boxes?"

The woman took one look at Annie's face and gasped. "Dear lord, what happened?"

"My ex is here," Annie murmured. "And he doesn't seem to be in the mood to leave us alone."

"You just point him out to me, and I'll have him escorted out. You don't need to leave."

"That's all right, ma'am," Gabe said. He flexed his right hand, noting a small cut on one of his knuckles. "At this point, I think it's best we head home."

"Understood. Dinner's on the house. I'm so sorry."

"It's not your fault, and that's not necessary."

The waitress brought out their meal in Styrofoam boxes, and when Gabe tried to pay the check, the hostess refused to take his cash, so he gave a forty-dollar tip to each of them instead—what dinner and the tip would've come to. From the corner of his vision, he saw Tom come in, his lip already swollen. Their gazes met again, and the dark gleam in Tom's eyes ignited Gabe's fury all over again.

"Shall we take our date back home, love?" Gabe asked.

She nodded and slipped her hand into the crook of his arm, then thanked the hostess and the waitress.

In the safety of his pickup, Annie turned to him. She chewed on her bottom lip for almost half a minute before she finally spoke. Her words came out in a teary burst. "I'm sorry."

He gathered her into his arms and hugged her tightly as hot tears streamed down her face. As they began to leech through his shirt, his chest constricted. "What the hell do you have to be sorry for?"

"Tom…. I don't know why he's doing this. I'm sorry."

"Don't you dare apologize to me for him. This is *not* your fault."

"I never thought he'd take it to the point that you would have to hit him. I'm sorry for that and for our ruined date."

"First of all, stop apologizing, Annie. I mean it. Secondly, our date isn't ruined. There's just been a change of plans, and as I recall, we didn't have any set plans to begin with."

She gazed up at him with rounded eyes. "How did you walk away like that? Because you looked like you wanted to kill him."

"It was easier than you might think." He sighed. "Even so, it would not be a good idea for me to go back in there right now."

After a few minutes more, Annie scooted over to the passenger side and buckled herself in. Gabe started the truck and drove away from the restaurant.

She was silent on the way home, and quiet while they ate dinner, and after, when they headed upstairs to bed, she didn't say anything until she dug through her overnight bag and realized she'd forgotten to pack her pajamas. Her parents had slipped something into her bag, however, and she held it up for Gabe's inspection.

He wasn't sure whether to laugh at Bill and Judy's not-so-subtle suggestion or beg her to put it on. It was a midnight-blue satin nightgown with delicate spaghetti straps and a flower-embroidered, net-covered slit that curved from the center of the neckline down to the top of the right thigh. The hem was more matronly than blatantly sexy and would skim the middle of her calves, making it quite a bit longer than her black dress.

Sensual. That was the word. He couldn't have picked anything that would've suited her better.

The brief amusement faded, and her brows again drew together.

"Are you sure you're all right?" he asked, taking her hands and pulling her into his arms.

She shook her head. "I never thought he'd do something like that."

"Go put that pretty little number on while I turn down the bed, and then we'll get comfortable and talk."

Within minutes, they were snuggled together under the horse quilt, and he listened to her talk as she idly traced random patterns across his chest.

"I was still talking with Jamie about you when Tom

came out. He said he wanted to talk to me alone, and I tried to tell him it could wait, but he insisted. And then the waitress came back out, and Jamie and Tad and Caleb headed in to the salad bar." She shivered. "He started off nice enough, asked how the auction went, offered to have Jim come up next week to clear a hayfield on that bench you pointed out. Then… he touched my arm and said we could have what we did that fall in Laramie, that he was sorry for ignoring me, and that he was finally coming to terms with having a b-bastard son."

Her voice hitched, and Gabe tightened his arms around her.

"He also said that he would start being a father to him… if I told you to leave. I told him to go to hell, that nothing he could offer would make me leave you."

"Is that when he said he was the right choice?"

She glanced sharply at him. "I didn't know you heard that."

He nodded. "You don't have to repeat the rest."

"I can't believe he grabbed me like that. What do I have to do to make him believe he has nothing I want?"

"Stand up to him. Call him out on his bullshit. And if you can do it with an audience so he can't deny it later, even better."

"I don't think I could do that at all. It's easy for you to say, but look at you. When was the last time you were afraid for your safety? I can tell you when the last time was for me. An hour ago, when Tom grabbed my wrists and I couldn't free myself."

That hit home. Hard.

"Christ, Annie," he murmured. "I'd say the last time I was afraid like that was when I was thirteen and Ezra pinned me down while we were branding and threatened to brand my face. That sense of powerlessness—of not being able to get away from him—was terrifying, but it's not the same. Deep down, I knew he wouldn't do it. I think you were right to fear Tom might hurt you. He's getting desperate."

He brushed her hair back from her face, and they were silent for a time. In the quiet, the rhythmic ticking of his bedside clock was loud, and it grated on him while thoughts of all the bones he'd like to break in Tom's body teased his mind. He wouldn't, of course, but it was damned appealing.

"He is exactly the kind of man that gives the rest of us a bad name."

"Yes, he is."

"As much as I want to, this isn't something I can do for you, Annie. It needs to come from you, or he'll never get the message." He straightened her pendant, frowning. "Think Cody might still be awake?"

"Probably."

He reached for the cordless phone on his nightstand and handed it to her. "Why don't you give him a call to say goodnight? Tell your parents to keep an eye out for Tom tonight and tomorrow morning."

"You think he'd try something?"

"At this point, I wouldn't put it past him."

From her end of the conversation, he surmised that everything was quiet on the home front. She briefly handed him the phone so he could say goodnight to Cody, and then chatted with her parents for almost half an hour about the awesome fort they and Cody had constructed in the living room and about her date with Gabe. By the end of the call, she was considerably more relaxed.

"I thought you might need that."

"I guess I did. Thank you," she murmured. Then she sighed. "You're right about me needing to confront Tom, but I'm afraid."

"Don't be. I'll be right there behind you. Tonight, tomorrow… every day you need me."

——Chapter Seventeen——

GABE HAD STAYED out at her cabin for several nights after their run-in with Tom as a precaution, but when it became clear Tom wasn't going to try anything sinister, his staying with Annemarie and Cody had become a habit, and she wasn't in any hurry to have him go home and leave her alone. For two weeks now, she'd been waking up beside him, getting ready for work and school together in the mornings, eating breakfast like a family, and coming home together in the evenings to talk about their day, and she loved it. She even enjoyed planning meals for three people instead of two, though that had taken some getting used to, particularly in adjusting her recipes and shopping lists.

More than once, she'd caught herself thinking of Gabe's comments about trying the idea of marriage on for size to see how it fit, and though he hadn't again stated his intent outright, it was clear he was still leaning that direction. The conversation at the dinner table frequently revolved around plans for the ranch, everything from which company to hire to drill the irrigation well to the benefits of hiring someone to plow versus buying a used tractor and plow equipment.

The idea of spending the rest of her life with him—it was a perfect fit. She wanted it.

"Isn't that the Tanners?" Gabe asked, interrupting her daydreams. "Getting out of that red car over there?"

She followed his gaze and grinned, spotting the familiar sedan a couple rows over in the supermarket parking lot. "Yes, it is. Hey, Cody, didn't you say you wanted to invite Caleb out to go riding?"

"Yeah! Can we? When?"

"Maybe today, if they have time."

He barely waited for Gabe to park the truck before he threw off his seat belt and jumped out of his seat. Annemarie almost didn't have time to get out of his way as he scrambled over the back of the seat, too impatient to wait for her to get out and open the suicide door for him.

"Slow it down, Cody," she chided. "Let's not ruin Gabe's truck, all right?"

"Sorry, Mom. Sorry, Gabe. Hey, Caleb!"

He waved enthusiastically, and she was surprised he didn't take off across the parking lot. Gabe took his hand and headed over to the Tanners while Annemarie grabbed her purse out of the truck. She had to jog to catch up.

"Fancy meeting you three here," Jamie greeted with a broad smile. "What happened that night at the

Stagecoach? We got back to our table and you guys were gone."

"We took dinner to go," Gabe replied. "I think Cody has an invitation for Caleb. Don't you, squirt?"

"Can Caleb come ride horses with me today?"

"Uh…." Jamie looked to Tad, who shrugged. "We didn't have any plans for the afternoon, did we?"

"Nope. We were going to wing it."

"So… can we?" Caleb asked. "Pretty, pretty please?"

"Yeah, pretty, pretty please?" Cody echoed.

"Sure," Jamie laughed. "Sounds like a blast. Can we bring anything for lunch or dinner?"

"Might be nice to have a barbecue," Gabe suggested.

"That sounds fantastic. Except that I don't have a barbecue," Annemarie remarked.

"We can grab mine on the way home."

Jamie and Tad exchanged grins.

Gabe chuckled. "Yes, you heard me right. Shall we head in and figure out what to cook?"

Because they would need charcoal no matter what they barbecued, that was the first aisle they headed to. After a quick debate, they settled on burgers—with hamburger from a Garrett Ranch Angus—and the usual fair of junk food with fruit salad to offset the less-than healthy indulgences. They divvied up the shopping list and went in separate directions to divide and conquer.

Annemarie cruised down the aisles, dropping items

with comedic flair into the cart Cody had volunteered to push. Her son laughed at her antics, which only made her smile more widely.

"You're almost giddy," Gabe observed.

"Well, this is sort of a first."

"You can't mean this is the first time you've had the Tanners out to the ranch."

"It is."

"Wait. What about other friends?"

"What other friends? Being a single mother in a new town hasn't exactly made it easy to make friends. Jamie and Caleb came over a few times when we lived in town, and vice versa. She invited us over a few times since we moved out to the ranch, but at first, the cabin was in no shape to be entertaining guests—not even another single mom and her son. Once I got it fixed up a bit and at least livable, she was newly married, which was a bit awkward for me. And…." She shrugged. "Habit, I guess."

"I hope this will be the start of a more solid friendship for you."

"Me, too. It'll be good for Cody to have Caleb around more often. And I enjoy Jamie's company. She's the closest friend I've had since high school."

"Lemme guess. Being a single mom didn't give you a chance to make friends in college, either."

"Nope. Most college kids want to have fun and party, and I couldn't do that." She nudged him with her elbow. "At least I had Cody as an excuse for being boring, but I get the feeling that you would've been the too-busy-studying type."

"What makes you say that?"

"Your work ethic."

He laughed. "You're probably right. Gus accused me more than once of sometimes throwing myself too hard into my work. He tried to tell me I needed to remember to live life once in a while, but that lesson didn't stick. Not until recently, anyhow."

"How recently?"

"Oh, I think you know."

"Good lord, if the last few weeks is us cutting loose, we really are a pair of fuddy-duddies."

They both laughed at that and laughed harder when Cody asked what a fuddy-duddy was.

"Someone old and boring," Gabe replied.

"But you're *not* old *or* boring."

"Thanks, squirt."

Annemarie noticed the cart coming around the corner just in time to stop Cody. "I'm sorry," she said, breathless with laughter.

Her smile vanished instantly when she saw who was pushing the cart.

"If it isn't the husband-stealing whore," Sandy Grant said with her lip curled.

Everyone within hearing fell silent, and a dozen shoppers stopped to stare. Annemarie ground her teeth.

"Just ignore her," Gabe whispered. "Don't let her ruin your good mood."

Annemarie started to do just that, even took a

couple steps around Sandy, but then anger shot through her.

"No." She spun on her heel and faced Tom's wife. "I am done ignoring it. I have shouldered the entirety of the blame for far too long. That stops *now*."

The older woman jerked back like she'd been slapped. Her eyes bulged and her mouth worked like a beached fish. The heat of satisfaction licked through Annemarie, and she smiled coldly.

"Anyhow, last time I checked, you're still married—happily or otherwise—to Tom, so I am not technically a quote-unquote 'home wrecker'."

"You're not seriously going to—"

"You bet I am. Right here, right now, and I don't give a damn who hears it. Because I didn't get pregnant by myself at eighteen. Because I'm not the one who blatantly lied about being married. Forget about just taking his ring off. He didn't have a tan line or an indentation from it, Sandy."

"Of course he doesn't. With the work he does on the ranch, it's not safe to wear it all the—"

"Horseshit," Gabe snapped. "My father hasn't taken his wedding ring off once in forty-seven years other than to have it cleaned."

"I beg your pardon." Sandy sniffed. "Who are you to speak to me like that?"

"The son of a rancher who does the same kind of work your husband does. So I say it again. Horseshit. Tom's a great big lying sack of it."

"How dare you!"

"*You* started this," Annemarie bit out. "Stop lying to yourself, Sandy. How many times has he cheated on you? I know I'm not the only one. Maybe I'm the only one you know of because I'm the only one with enough reason to ignore my pride and confront him."

"As long as we're airing out our dirty laundry to keep the whole town busy chattering about from here to Christmas, let's talk about how you moved halfway across Wyoming. Was it my husband you wanted or just his ranch? Hmm?"

"Neither. I only wanted Tom to help support the child he fathered."

"He's not—"

"Come on, Sandy. You've seen the paternity test with your own eyes. You *know* Cody is his son, and no amount of denying it is going to change that."

"I'm not his son," Cody muttered. "I don't want to be his son. Ever. I'd rather be Gabe's son."

"Shh," Gabe whispered. "We'll talk about that later."

"What in the hell is going on here?" Tom demanded, appearing around the corner of the aisle. He eyed the shoppers who pretended to be interested in the products nearby in a scarcely concealed attempt to eavesdrop. She almost felt guilty for unloading both barrels at Sandy. Almost. She was a victim in this, but she'd also chosen to ignore Tom's infidelity and lay the blame solely on Annemarie. And for that, Annemarie didn't care if their fellow shoppers heard it all and spread it all over town.

She'd endured the stares and the whispers for two years. It was Tom's turn to face their judgment now.

"Your wife and I are having a lovely chat about your marital indiscretions," she said at last.

"Indiscretions? There was only one. You. And I have apologized to Sandy and been nothing but—"

"Don't you dare say faithful." She pointed a shaking finger at him. "Don't. You. Dare. You were too good at it. Too practiced."

"You're causing a scene, Annemarie."

"Good! People deserve to know what you are, Tom."

Tom leveled his gaze at Gabe. "You might want to shut your woman up, Collins."

"I'm glad you're finally recognizing that," Gabe remarked casually. "But I think she deserves the chance to get this out. If you didn't want your secrets shouted to the town, perhaps you should've honored your wedding vows."

Sandy spun on her husband. "What did he mean 'finally recognizing' that Annemarie is his woman, Tom?"

"I have no idea, my love."

"He knows exactly what I mean."

"Why don't you tell your wife about the day you stopped out by my cabin, Tom? Or about what you said to me at the pizzeria later that night? Something about how I should come talk to you if I wanted to remember what a real man is. And let's not forget about the incident two weeks ago at the Stagecoach when you took advantage of Gabe stepping away for five minutes, pinned me against the railing, and tried to kiss me. Did he tell you how he got that busted lip, Sandy?"

"You said there was a deer… you slammed on the breaks… hit your face on the steering wheel."

Annemarie snorted. "I wonder, Tom. What lies would you have come up with if Gabe hadn't had the self-control to walk away?"

"You bitch," he snarled.

"Maybe that's what I need to be to make you understand that I am through letting you and your wife disrespect me. I'm here to stay whether you like it or not, and I think that was exactly your father's intent."

She was almost done now. Fury pounded through her, but the gas tank was draining fast, and the promise of a fun afternoon with Gabe and Cody and the Tanners had her itching to get away.

She drew her son close and linked hands with Gabe, then took a deep breath. "One last thing, Tom. If you *ever* touch me again or try to talk to me about anything other than ranch business, I will file harassment charges. You made me fear for my safety once. Never again."

Still holding Gabe's hand, she straightened her spine, took her son's hand, and walked away. An audible slap followed her, and she hesitated, unable to resist listening in.

"You lying son of a bitch," Sandy hissed. "You said you ended it with her years ago, before Cody was born!"

"I did. I swear, Sandy."

"Then why would you try to kiss her? Why, Tom? And then you lied to me about how you got that busted lip! Why should I believe anything you tell me?"

"Sandy, I'm sorry."

"I ought to divorce your sorry ass. Do you have any idea how humiliated I am?"

"Sandy, please. I love you."

"You've done a pretty poor job of showing it."

Annemarie dragged Gabe and Cody out of earshot. She'd heard enough. She didn't want to feel sorry for the woman who had made her cry and question her own worth, and she certainly didn't want to pity the man who'd gotten her pregnant and then refused to accept responsibility for his son. When they were safely several aisles away and out of sight, she stopped, doubling over as the adrenaline abated.

It was almost a minute before she was able to straighten.

Someone touched her shoulder, and she jerked around. A woman she guessed was around forty smiled reassuringly.

"I'm sorry for eavesdropping," the woman said, "but good for you, honey. It was all I could do not to cheer out loud for you. I was Tom's 'other woman' once myself, shortly after he and Sandy married."

Annemarie stared at the woman. "I-I don't know what to say."

"You already said it, honey." The woman patted her

shoulder, smiled smugly, and strode away.

With a finger under her chin, Gabe closed Annemarie's mouth, then kissed her soundly. "I am so proud of you, Annie."

Beaming, she replied, "I'm pretty proud of me, too. Not for unloading on them so publicly—even though you're probably right that that's the way it needed to happen—but for finally saying something. It feels great."

In fact, now that she was safely away from Tom and his wife, the adrenaline ebbed, and a curious energy pulsed through her. She wanted to be home on her ranch, clinging to the back of one of her horses and racing across the sage plain. Or laughing with her friends until the sun sank behind the wall of the Absaroka Mountains and the stars littered the sky.

"I think I have a new favorite smile," Gabe murmured. "What do you think, Cody?"

"About what?"

"About getting what we need for the barbecue and getting out of here."

"Yeah! We're gonna have so much fun today."

Annemarie nodded in agreement.

They finished their shopping, located the Tanners, and headed out to the truck. With the groceries piled in the bed, everyone buckled up, and Jamie and her family following, Gabe pulled out of the supermarket parking lot. Annemarie glanced out the window at the front of the store just in time to see Sandy storm out carrying several sacks with Tom hurrying along behind her. Even from the distance, Annemarie noted how stiffly Sandy walked and the uncharacteristically hunched and submissive way Tom followed her. She wondered if Sandy would finally leave him, then shrugged. Not her problem.

They stopped by Gabe's just long enough to grab his barbecue—he promised to show Jamie the inside later—and drove north out of town. The sense of relief that had brushed away the last of the anxiety and righteous indignation deepened as they neared home. She sank into her seat and sighed, watching the landscape now dusted with spring green roll past.

She wasn't naïve enough anymore to believe her troubles with Tom were over, but she knew now that she wouldn't tolerate his bullshit or Sandy's anymore, and there was a lot of peace to be found in that.

After a moment, she closed her eyes and smiled.

"Hey, Mom?" Cody asked.

"Yes, pumpkin?"

"How are we all supposed to go riding? Since we can't ride Diamond Dot yet, we only have River and Sundance."

"Well, we have the two four-wheelers, too."

"Yeah, but that's not as much fun. Caleb really wants to ride the horses."

"Jamie and I can ride the four-wheelers and you and Caleb can ride double with Gabe and Tad. How's that sound?"

"I guess."

"Think Thomas would let us borrow a couple

horses?" Gabe inquired.

"Probably, but I don't think it's a smart idea to be showing my face at Grant Ranch right now. Especially since I don't know when Sandy and Tom will be getting home. Knowing my luck, they'll have beat us home and have set up a road block."

Inexplicably, Gabe chuckled. "I don't think that'll be a problem. We could call, ask Thomas, and have Jim bring them up."

"It's Jim's day off."

"Something tells me he won't mind."

She frowned at him. "All right, out with it. What's with the…" She gestured to the whole of him, searching for the right term. "…that? I'm not sure you could look any more pleased with yourself, so what's going on?"

"You'll see."

No matter what tactic she tried to pry the secret out of him, he only smiled. She crossed her arms and pretended to pout, but that didn't last long. She was too curious and too excited about the prospect of spending a lazy day on her and Cody's ranch with their friends.

She jerked upright. "Um, Gabe… you missed the turn."

"No, I didn't. We're taking Garrett Ranch Drive."

"News flash. It's washed out."

There was that sly smile again.

Several miles later, Gabe slowed and turned left off the highway.

She gaped.

She barely recognized the road. A brand new log gateway arched over the freshly graded gravel road, and hanging from it were iron letters that spelled out Garrett Ranch. It was plain compared to the main gate of the Grant Ranch or even the Collins Ranch, but Annemarie loved it. It suited her home just fine; Garrett Ranch wasn't anything fancy, either.

Just through the gateway, Gabe parked off to the side, rolled down his window, and waved Tad and Jamie forward. They pulled up alongside.

"Would you mind meeting us at the house? I have a feeling I'm about to be skinned alive, and I'd prefer not to have an audience."

"Um, sure. How do we get there from here?" Jamie asked.

"Just follow the road and turn right in about half a mile—only right turn you can make—and you can't miss the cabin. It's the first building you'll see, by the pond. Door's unlocked."

"All right. See you all in a few."

Annemarie didn't wait for Gabe to roll up his window. "Out with it. How much did this cost you?"

"Just a couple hundred bucks for the sign. Sam and Isaiah cut the logs off our ranch, and I called in a favor for the road."

"Who would owe you that kind of favor?"

"A friend whose shop I wired back when I was still with Leigh. We struck a deal just like the one you and I struck."

"And you wasted your favor on me."

"As I see it, I didn't waste it at all. There's something else I want to show you."

"More?"

"Well, it's part of this. I don't think you'll have to worry about the road washing out again now."

She sat quietly in the passenger seat as Gabe pulled back onto the road and waited patiently for them to reach the part of the road that had washed out this past fall right after she and Cody had moved out here. Where there had once been a decrepit culvert was now a sturdy timber bridge plenty wide enough to accommodate even the biggest cattle truck and trailer. She pressed her knuckles to her lips, but that did nothing to stop the tears from burning her eyes.

Gabe parked the truck again, and she slid out to walk the new bridge with her lover and her son following a few paces behind.

No more dreading the drive home. No more unexpected and anxiety-triggering run-ins with Tom and his wife. No more feeling like a trespasser.

She'd never have to cross the Grant Ranch again to get home.

"Thank you," she whispered, turning to them. "But you shouldn't have. I'll never be able to repay you."

"Sure you will. The way I see it, this is an investment."

"It is, is it?"

"Yep."

She frowned at him, and it didn't click in her brain what he meant until at least ten seconds after he sank to one knee on the bridge and Cody handed him a tiny box. She took in the bright-eyed hopefulness on both their faces and the way her son tucked his arm around Gabe's neck and leaned into him. How long had they been planning this together? And good lord, they were in on it together. *Together!*

"The only payment I need or want is your heart, Annemarie Elizabeth Garrett," Gabe said softly.

She couldn't recall ever telling him her middle name. "How did you…?"

"Your parents told me. Right after I asked for their blessing."

"You…?"

"I told you. I want to be a gentleman because you deserve to be treated like a lady."

"So you did."

"Will you do me the honor of sharing my life? Will you marry me?"

"Please say yes, Mom," Cody said. "So we can be a family. The three of us."

The tears spilled over then, and she embraced them both together, laughing. She kissed the top of her son's head, then turned to Gabe and kissed him fiercely. "Yes. Unequivocally yes. Oh my God, I love you."

"We love you, too," Gabe and Cody answered together.

She laughed as the tears streamed down her cheeks,

and she buried her face against Gabe's neck. After a minute or so, she leaned back, frowning. "Either you think I'm mean, or there's something else you haven't told me yet. Why did you tell Jamie I was going to skin you alive?"

"The road, for one," Gabe replied.

"For one? What else have you done?"

"I hired Jim. Full time. He's going to move into that little cabin down by the soon-to-be hayfield as soon as we can make it livable, and he's even agreed to help me get it there."

"I can't afford that, Gabe."

"No, but I can. At least until the ranch is making enough money to cover it. And it'll get to that point a lot faster with a full-time hand. You're not in this alone anymore, Annie."

He took her left hand and slid the ring onto her finger, and she finally looked at it. It was simple but beautiful—a solitaire triangular diamond set in a band graced with antique-style engraving that reminded her of the Old West.

"We might want to wait until Tom's had a few days to calm down before we tell him we're stealing his best hand," Gabe mused.

"We," Annemarie murmured. "I don't think it's going to take me long to get used to that."

"In that case, *we* should probably hurry down to the cabin."

Back at the house, Annemarie called Thomas about borrowing two horses and saddles. He had no problem with that as long as he got to tag along, and *she* had no problem with *that*. Jamie put groceries away while Gabe and Tad got the barbecue ready for later in the evening. The two boys raced around the cabin in a riotous game of tag with their dads as soon as they were done with the barbecue. Annemarie's lips twitched into a smile. Might as well get used to referring to Gabe as Cody's dad now that it was blatantly apparent he wanted the job. She covertly studied the beautiful piece of jewelry now adorning her left hand and smiled coyly.

She and Jamie joined the menfolk outside, and together, they headed down to the barn. Thomas arrived with three horses already saddled, and the first thing he noticed was the new ring on Annemarie's finger.

"I should've bet you money, Gabe," he remarked, taking Annemarie's hand and holding it up to inspect the ring. "You have a good eye. It suits her."

"What suits…?" Jamie's voice trailed off, and she snatched Annemarie's hand from Thomas and let out a squeal. "Oh, my God, Annemarie! It's gorgeous! Tad, lookit!"

Annemarie shifted her weight. She wasn't completely ready to share this yet. It was too new and too wonderful, and she wanted to keep it all to herself until she had quiet time with just Gabe and Cody to fully process everything that glittery ring meant. With the horses all saddled, she shooed everyone away and climbed into Sundance's saddle.

Gabe and Cody led the way on one of Thomas's

horses, and Annemarie rode beside them. Peace settled over her, penetrating her more fully than any she had felt in maybe ever, and she breathed deeply. With the sun warm on her back and shoulders, fresh, sagebrush-scented air in her lungs, and acres upon acres of wild land that was all hers and Cody's and soon Gabe's, she embraced the true meaning of home. There would be struggles, but she didn't have to face them alone anymore.

Reaching over, she took Gabe's free hand, smiling when he turned his head to meet her gaze.

"I guess my mom is right. Looks like guardian angels exist after all."

"Do they now?" Gabe asked. "And what changed your mind?"

She leaned precariously in her saddle to kiss him, and he met her halfway. With a hand on his shoulder for balance, she gave him a grateful squeeze. "When I most needed one, you showed up."

* * * * *

About the Author

Suzie O'Connell is the *USA Today* bestselling author of the Northstar romances. The series is the product of a love affair with Southwestern Montana that began with a two-week adventure to her stepsister's rustic cabin in her teens and shows no signs of abating. She also has another series started—Sea Glass Cove—that harkens back to her Pacific Northwest upbringing and the salt-water running through her veins courtesy of her "Salty Dog" grandfather.

When she isn't writing, you'll probably find her in the mountains with a camera in hand and enjoying the beauty of Montana with her husband Mark, their daughter Maddie, and their golden retrievers Reilly and Angus. Or spoiling their three cats and their flock of chickens.

For more information about Suzie and her books, find her online:

www.suzieoconnell.com

* 9 7 8 1 9 5 0 8 1 3 1 0 0 *